USA TODAY BESTSELLING AUTHOR
CARMEN JENNER

KICK
Copyright © 2015 Carmen Jenner
Published by Carmen Jenner

All rights reserved. No part of this publication may be reproduced, distributed, or transmitted in any form or by any means, including photocopying, recording, or other electronic or mechanical methods, without the prior written permission of the publisher, except in the case of brief quotations embodied in critical articles or reviews.
This is a work of fiction.
Names, characters, businesses, organisations, places, events, and incidents are either of the author's imagination or used in a fictitious manner. Any resemblance to actual persons, living dead, or actual events is purely coincidental.
This book is licensed for your personal enjoyment only. This book may not be re-sold or given away to other people. If you would like to share this book with another person, please purchase an additional copy for each person you share it with. If you are reading this book and did not purchase it, or it was not purchased for your use only, then you should return it to the seller and purchase your own copy. Thank you for respecting the author's work and for not making me set some very pissed off Savage Saints MC bikers on you.

Published: Carmen Jenner January 19th 2015
carmenjennerauthor@gmail.com

Editing: Lauren McKellar
http://laurenkmckellar.com/hire-an-editor/

Cover Design: © Arijana Karčić, Cover It! Designs
http://coveritdesigns.net/

Formatting:

www.emtippettsbookdesigns.com

"What matters most is how well you walk through the fire."
   – Charles Bukowski

For any woman who has ever had to walk through the fire.

For my Brothers — yes, both of you — thank you for an amazing childhood, and for showing me what a brotherhood was.

Dear Reader,

I'd like to thank you for picking up this book, but before I let you get all acquainted with my boy, I feel we need a warning first.

KICK is not for the faint of heart. It's not a hot romp through a magical world of sweet bikers, soft leather, hooker heels and cupcakes, and we are definitely NOT in Sugartown anymore, Toto.

KICK is brutal, it is graphic, and it is probably going to make you question my sanity – to be honest, I've been doing that for a while now, so don't feel bad. There will be situations that will be hard for you to read; they were hard to write. Some of them gutted me.

You might be wondering why I'm giving you this warning – and it is a warning – because if you're reading this and trying to determine if KICK is the book for you, then I'm going to say this: it will challenge you, it will probably break your heart, and you will find some of it distressing. I didn't write this book as a gimmick, to be controversial, or to push boundaries of what people find acceptable and what they can live with themselves enjoying – though in my defence, if I'm not making you feel, if I'm not forcing you to keep a white-knuckled grip on your e-reader or paperback, or leaving you with your heart beating in your throat, then I'm not doing my job properly. I just wanted to write something that felt honest and true to the subject, not something that glorified it, and made MC life pretty. That shit is not pretty; it's brutal.

If you've read my previous books, you will know that KICK played a large part in Greetings from Sugartown (Book #3) and you will already know a little about Kick's past with Elijah (Ethan). But for those of you who haven't read Sugartown, don't fret. Kick is a standalone spin-off told in a series of present day events and flashbacks, and each chapter gives us a little more insight into our messed up, tormented leading man. His present day takes place after the events in Greetings from Sugartown, but his past takes place in the years between Welcome to Sugartown and Greetings. Confusing, right? Try writing that shit!

To those of you who do move forward after reading this very dreary preface where I prattle on for far too long, I say this: sometimes you choose to write a book, and sometimes that book chooses you. I couldn't be more proud of KICK. Even in all its raw and gritty horror, I still think there's beauty in it, and that Kick's is a story worth telling.

I hope you love my insanely fucked-up, damaged biker as much as I do.

Carmen

xoxox

PROLOGUE

The metallic click of a bullet sliding through a chamber wakes me. My eyes spring open, but the bite of cold metal against my temple forces me to hold completely still.

Until I see her, bound and gagged on the worn motel carpet.

Her eyes are wide with fear. Her body quakes as Tag kneels behind her. Her face is contorted with pain. Tears stream down her red cheeks. Her mouth gapes open in horror around the gag. Her eyes stare accusingly at me.

I explode.

I don't think. Just act.

Too damn bad I wasn't quick enough.

Too bad I wasn't enough to save her.

KICK

I jolt upright. Sweat beads my brow and I wipe it away with the back of my hand. Ivy sits up, her long dark hair trailing over my shoulder as she wraps her naked body around me. She kisses my neck, presses her warm tits into my back and slides her hand around to my cock, which is harder than fucking concrete. That's the really sick thing about it. No matter how many times I relive the dream, the end result is always the same. Has been for years. I see her bound and gagged with a gun at her temple and I wake up hornier than a fucking bitch in heat. I shove at Ivy's small, expert hands and stand, causing her to lose her balance.

I grab a pack of smokes from the bedside table and light up. Down the hall, the party's still going strong. Who am I fuckin' kidding? At the Savage Saints clubhouse, every night is a fuckin' party. There's always an endless supply of hard liquor, even harder drugs and slippery pussy that'll ride your cock until you can't get hard no more.

I look at the club whore in my bed. Perfect tits, perfect arse, perfect fucking face. She coulda been a model, or a Hollywood starlet. Instead she's passed around between the brothers, used and abused. And what's more? She fucking loves it.

"What are you doing here, darlin'?" I ask, 'cause I can't for the life of me see how hanging around a club full of arsehole and degenerate criminals is the kind of career move a smart young woman should make.

"Hoping you come back to bed." Her eyes follow the line of my torso, rolling over every inch of hard-won muscle. She holds out her hand for my smoke, but I just laugh and shake my head. She pouts.

"Get up. Go home." I throw a short leather skirt and a ripped up Harley-Davidson top at her. I can't find her underwear, but then again, Ivy doesn't ever really wear it. "Go and get a job in a fucking coffee shop, or some shit. You need away from this club, sweetheart."

"I happen to like this club," she says, tossing that shit she calls clothing aside and coming up on her knees. Her hand wraps around my lagging dick, sliding over the barbell in my frenum. She smiles triumphantly when my cock hardens in her soft grip. "And I'd rather get you up."

"You like being treated like a whore, darlin'?" I nip at her neck as she strokes me, faster, harder.

"I like being treated like your whore."

"Stupid girl." I grunt and take a drag of my cigarette, cupping her nape in my hand. I pull her close and cover her mouth with mine, blowing smoke into her lugs. She gags and wrenches free, her eyes watering.

"I hate when you do that."

"I know." I chuckle.

"That bitch really did a number on you, huh, Kick?"

My hand shoots out and slips around her throat. "You don't get to say shit about her, you got me?"

Ivy swallows. The muscles of her throat bob against my hand as I tighten my grip. Her eyes widen in fear. I smile. "Don't worry, sweetheart. I'm not gonna strangle you. It'd be more trouble than it's worth, trying to get rid of the body." I slide my free hand over her tits, twisting her nipple, hard.

"You're hurting me."

"But that's the way you like it, isn't it, baby? Rough and hard. Just the way your daddy used to give it to you." I squeeze her firm arse, raking my blunt fingernails across her smooth flesh. She arches into my touch, her tits thrusting forward, firm nipples brushing my chest.

"Oh, yeah." She moans. "Hurt me, Daddy."

"You're one sick bitch, Ivy, you know that right?" I shake my head, sliding my fingers down the seam of her crack. She spreads her legs wider for me. I thrust a dry finger in her arse, and my thumb inside her cunt. She moans and rocks against my hand until she cums, slapping and scratching at my bare chest. I tighten my hold around her neck, watching her gasp for air as she rides out the remainder of her orgasm.

With my hand wrapped around her throat I pull her closer, smother her mouth with my kiss, and then I fuck her. For hours. In every hole she possesses, and in every position possible because the bitch is hot, and not just that, beyond the gorgeous tits, and hair, and that broken down look she gets in her eyes right before she cums, squeezing my cock with her pussy harder than a vice. It's because I recognise something in her. Something more than her fucked-up daddy fantasies and her innate need to be used up. I recognise loneliness. And the fact that she may just be the one other person inside this clubhouse who is as fucked in the head as I am.

My brothers kick her out when she begins sobbing like a little girl. They can't wait to be rid of her. After they've used up every hole she has to offer, they discard her like trash. But not me. I like to watch her cry. I taste her tears. I relish them. Because pain is beauty, at least in my world. And everything in my world is pain.

Has been since the morning I woke with a gun pressed to my head.

Since *her* life was snuffed out.

KICK

I shrug off the frosty fuckin' reception I receive from Prez and my brothers as I walk into church, and I flop down in my chair beside Tank, a dude with short dark hair, bright blue eyes and a frame a hell of a lot bigger than any other I've ever seen, way bigger than Moose ever dreamed of being. I'm late because after fucking all night, Ivy had decided she wanted to snort coke off the end of my cock at the arse crack of dawn. It took forever to cum.

Prez glares at me, his no-nonsense stare pinning me to the back of my seat. I sniff and feel a wet trickle of what I think is snot dripping from my nose, but after wiping it away with my sleeve I quickly realise I'm bleeding. Tank smacks me upside the head.

"You fuckin' high, Kick?"

"It's a party isn't it?" I shrug, but know I've said the wrong shit as soon as Crazy, Tank and Killer shake their heads.

"No, arsehole, it ain't a fucking party," Prez roars. "Last night was a fucking party, today we got business. And I don't need your spoiled little newbie arse fucking my shit up. So you'd better sober up real goddamned fast. Or do you need me to beat that shit outta your bloodstream?"

I hate when he refers to me as a goddamned newbie. Prez is ten years my senior. He's a bad-arse motherfucker—don't get me wrong. But he wasn't indoctrinated into the life. He stumbled upon it after a stint in a Sydney jail fifteen years ago. He built this club from the ground up, and I gotta give him props for turning it into one of the most notorious clubs in Australia in such a short amount of time, but I was born into the club life. My father was an Angel, and my grandfather before him. I was birthed by a club whore, suckled at the breast before the bitch ODed. I was chewed up as a sweet, blue-eyed baby boy and spat out a man. I took down every bad-arse motherfucker in my chapter when they turned against me. I did my time as a prospect for both the Angels and the Saints, and I patched into both early by doing the really fucking dirty-arsed shit no one else wanted to do. I was not a fucking newbie. I never had been, because I'd never had another choice.

"I'm sober, Prez," I say quickly.

"Good, then go clean your shit up before you ride out. You and Tank are going to pay our friendly neighbourhood dentist a visit. Bastard fucked with Raphe's old lady. Been putting the moves on bitches while they're under sedation. This time he picked the wrong bitch to fuck with."

"Raphe doesn't want a go at him?"

"Why the fuck do you think he isn't at church? He already had a go, landed his dumb arse in jail because of it. Told him we'd have a little Kinder Sur-fucking-prise for him to play with when he got out."

There's a timid little knock on the door, and Prez leans back in his seat, scrubbing his hands over his face in agitation.

"What?" he yells, and then his eyes widen a fraction when the door swings open and he sees Raine, a pretty blonde with a bangin' body and an even sweeter disposition, standing on the other side. "Come on in, darlin'."

"Sorry, I'm interrupting," she says, staring nervously between Prez and the rest of us sorry sons of bitches. She's carrying a steaming cardboard cup of coffee and one of those little white bakery bags. She sets them down on the table in front of him. "I stopped by the bakery near my house this morning. It's a warm crème brûlée muffin. They're really good."

"She wants you to eat her warm, sweet muffin, Prez," Trigger says, waggling his eyebrows like a fuckin' geriatric douche. His boyish good looks are mis-fucking-leading, because the dude is motherfuckin' crazy. He's like a kid with ADHD. On speed.

Prez glares, and Trigger quickly shuts up.

Prez took Raine on as a bar wench and occasional cook after she lost her job a few months ago at the local café we frequent. Most of the brothers take care of their own meals, and some of the lucky bastards head home to a cooked meal at the end of a long day and the same familiar pussy in their beds at night. And some of us eat take-out twenty-four fuckin' seven. But food doesn't prepare itself for club meets, and that's where Raine comes in.

Far as I know, she's alone in the world; no family and no friends, except a club full of criminals. Raine tiptoes around this place as if at any moment she's afraid Prez is gonna turn her out on her arse, but he wants up inside that pussy bad; I'd seen it the first time I tagged along to the coffee shop with him, and I still see it every damn day. Prez is hard up for the vanilla bitch who makes his coffee and cleans his office. And I'd bet my last dollar that he's wishin' and hopin' she could start cleaning his pipes, too.

"Well, I'll just..." She points to the door, and scurries away like a little mouse.

"Sweetheart," Prez calls to her, and she turns. He grins like the fuckin' Cheshire cat. "I'll savour every morsel."

Raine's eyes light up like a fuckin' Christmas tree. She blushes and then leaves the room as silently as she entered, closing the door behind her. My brothers and I practically bust our nuts laughing. All except Grim. Dude needs his fuckin' head checked 'cause Prez is gonna rip it off his shoulders if he catches Grim starin' at Raine the way he does.

"Shut the fuck up," Prez hollers, as pissed off as a fuckin' cut snake. "Tank, don't come back without that dentist."

Tank nods. He's a douche of few words.

"The rest of you," Prez says, "we've got Bandits to meet with." He bangs the gavel against the table and the room is filled with the sound of shuffling feet and shifting leather. I sit in my seat long after the others have piled out.

"You got somethin' else you need to be discussing with me, Newbie?" Prez is standing in the door way, looking back at me with a pissed off expression on his face.

"No, Prez," I say, and rise from my chair.

"Then get the fuck outta here," he says, but before I can pass, his arm shoots out and stops me in my tracks. "Wait."

"What's up?"

"You been with Ivy?"

"Yeah."

"I know why she's a coke whore—the whole fucking club knows that kid is messed up—but you're the only one that'll let her whiny arse stay the night. Why is that?"

"'Cause I don't care if she cries. She gets what she needs, and I get what I need. It works."

"You gonna put her on the back of your bike?"

"Hell fucking no."

"I like fucking her as much as the next brother, but that bitch is damaged goods, and not even you can tape that shit back together."

"I'm not looking for an old lady, Prez. Made that mistake once before."

He shakes his head, running a hand through his greased-back blond hair. "Life's too fucking short for the same old pussy day in and day out, kid. Thank fuck for club whores or else my dick would have fallen off years ago. My old lady hasn't let me inside since she found me in this very room, eatin' out two pussies at once."

"Can't say I blame her, Prez."

"Shut up, arsehole," he says and clips me on the back of the head as I walk towards the door. "Kick? Do the blow on your time, yeah? I don't need you falling off your bike and getting your stupid arse arrested while you're wearing my patch."

"Yeah, Prez."

I stalk through the door to find Tank leaning against the wall outside church. He slaps me upside the head too, but this time I'm quicker with my retaliation. I punch him in the side and shake out my fist when he doesn't even flinch. He's one hundred per cent muscle mass. *Fucking giant cunt.*

"Clean up your face, fuck-stick. You look like you've been eating clam with red sauce."

"Makes sense." I shrug with a wicked grin. "I about punched a hole through that perfect cunt into her stomach, and then I kissed it better, but what's a little blood between brothers?"

The warehouse sits empty, save for Dr Calder. No surprise there. It's 2:00pm on a Sunday in a quiet part of Erskineville. We sit in an unmarked van with blackout windows and fake plates. We sit and we watch. When it looks as though no one's coming or going, Tank revs the engine and we pull up to the back entrance and slip from the van in plain, dark clothing, hoodies covering our faces.

Tank kicks in the door. It takes him all of three

seconds for the thing to splinter off its hinges. We're under instructions to collect the Dentist, deliver him to the club, and keep him safe until Raphe is out of lock-up.

Easy enough. Right?
Wrong.

The music hits me first, some fucking classical shit played way too loud. I can't hear fucking jack over the noise, but it's the scent of blood—a lot of blood—that sets off my twitchy trigger finger. When I see him, bent over a rusty surgical chair, a flash of long chestnut hair behind him, and I feel more so than hear the screams coming from the woman that's strapped to the seat, I explode. The coke high wore off about two hours ago. I feel a little like shit warmed up, but I have all my faculties about me. I'm thinking one hundred per cent clearly when I raise my gun and shoot him point blank in the back of the head. The dentist lands in a heap, a pair of shiny, blood-drenched dental pliers falling from his hand and onto the putrid concrete floor. The tooth he's extracted skitters across the ground. It reminds me of the games of Knuckles that Ethan and I would play with the other MC brats at clubhouse parties.

The naked woman beyond him had gone completely still when she watched the dentist fall, but now her screams start up again.

"What the fuck? You still fuckin' high, motherfucker?" Tank says, shaking his head. "Prez is gonna bust your balls in a fuckin' vice, brother."

He raises his gun and aims it at the brunette's head.

"No!" I shout and throw myself in front of her, knocking over a tripod with a video camera attached.

KICK

The camera comes lose and slides across the floor. The brunette continues to scream like a fucking banshee.

"Jesus Christ, what the hell is wrong with you?" Tank lowers the gun. I turn and face the woman, who begins thrashing against her restraints.

"I'm not gonna hurt you." I whisper, but I guess the fact that I just shot a man in cold blood three inches from her face might sort of imply otherwise — she is covered in his brain matter, after all. A gob of something white and globular slides over her collarbone and off her nipple, landing in her lap. Her body quakes with fear, her tits jiggle with the jagged, panic-filled rush of air into her lungs. I close my eyes, trying to get my cock to sit the fuck down. I'm all kinds of fucked up; I know this, but there's a scent to a woman's fear, and my dick is all too keenly aware of and enamoured with it. It's fucked up, but it is what it is.

"Snuff it out, Kick," Tank says behind me. The motherfucker sounds bored shitless, as if he can't wait to be done here so he can go and grab a fucking Big Mac. "She's seen too much."

"I got it. Shut up, man," I say. "Do something useful and wrap that sick fucker in that plastic tarp."

"Do I look like your bitch, Kick?"

"Just fuckin' do it."

He holsters his piece and pulls the tarp closer. I turn back to the girl. Her face is a fucking mess, and she's yanking on her restraints and staring at me with wide, terrified eyes. Her cheeks are swollen and bloody.

"I'm gonna untie you. Okay? I'm just here to help you. I'm not gonna hurt you." She thrashes against the stirrups, trying to free herself. "If you scream, I'll be forced to put a bullet between your eyes. You don't want that. I don't want that."

She shakes her head.

"Jesus H. Christ," Tank moans. "Don't fucking untie the bitch."

I lean over and unfasten the buckle strapping her head to the chair. She lets me, and then she lurches as far forward as her restraints will allow, and head-butts me.

"Fucking bitch," I shout. Backing away, I press a hand to my bleeding lip.

"Oh, I like this one." Tank chuckles. "Shame we gotta put her out of her misery."

"Shut the fuck up," I say, and then press my gun against her temple. "Do that again and I will put a bullet in you. Understand?"

She nods, carefully. Not so fucking brave now that she has a gun aimed at her brain, though I have to admit, her fight has me rock-fucking-hard in my jeans.

"Kick," Tank warns. "Put her down, or I will."

"You think she's gonna talk? That fucker was ripping her teeth out. Bitch ain't gonna talk."

I close my eyes and remember a scene only a few short years ago in a cane field in the arsehole of nowhere town. The dude I'd loved my whole life like a brother, standing before a bitch that'd seen too much, begging him to spare her life.

How the mighty have fallen and become fucking pussies.

I can't believe I'm begging to save her life the way Ethan did with that whore. "We're taking her with us."

"The hell we are." Tank says. "Prez is gonna grind your balls for his bread over this shit." He waves his gun at the plastic-wrapped body of the dentist. "You can't bring a civilian into the club."

The woman takes that opportunity to scream. I clamp my hand down over her mouth, wincing when I touch the cracked and swollen flesh beneath my fingers. She bites down. I yank my fist away, the pain in my hand acute and searing. "Fuck me, bitch! I'm trying to save your goddamned life here and you're doing a hell of a job trying to fuck that shit up."

"Kill me," she growls. "I'd rather die than be passed around between filthy fucking bikers."

"Oh, that can be very easily arranged, sweetheart," Tank says, lifting his gun and aiming it at her head. I hold up my arms and ease in front of the rabid bitch, protecting her. Who the fuck knows why? Certainly not me, that's for sure. I just can't walk away. I can't look at her face, all beaten and bruised, and put her down like a dog.

"Do it," she screeches. "Fucking do it! Do it! Do it!"

Tank looks as if he's about to put a bullet through me in order to stop this bitch's screaming. I've had enough. I snap. I lash out and strike her on the temple with the butt of my gun, rendering her unconscious.

I stare at her face for a long time. Swollen and bloodied as she is, there's no telling if she's beautiful, or is she's as ugly as a hat full of arseholes. Her hair is filthy, her body is covered in crusted blood, and shit, she smells like shit too. How fucking long has she been here? Locked away in an empty warehouse, the plaything for a sick, twisted fuck. Hooked up to an IV that I'm guessing fed her sedatives and other more potent drugs, instead of nutrients. I rip off the tape and yank the needle from her arm, then shove away his tray of torture devices.

All gleaming, shiny dentist tools, or they would have been gleaming and shiny, if they weren't covered in the fucker's brain tissue and tiny fragments of his skull.

Lifting a syringe and a tiny vial labelled morphine from the tray—which I'm sure he uses in order to knock her out rather than ease her pain—I push out the air from the needle and tap the crook of her elbow, finding a vein to drive into.

"What the fuck are you doing?" Tank asks, but I ignore him as I place the needle back on the tray, and run my fingertips across her shoulder. I lift a limp strand of matted hair to my nose. It's sweat and blood, fear, and general human filth. My gaze rolls over her from head to toe. There are bruises everywhere, but it seems as though he only liked to really mess up her face and mouth.

"She's not Lauren."

I close my eyes. "Don't say her name. Not here."

"End it, Kick."

"Fuck you."

Tank lifts his gun and aims it at her head. I move on autopilot. I don't even think about what I'm doing. I just do. Like in all the important decisions I've made in life, it's as if my brain flips a switch and someone else takes over. Someone who isn't me, but cares as much for self-preservation as I do. Cares for life. Cares for others who can't muster a shit of care for themselves. I pull on him, gun aimed and at the ready, my finger hovering over the trigger.

"You fucking pulling on a brother?" Tank demands with seething, narrowed eyes. His jaw ticks.

"We're not killing her," I say, though the words feel

as if they're being pulled from me, wrenched from some alien place in the pit of my gut. "Not today."

"What the fuck's gotten into you, man?" Tank says. He hasn't lowered his gun yet, so I don't lower mine either. I can feel the fury radiating off of him. If another brother had pulled on Tank this way, he'd already be laid out on the floor, a bullet between the eyes, blood oozing out from the hole in his skull. I don't know why he hasn't put me down already like the rabid dog I am. A part of me wishes he'd quit fuckin' holdin' back.

"She's not her."

"I know," I whisper. I don't know why I'm fighting for this. Bitch is probably crazy—not that I'd blame her—and I'm the last person who should be attempting an act of decency. I'm not the hero in this story; I'm the motherfucking villain.

Tank shakes his head as he lowers his gun and tucks it into the waistband of his jeans. He may have decided not to shoot me today, but there's venom in his tone when he says, "You pull a piece on a brother again, and I'll put you to fuckin' ground."

I nod.

Tank crouches down and hefts the dentist's body over his shoulder. He might be wrapped in plastic but blood still pours out from the clear tarp and leaves a trail across the floor. Once Tank has cleared the room, I bend and pick up her tooth from the floor. I take a moment to roll it across my palm and then pocket it before I turn back to the woman in the chair, and unbuckle her restraints. I lift her in a groom's hold and carry her out into the sombre grey Sydney day. I climb into the back of the van and Tank shoots me a questioning look from the driver's seat.

"I wanna be close if she wakes up."

He glares at me.

"Can't have her busting open the doors and streaking around town like a madwoman."

"If we'd shot her in the head, we wouldn't need to worry," he says without preamble and throws me an *"I'm not fucking buying your bullshit excuses"* glower over his shoulder as he shifts the van into reverse, forcing me to clench my body tight to keep from toppling onto my ripe-scented new plaything. I glance down at the woman in my arms. She's sleeping soundly, probably for the first time in a long time. Her body is covered in bruises. Yellow, purple, blue-black, head to toe—there isn't a single part of her thin frame that hasn't seen some form of torture. It makes me wonder—if this is what she looks like on the outside, what the fuck kind of damage did he do to her insides?

I don't know what the hell I was thinking.

This bitch needs a hospital, or a mental institution. Not a fucking bikey.

I stare at the plastic-wrapped body of the dentist. I wish I'd made him suffer a little more. I wish I'd made him pay, not just for this woman in my arms, but for all of them. I wish it was me wrapped in that tarp, because the things I've done, the things I want to do make me no better than him. Just smarter, because I was the one holding the gun instead of a pair of fucking dental pliers.

KICK

"Killer's bike's here, but it don't look like no one else is back yet," Tank says as he punches the code into the gate. The loud metallic grinding against concrete alerts me to them swinging open, and oddly—even though I'm likely to get my balls handed to me in a brown paper bag for going against the Prez's wishes—I feel a sense of relief.

Fat Boy, a huge black pit bull dumber than the shit that comes out its arse, barks as Tank eases the van into the compound.

"Where's the fucking dirty bastard that touched my woman?" Raphe's booming voice filters through the closed van doors. *Fuck.* They let him out of lock-up sooner than I'd thought they would. My relief is short-lived. "I'm gonna skin his dick and roast it on an open fire, and then feed it to him."

Tank shoots out of the front seat and intercepts him before he can open the door and find his dentist dead as a doornail. "There was a complication, Brother."

"What fucking complication?" The doors are yanked open and sunlight floods the van, blinding me momentarily. All I see are two massive black shadows looming over us.

"Who's in the tarp?"

"That would be our friendly neighbourhood dentist," Tank says.

"Jesus fucking Christ," Raphe shouts. "You boys had one fucking task—deliver that little cock-fuck to me and I'd rip his head off. What the fuck happened?"

"Kick happened." Tank mutters, folding his huge arms across his broad chest. "Went in there guns blazin', just like Trigger, and punched a whole in the motherfucker's head."

"I oughtta punch a fuckin' hole in his head." Raphe pounds his fist against the roof of the van. It causes the girl in my arms to stir, and I really want to get her locked away in my room before Prez gets home and she starts skitzing out. "Who's the bitch?"

"Kick's new toy," Tank supplies helpfully with a shit-eating grin. "Pretty, ain't she?"

"She smells like shit."

Tank threads an arm around Raphe and walks him away from the van. I deposit the girl beside the body of her attacker and ease out of the back. Then I shrug off my hoodie and dress her in it while she lays there unconscious. The hoodie swamps her, but it doesn't completely cover the length of her body. I take an anxious look at her face, making sure she's still asleep before I nudge her knees apart with my hands. There are no gashes or even blood, but beneath the filth coating her flesh she's bruised, pretty badly. I want to know what he did to her. I want to know because a part of me wants to harm her, too. A part of me wants to bruise and mark her flesh, see her writhe and twist and scream beneath me.

I trace my fingertips over soft flesh, marvelling at how easily it bends to my will, at how goose bumps slowly creep over her exposed skin.

Standing behind me, Tank clears his throat. "You wanna move this to your bedroom, brother?"

That's the thing about Tank; nothing ever fazes him. He gets in, gets the job done. He feels nothing. And he sure as hell doesn't lose any sleep over it. Tank is an ex-Angels nomad. When that shit went down in Sugartown and our whole chapter was slaughtered in a farmhouse in the middle of Bumfuck, Nowhere, he didn't bat an eyelid.

I went to him because I knew he wouldn't have any qualms about killing me. He knew the betrayal I had brought upon the club, he knew what they'd done to me months earlier, and he knew what they had done to *her*. He knew everything, and he wasn't the least bit surprised when I showed up, bleeding all over his doorstep. He'd just laughed and handed me a beer while my guts were spilling out all over the place, and then he called in the good doctor to patch up the stitches I'd busted open while trying to flee the cops at the hospital and hitch a ride back to Sydney.

And then he brought me to the Saints. He convinced Prez to take me on as prospect and burned the Angels insignia from my arm with a fucking cattle brand before the Saints could see it. He knows about my fucked-up arrangement with Ivy, knows that after Lauren I can't get off any other way than by hurting, bruising, or punishing when I fuck. He knows and couldn't give a shit. He doesn't feel anger or remorse, fear, pain or torment. He feels nothing. And that's what makes him truly terrifying. When you have nothing you care about, nothing to lose, you're indestructible.

I remove my hand from the woman's thigh and scoop her up in my arms. She's still unconscious but it feels as if she's snuggling into my chest. Or maybe that's just too many drugs thinking.

Fat Boy jumps up all around us, licking at the girl's legs and nipping at mine as we walk around to the front entrance. The clubhouse is quiet with most of the brothers gone. Though maybe quiet is the wrong word, considering the banshee screams of pleasure coming from the whore that Killer has bent over the couch. He shoots me a curious look as we pass, but I quickly avert my eyes and continue on to the hallway. Tank follows. His room sits right beside mine, though it only ever gets used when he can't be bothered riding back to the mountains. I fish out my keys with one hand and Tank opens the door for me, because I have mine full of crazy.

Ivy is spread out on the bed. A mirrored plate with three neat little white lines, all running parallel to each other, sits nestled in sheets that I've needed to change for far too long. Ivy blinks up at us and runs a finger over her gums. Cocaine dusts her chin and chest.

"From one fucked up bitch to another." Tank chuckles and turns to me with a look of disbelief. "What are you, collecting them?"

"Jesus Christ, Ivy. How many lines have you done

today?"

"Who's the girl?" she slurs accusingly. She looks like fucking shit, all strung out and shaking with bloodshot eyes and a bad case of bedhead. Ivy knows how it is between us; she knows she ain't ever gonna be riding on the back of my bike, but she still makes out like it might one day be a possibility.

"No one."

"Why is she in your arms if she's no one?" Her eyes close and she sighs as she chases her high. A smile only meant for the things inside her head plays on her lips. She comes up on her knees and tugs at my belt. Her hands are weak and fumble twice before she can get it undone. I roll my eyes and edge away from her. "I need to be fucked, Kick."

"No, sweetheart, you need a stint in rehab."

"I got your rehab right here, baby," Tank says, clutching the bulge in his jeans. Ivy licks her lips and smiles like the cat that got the fucking cream. Tank throws her over his shoulder, smacking her arse as he carries a shrieking Ivy from the room.

I lay the woman down on my bed, quickly moving Ivy's little party treats and setting them on the dresser before covering her with a sheet. I go to my cupboard, where Ivy stores all her shit. Unlike the other brothers, this is my home. I don't have some fancy fuck-off house in the mountains like Tank or Prez, or even a shitty rundown apartment in the city like Grim. This room contains everything I own. This room contains everything Ivy owns, too. I never thought about that before, but as I rummage through her bags and pull out an unused needle, it hits me. I've let her become too familiar with me. Ivy's gorgeous; not just because of the way she looks outwardly but she's so beautifully broken that I just gravitate towards her.

I love the broken ones because for a brief second, in the heat of the moment, I can forget how fucked up I truly am inside. I can forget about the darkness that I crave. I can forget who I am and focus on someone else's pain, because that has to be infinitely better than wallowing in my own.

And I have so much of it, seeping from every pore in my body. So much pain, and betrayal, and fucked-up-ness. All of it.

I am the king of shit, and my throne is built upon the bodies of all I have betrayed; my crown is made of her teeth and tears.

I wasn't always this way though. Once upon a time I was happy, content with my swift slide into a life of criminal activity and debauchery. And now? Now I'm just bitter and hollow. Soulless. Fucked up.

I walk over to the bed, pulling the cap off the needle with my teeth. I wrap my belt around the woman's arm and cinch it in tight. Grabbing a spoon from the kitchenette that I built into my room, I sprinkle a little of the coke onto it, and then flick my lighter beneath it, waiting until it bubbles and becomes liquid. I pull back the plunger and draw it up through the needle, and then I release the air. The woman's eyes open drowsily. She glances at the needle in my hand and shrieks, kicking like a wild animal, despite her injuries. She struggles against my hold, screaming. I cop an elbow to the face. Her nails rake the skin over my bare chest, but I lunge onto her and lean my weight against her body. I can't reach her arm without copping a kick to the face, so I plunge the needle into her neck, instead.

She sobs as her weak hands pound against my back. I ease off of her and watch her wide, panicked eyes lose the fight against the drug coursing through her veins.

"I hate you," she spits, barely able to keep her eyelids open.

"I saved your life."

"You should have killed me." She laughs. It's a weak and worthless sound. "The first chance I get, I'm going to put a knife in your heart."

"Shh," I whisper, stroking her disgusting, matted hair as I lie down on the bed beside her. She flinches and tries to pull away, but the coke makes it a lost cause. She's weak from malnutrition, coke, and whatever drugs he's been cycling through her system for who knows how long. When she slips under, her breathing is light but fractured, as if she's nursing a broken rib.

I study her face. I wish I could sink my fingers inside her skull and pull out all the memories she'll spend her life trying to repress. I wish I could run a feed from her mind to mine and see exactly what the dentist did to her.

I follow the curve of her lips with my fingertip, trace her thick, black lashes. She has a sweet, slightly upturned nose, and I know now why he took her. She may be skinny, but the bitch is fucking gorgeous. Even beneath the dirt and the fresh layer of beaded sweat on her skin, the swollen cheeks, the tangled hair, she's beautiful. Maybe she's beautiful because she looks like she went ten fuckin' rounds in the ring with Tyson and she's still comin' out swinging. The longer I stare at her, the more I come to understand this. I begin to understand why I saved her, because on some level I saw in her what I've only ever seen in one other person: fight. Not self-preservation, or the need to beat the shit outta someone like my brothers do on a daily basis, but fight, as if every cell in her body was made up of it, and it's fucking glorious. Even bruised and filthy and as physically defeated as she is, this crazy bitch is beautiful. Even in sleep, her fight is undeniable. And I am harder than I can ever remember being. I strip off my jeans and slip beneath the covers, then I wrap my arm around her, pull her close, and close my eyes.

KICK

TWO YEARS AGO

I'm always nervous at rallies like this. Opposing clubs come together with a bunch of stuffed teddy bears strapped to our bikes and pretend as if we're not secretly plotting to off one another in a different setting, with much less media coverage. We play nice with arseholes that we'd likely gut on the street given the chance, and it's all in the name of the kiddies.

It's not the opposing clubs that are the problem though, or at least it's not the other clubs that are making me nervous. It's that members from the Banditos chapter in Byron are here. Members I falsely accused of ambushing us a year ago when I saved my best friend's arse.

Ethan—or Elijah, if you want his pansy-arsed new name given to him by the state after he was released from prison with a government issued "get out of jail free" card—and I had grown up brothers. Our fathers belonged to the Angels, still do, and they indoctrinated us into the family when we were barely old enough to ride a goddamned push bike, let alone a motorcycle. But Ethan had been sent to jail; he took the wrap for me, and when he was let out early on good behaviour he disappeared without a trace, Prez had sentenced him to a date with the reaper.

Course we had to find him first. We hadn't even been looking when Rocker and I were on a run up north and spotted him and his old lady at some quiet country-town parade. Every fibre of my being wanted to beat down my brothers in order to allow Ethan to get away, but my hands were tied. When push came to shove, I chose Ethan. I shot my VP in the back and chose the brother who had abandoned me over the brotherhood I had patched into. I had two options—spend the rest of my life running, or fake an ambush and ride back to the club with my tail between my legs and some bullshit story that would cost a lot of people their lives. Prez had gone in, guns blazing. We'd invaded the Byron chapter and shot up every last motherfucker in that club, women too.

Other charters heard about it, ties were broken and business deals were hard won. And from what I hear, the big bad B's are still out for blood. So fuck yes, rallies like this make me un-fucking-comfortable, to say the least.

"You keep staring over there and some fucker's gonna come beat in your head in front of all these cute kiddies here," Tank says, smacking the back of my skull. He holds out his hand and I clasp it as he pulls me into a one-armed hug, striking my back with a loose fist in a show of brotherly affection.

"Hey man, where you been?"

"Brisbane, Gold Coast, out west, and every shit hole town in between. Prez's got me tied up in so much shit I'm starting to reek of it."

Tank is the closest thing I've had to a friend since Ethan left. But he's not Ethan, and I'm not the same stupid kid I was. "Hit me up next time then. I could use some time away from the club; old man's breathing down my neck. Can't take a piss without him popping up to put the fuckin' chokehold on about where I am in the club and where he was at my age."

"You're a ballsy little fucker, I'll give you that, but you're not cut out for the jobs I do, man. You're too fuckin' sensitive."

"I am not fuckin' sensitive."

"Yes, ya fuckin' are." He grins. "Ain't nothing wrong with that, brother. You're just a pussy, is all."

"Fuck you."

Tank sweeps his huge arm out and playfully tags me in a head lock. I buck and writhe in his grip. With a little more pressure and a twist of his bicep he could decapitate me in the blink of an eye. I make a mental note not to ever do anything to ensure I'm handed over to his tender loving care in the future.

I'm busy looking at the ground when a pair of spiked heels attached to very long leather-clad legs stop in front of us. Beside the perfect pins, an overly-tanned pair of much shorter legs stand on equally high heels. I follow them up past a mini skirt, a midriff pink top and an average pair of tits. Her face is made up with too much gunk—too dark, too orange, too fucking Oompa Loompa. Her friend on the other hand, is the shit *Playboy* is made of—sweet curves to her hips, a toned stomach, big, fucking perfect tits nestled into a vest that's far too tight so they spill out in front. *Fuck me*. Rolling my eyes up further, I'm met with a long neck, shiny brown hair and clear brown skin—not that fake-tan shit her friend's wearing, but a creamy café au lait colour. She looks like one of those fancy fucking lattes, and I am a man dying of thirst. Pale blue eyes glare at me, but the corner of her mouth tips up in a seductive smile. I thump Tank in the kidneys again and he quickly releases me.

"Excuse me, boys," the brunette says, and Christ on a crapsicle, she has a voice like whiskey and melted butter combined. It's soft, but husky all the same, and it immediately makes me think of shoving my cock in between that perfect, full pout. A beat passes. One in which we both just stare at one another, and then, feeling some of my wits return, I quit staring and take a step towards her. She doesn't back up. We're face to face, chest to chest, fucking cock to pussy, and all I want to do is shove myself so far up inside her that I poke a hole out the other side and see daylight.

She smiles with her eyes. She smiles with every single muscle of her face. I exhale sharply. "You might wanna give me some breathing room"—She glances down at my cut, to the nametag sewn into the soft leather—"Kick."

"Baby, the only breathing room I wanna give you is when you're coming up for air after sucking me off. And even then I'd rather you just gag on it."

She laughs, but there's heat behind her gaze, and I'd bet my left nut her panties are as soaked as my dick is hard. *This bitch wants me bad.* And I'd about give my right nut to have her rolling around between my sheets, taking my cock in her mouth, and my cum in her cunt.

"You bikers are all the same. My friend Cece and I were just trying to get out of the heat and grab ourselves a drink, and here you two are, spoiling our fun with your pathetic display of machismo."

"Pathetic?" I give her an incredulous look and turn to Tank, but he and the petite blonde are already dry humping one another up against the pub wall. *Damn, that fucker works fast.* "Looks like your friend found refreshment in my brother's mouth."

"Jesus," she mutters and glances across the road to the Severed Sons MC charter, where their president — who looks about ninety in the shade — stands, arguing with a big burley dude in his thirties. His long black hair is tied back, bringing attention to his hook-like nose. Several of the Sons turn to face us.

"You an old lady?"

"No."

"Then I'm not gonna get my head beaten in for doing this?"

"Doing what?" she asks warily.

I snake my hand around her waist and pull her to me, covering my mouth with hers and kissing her with brutal force. She doesn't fight like I expected her to; instead she kisses me back, driving her tongue into my mouth before shoving me away from her and punching me square in the jaw.

"Ow!" I cup my aching jaw, flexing it side to side to ease away the sting. "What the fuck was that?"

"I didn't give you permission to touch me, much less clean out my oesophagus."

The old man and the greasy Italian dude who were arguing only moments ago, shove her out of the way and get up in my face, ready to beat my head in. "You touching my daughter, motherfucker?"

"*Your* daughter?" I glare accusingly between her and her old man. "You're a club brat?"

"Don't fucking talk to her, arsehole," the old guy says, and I'm not gonna lie, the dude's still pretty fucking scary. "Talk to me."

"I didn't know. She said she wasn't an old lady."

"Because she's the fucking Prez's daughter, you fuckwad. No dirty Angel scumbag is good enough for our girl." The big Italian dude steps closer to me, and then he glances at his president. "Can I kick his head in now?"

I give her a once over and shake my head. The bitch just fucked me silly sideways. She may not be an old lady, but she's an MC brat, and not just any MC brat, but the fucking Severed Sons' princess, which in some ways is worse than hitting on someone's old lady.

"You set me up," I accuse. She smiles again, and her whole fucking face is in on the seduction: eyes, lips, a single dimple in one cheek, everything. I gotta get this woman on the back of my bike and in my bed, because I haven't met a bitch yet that can best me at my own game.

Or I hadn't.

Until her.

"I'll get you back for this, and you'll be beggin' for me to ram my co—" I don't get to finish that sentence because the next thing I know the old dude's meaty hook is pounding in my face. He has a fist full of heavy silver rings, and I feel the sharp edges of every single one of them.

Tank is beside me in another beat, throwing full-grown men away from him. The ruckus attracts the rest of the Angels, not just our chapter, but our associates too. My dad is suddenly beside me, pulling the old coot away from me as he pounds his fist into the old bastard's face and screams, "Couldn't keep your fucking nose clean for one goddamned rally, could ya, kid?"

I king-hit the Italian, bringing him down with one hard blow to the head and glance around for the girl. I can't make out anything, not the patches of my brothers, or those from rival gangs. I turn around and see her and her friend huddled against the outside of the pub. I should leave them there. It would serve the bitch right. She doesn't look at all fazed by the violence, but her friend is squealing like a frightened piglet.

The cops are already moving in, hosing us down with a shower of batons and pepper spray. I can't see Tank anywhere in the fray, so I flee in the opposite direction, heading for the girls and taking down two motherfucking Sons that get in my way. I don't even stop when I reach them—I just clasp Blondie's hand with the princess and drag them off towards the alley. Or at least, I try to drag them off towards the alley. Princess has other ideas.

"Let go of me," she demands snatching her hand from mine.

"I'm trying to fucking help you, bitch."

"Oh, I can see that," she says caustically.

"Your dad's having some pretty new jewellery slapped on his wrists right now, Princess. What happens when a fucking hot bitch like you gets left alone with no club protection at a biker rally?"

"She screams for help," she replies, and she deafens me with an ear-splitting shriek that brings the cops running.

Motherfucker.

I go down on my knees, my hands clasped behind my head before the cops can even reach me, but the dumb fucks beat me into submission anyway. She winks at me as I'm hauled to my feet and dragged off to the paddy wagon. Fucking MC brat.

Shoulda known.

Prez, Rocker, Frogger and me spend the afternoon in lock-up while our brothers do damage control on the outside and try to bail our sorry arses out. When we're finally released around nine pm, Prez pulls me aside as the others walk towards the van. He rests two meaty hands on my shoulder and looks into my eyes.

"That shit you pulled just cost me a lot of favours, kid."

"I didn't pull any shit. One minute she was comin' on to me, and the next she just flipped and her club was laying into me. I didn't know she was the fucking princess of the Severed Sons. I mean fuck me, did you see her? How the fuck did that come from someone like the old dude?"

"Slayer had more than his fingers in some sweet ethnic pussy pies, that's how. Listen, there are bigger things in play here than you wanting to see that little bitch bouncing up and down on the end of your dick. The Sons have recently been making life hell for us. He glances at the brothers filing into the van, then lowers his voice, his eyes back on me. "See, they've taken a good deal of our profit away from that drug bust last month, they got the bitches in blue in their pocket and it's affecting Angel deals. With that shit the Banditos pulled up north, our hands are fucking tied. And that means you gotta keep clear of that pussy."

"Jeez, Prez, I'm looking to get my cock sucked. I wasn't planning on marrying her," I say, shrugging out of his hold, though truth be told, I'm fucking angrier than a cut snake. I don't know why, the bitch is no one to me, but that doesn't stop this irrational rage welling inside me at my prez's demands. I stalk towards the van and climb into the back. Tank, who'd driven out from the mountains to bail our sorry arses out, slides the van door closed as he piles in with us. Frogger, a middle-aged brother as ugly as homemade fuckin' sin, with big googly green eyes, raises a quizzical brow as he asks, "What the fuck's eatin' your knickers, boy?"

"Your old lady. I make her lick my skid-marked jocks before she reams me out." A beat passes in which Rocker bursts out laughing, and then Frogger launches himself at me, crashing us both into the side of the van. His hands slide around my throat and he smacks the back of my head into the metal siding. I laugh as he punches my already bruised face.

"Fuckin' knock it off or I'll strip both your patches," Prez yells from the front of the van as he brings us to a skidding stop, probably no more than two hundred metres from the cop shop. Tank is the one to pull Frogger off of me. His big, meaty fist yanks him back by the curls at the nape of Frogger's neck, and he slams his body into the side of the van the way Frogger just did with me. Only seeing as it's Tank, I'm guessing it was a lot harder than the way Frogger had thrown me around.

"Say fuck about my old lady again and I'll gut you in your sleep, you little prick."

I open my mouth to speak, but Tank gives me a warning look and I wind up spitting out blood onto the steel van floor instead. Tank is one huge motherfucker, and I'm not scared of him—I've taken him on before, fucking around at the Clubhouse after having a few drinks—but after having the shit kicked out of me by the Sons, taking a police baton to the head and letting Frogger give me a few good hits to the face just now, Tank would hand me my arse in three seconds flat. I'm done fighting today. I just wanna head back to the clubhouse, grab the first available bitch and let her nurse me back to health with a long, hard fuck.

And that's exactly what I do. Cindy, a skinny club whore with long dark hair, who I've never really looked at twice before now, is the first bitch I lay eyes on. I walk right up to her—as the rest of the club cheer and applaud our return from lock-up—and take hold of her hand, sliding it down into the waistband of my jeans as I kiss the corner of her mouth. My fat lip stings like a bitch, but I relish the pain anyway because it makes the pleasure of her tiny hand stroking my cock that much sweeter. I lead her to my room and I fuck her every which way possible, imagining all the while that it's that mouthy little bitch's cunt I'm driving my dick into. I punish Cindy, or Carla, or whatever the fuck her name is, the way I want to that Severed Sons club brat, and vow that one day it will be her bouncing up and down on my cock, despite the fact that my Prez just forbade it.

I gotta get inside that woman, even if I have to take a bullet to the gut for betraying my club.

I gotta get inside.

KICK

I wake to a pounding on my door and Prez's angry voice bellowing for me to open up or he's gonna kick it down, and then he's gonna kick my head in, too. I slide my arm out from underneath the woman's filthy body and stumble to the door, buck naked. I push back the lock and Prez comes barrelling into the room, bailing me up against the wall.

"You had one simple order: bring the dentist back alive, and you disobeyed it. For what? Some filthy little whore who should have been put down?"

"I know," I throw my hands up to ward him off. "I fucked up. I know. But I couldn't shoot her. I couldn't let Tank shoot her either."

He pulls a piece from the back of his jeans and turns it on her. "It's pretty fucking easy, Kick; you just aim and pull the trigger."

"Don't. Please?" I beg. I actually fuckin' drop to my knees and beg. I shake my head, knowing that I've hit an all-time low. I don't even know this bitch and I'm throwing myself at my prez's feet, begging him to spare her life. Jesus Christ, I'm a worthless, sorry fuck.

"Christ, get the fuck up." He shakes his head at me. "Saints don't fucking bend the knee for anyone. Why is this bitch so fucking important to you?"

I open my mouth to speak, but nothing comes out, because the truth is I don't know. I don't know why I saved her from one monster only to be taken into the care of another. I don't fucking know anything anymore. And I don't like it one fucking bit. I shake my head and say, "I knew someone like her once."

Prez laughs and tucks his gun away, scrubbing a hand down over his tired face. "Let me guess—this is your way of making amends for not saving that someone?"

I nod. "She needs a doctor. I shot her up with some coke so she'd sleep soundly, but it'll wear off soon, and she'll feel worse than before. She has bruises everywhere, maybe a few broken ribs. There's no telling how long he had her there."

"Fucking long time by the smell of her," Prez says. "I'll call the Butcher, but it's gonna fucking cost ya. And you're keeping her: food, clothes, all of it is on you. I can't have her running scared and straight into the open arms of the pigs. The minute she tries to run, she gets a bullet to the head. It's your job to make sure she doesn't run. You got it?"

"Yeah," I say.

He looks down at my naked body and shakes his head. "Put some fuckin' clothes on. If you're fuckin' lucky I can get the Butcher here within the hour, and you gotta get her smelling a little more like roses and perfume than shit before he'll touch her. You know he's fuckin' weird about shit like that."

"Yeah," I mutter, wondering how the hell I'm going to clean her up without losing my nut-sack.

Prez makes for the door, but he turns with his hand on the knob. "Ivy's having a full meltdown out in the fuckin' hall. You know no one can handle her shit the way you do."

Fucking Ivy. That girl doesn't need me, she needs to get clean and get as far away from men that use her up as fast as possible. She needs a rich man to keep and care for her, and she needs the best fucking psychiatrist money can buy.

I haven't slept properly for three days straight, with the exception of the nap I just took, that is, so Ivy on a comedown is the last thing I feel like dealing with today. I grab a pair of jeans that haven't seen the inside of a washing machine for far too long off the back of the recliner and pull them on. Prez turns to leave, throwing one last pitiful look at the girl in the bed.

"Prez," I say. "Thanks."

"You'll be doing a lot more than thanking me, brother. You're gonna be my bitch for the next three weeks straight for disobeying an order." When he opens the door, the sound of Ivy's screeching as she comes down fills the room. "If wishes were bullets," Prez mutters as he stalks out and walks in the opposite direction of the noise.

I step out into the hall. Ivy is rocking on the balls of her feet, her hair hanging down in sweaty limp strands in front of her face. She's shaking and chanting into the

KICK 41

crook of her arm. "Don't touch me, don't touch me. Please, stop."

I crouch down in front of her, taking hold of her arm. She yanks it away and presses herself back into the wall. "Don't fucking touch me."

"Ivy," I command in a voice that's not really my own, but some weird persona of authority that she responds to when she gets like this. It's the only fuckin' voice she responds to. You could scream and shout and even strike her, as some of the others have done when she flips out, but she just retreats further into herself. Only when I use this voice does she sit up and pay attention like a good little girl. She's told me bits and pieces of what her father did to her growing up, but none of us know the full extent of it. "Ivy, come here."

She stares at me through her tears and then scampers on her hands and knees into my lap. I stroke her hair and marvel that this is the second naked broken chick I've comforted in my lap today. I'm beginning to feel like the fucking psychotic woman whisperer. Ivy sobs into my lap, clutching my jeans and leaving a wet patch from her tears. "What happened, baby?"

"Don't leave me, Kick. Don't replace me with her. I'll do whatever you want. I'll be whoever you want, but don't replace me. Please? I'll die without you."

I stroke her hair and sigh. She doesn't mean it. This is the comedown talking. It's the same every time, only most of the time she calls me *daddy* and begs for me to put her over my knee to show her how much I really love her. I don't say anything; how can I? By allowing her to behave this way, by taking her the way I do, by being the only brother who will care for her after I've fucked her senseless, I know I've enabled her behaviour. I've allowed it. Encouraged it. I've become her crutch.

The problem is that I've never seen Ivy as a long-term fixture. I've never looked at anyone but *her* that way. It's not my intention to replace Ivy with the woman in my bed; I don't even know if the woman in my bed is going to be stable enough to endure a friggin' conversation, let alone a lifetime in the MC. One thing's for sure, though—if she can't abide the life, she's as dead as she was in that warehouse, because there ain't no way Prez is letting her leave this compound. I should have killed her. Instead, I've condemned her to a life of monsters, of turning to drugs to dull the pain. And while I didn't do these things to Ivy, she came to the club of her own accord, I certainly haven't helped her in any way. I gave her what she needed because it benefitted me. I could get my dick sucked and live out my wretched rape fantasies with someone who couldn't get off any other way, but that's not the same as helping her.

I sit on the worn carpet that reeks of years' worth of soiled boots and smoke, and I rock her in my arms. I stroke her hair until she falls asleep, and then I scoop her up and tap on Tank's door.

He opens it, a beer in one hand and an unimpressed look on his face. "What?"

"Can she sleep here?"

"If she's finished fucking wailing like a little kid she can. I can't do strung-out bitches with tears."

"Don't be a fuck-stick, man. She's messed up."

"She's a drug addict, Kick. She might be better looking than the junkies you find on the street, but she's still fucked every which way from Sunday if she doesn't get a hit."

"She means a lot to me, Tank." I lay her down on the soiled covers and step back from the bed. "I don't expect you to understand that shit, 'cause you've never cared about anyone but yourself—"

"I cared enough about you not to blow your head off when you said you'd gunned down our entire chapter of the Angels, didn't I?"

I scrub at my beard. "I still haven't worked out why that was. But yeah, I guess."

"I get it, you have this hero complex with these bitches, but you gotta know when to cut your losses. She's a great lay, but she'll fuck with your head, brother. They all do. And neither one of these bitches is Lauren. We both know that."

"I'm not fucking substituting," I shout, and then I lower my voice when Ivy jolts in her sleep. "I know they're not her. No one knows that more than me."

"I'm just lookin' out for you, brother." He shakes his head and grins, pointing towards Ivy's naked body. "You already got your hands full with this one. Another bitch in your bed isn't going to help anyone."

"Let me worry about who's in my bed."

He holds up his hands and flops down beside Ivy, slapping her bum. "She does have a fucking incredible arse, though."

Tank unzips his fly and shoves his jeans down his legs. He climbs on top of her body, engulfing her tiny frame completely, and ignoring her sleepy protests as he spits on his dick and rubs himself between her arse cheeks.

"You gonna watch, brother? Or are you gonna get

the fuck out?"

"Don't kick her out this time, arsehole. Try being fuckin' human for once." I shake my head and retreat to my room.

Opening the door, I see she's still asleep, so I deadbolt it behind me and set the keys on the table. I pick up a cup of cold, stale, black coffee and chug it down. It tastes like shit, so I screw the cap off of a bottle of Jack and chase the black filth with the burn of amber. I set it back on the table while the familiar click of my gun being cocked echoes through my small room. I laugh. *Fucking ballsy bitches make me hot.*

"Hands in the air, and turn around. Slowly," the woman says through a scratchy throat. I do as she asks, mostly because I want to keep my spine intact, but also partly because bitches with guns are fucking hot, and I'm hard as a rock just thinking about the way she's gonna look with a pistol trained on me.

She's been busy while I was out, rummaging through my drawers and finding a pair of loose tracksuit pants. They're rolled at the waist, so much that it makes her look pregnant. That, combined with her crazy fuckin' cat lady hair and the filth covering her body, makes her look like a homeless person.

I smile and clasp my hands behind my head. Her eyes rove over me, taking in my size. She's checking me for the arsenal I so obviously have stashed away in my fucking worn, faded jeans. She's not checking me out and dreaming about me taking her rough and hard on my fucking scratched-up dining table, but I still get a fucking boner out of having her eyes roam all over me.

"Pick up the keys, and open the door," she

commands.

"If you run, they'll shoot you."

"Pick up the fucking keys."

I snatch up the keys and lob them at her, hard enough that she has to twist out of the way. She cries out as she does, proving to me that her ribs are definitely injured, maybe even cracked. I lunge at her. Shoving her back against the bed, I land on top of her, warding off her blows with one hand and squeezing her wrist with the other until she drops the gun on the floor.

"Get off me!" she screams.

"You're not leaving this clubhouse," I whisper in her ear as she struggles beneath me. "The best you can hope for is to play nice and I might decide to keep you as a house mouse. But if you piss me off, and if you pull on me with my own gun again, your life will be so much worse. You thought the dentist was fucked up? Baby, you haven't seen anything until you've lived inside my fantasies for a day. So if I were you, I'd be really fuckin' careful about how you play your next move."

She stops kicking, and I push up and off the bed. She's gasping, her face twisted in pain, her body practically fucking vibrating with fury as she glares up at me.

"Get up," I command. "You smell like shit."

She rears her leg back and kicks me in the stomach, I stagger back, thankful that her aim is shithouse and that she didn't get me in the nuts. Twisting on the mattress, she reaches for the gun, but I'm on her before she slides her arm over the bed. I twist it back behind her, pushing the weight of my knee into her back. She screams. I hate that it makes me harder than fucking diamonds, but that fucked up part of me loves it too.

"I will fucking end you, bitch," I whisper as she sobs into the filthy bed sheet. Keeping her arm twisted up at a painful angle, I stand and pull her up with me. She screams as her ribs and likely her whole body protest the movement. Looping my arm around her waist, I heft her against my chest and walk her forward to the bathroom as she bucks and kicks her feet out at thin air. She thrusts both arms out and latches onto the door jamb, trying to gain traction. I push forward. Right now, I don't give a shit about her injuries. I shove her into the bathroom. She loses her balance and falls into the wall beside the toilet. Slamming the door with my foot and locking it behind me, I keep my eyes on her as I run the shower. She's trembling, but there's also a fierce determination in her eyes as she glares at me while she sobs.

"I can do this all day, sweetheart, so either you get over here and get in the shower like a civilized human being, or I drag you in, but either way you're getting naked and cleaned beneath that spray."

"Fuck you."

"Not while you're smelling like that, Little Spitfire."

"You should have killed me, when you had the chance."

"Oh there's still time." I lunge for her, pulling her up by her midsection, dodging the way she thrashes and strikes out with her small fists and bony elbows. I struggle with her all the way to the shower and then I shove her inside the tub and under the spray. She lurches forward, but I'm done playing games. My temper is never very far from the surface these days and this bitch is pushing all my buttons. I climb into the tub with her, not caring that I'm getting soaked in my jeans. She tries to run, but I slam her lithe body up against the tiled wall, wrapping my hand tightly around her throat. "Listen to me. I'm trying to help you. If you walk out that door, there's ten men ready and waiting to put a bullet between your eyes. You'll be dead before you can clear the clubhouse parking lot. I'm your only fucking chance at survival; you got that?"

I grab the hem of the hoodie and yank it up over her head. She begins screaming again, thrashing and raking her nails over my hard chest. I don't blame her, but I don't let it faze me either. The butcher won't look at her if she isn't clean, and for a doctor who had his medical license revoked for dismembering female genitalia, he's pretty fucking weird about that shit.

I throw the soaking hoodie towards the bin and yank off the pants. They fall around her ankles, almost tripping her up as I shove her back underneath the shower. My hand wraps around her delicate throat as she thrashes beneath the stream. Water invades her mouth and nose. I pull her towards me and whisper, "Either you can behave like a big girl and wash yourself, or I'll do it for you, but either way this shit is getting done."

"Go fuck yourself." She spits, like actually motherfuckin' spits in my face. Seething, I grab the soap, and rub it vigorously over her bruised body as she shrieks and fights against me. Her screams hurt my ears in the small bathroom. I shove the cake of soap in her mouth and hold her jaw tightly closed with my hand clasped over her lips and chin, gagging her with it.

"Shut. The. Fuck. Up," I say and wrench my hand free. She coughs, spitting out the soap and retching up the empty contents of her stomach. I don't let that stop my assault. I yank her head back and scrub the soap over her neck and shoulders, aggravating the tender wounds, and poking deliberately at old bruises that show their distaste for being touched. I rub it over her swollen face as she sobs through her hair.

Reaching around her to the shower caddy I pull the shampoo from the shelf. It's only that two-in-one generic shit from the supermarket, but it'll do the job. I empty the shampoo into my palm and rub my hands together, and then I do something I've never done for anyone. I wash the bitch's motherfucking hair. It's not like it is in those cheesy fucking romance films. It's disgusting, and it takes two times through of vigorous scrubbing to get the crusted blood and filth out, and my dick is hard as fucking nails the entire time. I think of wrapping her hair around my fists, jerking her head back as I shove my cock inside her from behind, and I have to step away from her bruised body before I give in and take whatever the fuck I want, *however the fuck I want.*

Her hair is a deep chestnut, and now that it's not matted and sticking out at all angles, it's glossy and plastered to her back. I reach out and run my fingers through it. She stiffens, and I can almost taste her fear. I pull her into me, wrapping my arms tightly around her waist. She tries wrenching herself free, but I tighten my hold and grind my hard-on against her arse. I use my free hand and drive my fingers between her legs, separating her lips. I could pretend I'm just washing her pussy as thoroughly as I washed the rest of her body, but we'd both know that's not true. I soap up my hand and circle her arse with my fingertips. She flinches. She fights. Of course she fights. That's the thing that made me want her in the first place. Her defiance. Her fight.

She gasps for breath, a visceral, wounded animal sound tearing from her throat. I loosen my hold. Her hands claw at me, scratching, seeking flesh to inflict pain upon. That's a feeling, a need I know well. And I let her fulfil it, because I know better than anyone that that need doesn't ever go away, not once you've been arse raped by the world, not once the violence seeps into your pores and under your skin, blacking out all of the goodness within.

"You should have left me there. You should have let me die," she sobs as she turns away from me and sinks down to the bath floor, sitting in the pool of filth as the water beats down over her head and washes her clean. "I just wanna die. Just let me die."

I stare down at her, feeling like an arsehole for not having been able to put a bullet in her brain when I found her there in that chair. It would have been kinder. I freed her and brought her back to the club with me because I'm selfish. I'm fucked up. I'm a vicious cunt who thinks only of his own torment and pain.

Leaning over her, I press my forehead into the wall. Ending this misery for her would be as simple as opening the door and letting her walk out into that clubhouse, but I can't. I can't, because I didn't save the one woman who mattered. I can't, because I don't want to. I can't, because the same thing inside me, inside Ivy, is inside this woman too, and she might hate me for now, but she'll come to realise quickly that the fucked up ones gravitate towards each other like magnets. Darkness doesn't seek out the light. It smothers the light, and it revels in the light's death. And there is nothing more dangerous than darkness that doesn't have an outlet.

I am a monster. Not because I'm a product of my environment, or because I like to hurt women. I am a monster because I choose to embrace my darkness—I revel in it and nurture it like it's a newborn. I feed it regularly from the suffering of others, because that's what I do: I make those I love suffer. I betray everyone who ever wrongly put their trust in me. And at the end of the day, this girl will be no different.

Because that's my special power; that's the one thing I'm truly good at—betrayal.

KICK

I don't know how long we stay beneath the spray, with me bent over her body protectively. It'd be nice if I could protect her from myself, but that's about as likely to happen as me coming clean to the club about killing the Angels. After a while I grab her wrist and pull her up to a standing position. She flinches and tries to struggle free, but I only tighten my grasp.

"I know you're hurt. I can help you. You just need to trust me."

She laughs. An outright, motherfucking, this-bitch-is-crazy laugh. She laughs until she breaks down sobbing again, her tears washed away by the warm water pounding us. Her face is frozen in a mask of anguish—her mouth open and eyes tightly shut. Saliva runs out over her chin, but that too is washed away. I want to comfort her; I wanna tear at her flesh, slam her up against the tiles and fuck the shit out of her bruised cunt, but I don't do any of those things. I just stare at her, not knowing what the fuck to do.

Finally, I decide kindness is probably much worse in this situation than brutality is. She's used to brutality. I'd say it's all she's known for a good long while now.

I shut off the water and climb from the tub, throwing the only available towel at her. It's old, and drying yourself with the scratchy fibres sucks, but this ain't the fucking Ritz. She just stands there; she doesn't even catch the towel and it falls into the bath, soaking up the remaining water in the tub. I shuck off my soaking wet jeans as she covers herself from my view with her bony arms.

Did she forget I just had my rough calloused hands all over her tight little body? I reach for her, and she skitters back against the wall. I sigh. Jesus Christ. I'm gonna start fucking shooting up like Ivy soon just to be able to deal with this shit storm.

The woman slaps at my arms to ward me away, but I clench my jaw, wrap my hands around her waist and yank her towards me, and out of the bathtub. I set her down roughly on the mat as I unlock the door and shove her into the room. I stalk naked over to the edge of the bed and pick up the gun, then I empty out the magazine and set the gun and the clip on the table.

The room is always stifling after a shower. With no windows and a pretty shitty central air-conditioning system the clubhouse is stuffy as fuck, and we have to rely on the small ventilation fan above the shower to suck up the steam. Of course I didn't remember to turn that fucker on because of the crazy bitch I had to wrangle into my shower.

I turn to the beaten-up old dresser and pull out a

new pair of jeans. Sliding them on, I turn and look at her. Her eyes are downcast, her arms still attempting to hide her body from view. "What's your name, Little Spitfire?"

She glares through bloodshot, puffy eyes, dropping her gaze to the gun. I quirk a brow and tilt my head towards it, daring her to take it. She doesn't; she just glares at me.

"What's your name?"

"Go fuck yourself," she whispers. A beat passes. One in which the old wounds left by *her* open up again, rending my heart open. I'm reminded of a conversation I had with a girl that sounded very much like this one, and looked almost exactly like this one, too. Only her skin was a pretty latte colour, and this girl's is pale.

"That's a nice name," I whisper, echoing words from what seem like a lifetime ago.

KICK

TWO YEARS AGO

I push Cindy, or Kim, or whatever the fuck her name is off of my dick the minute I finish cuming and collapse on my bed beside her. She lets out a sexy little moan and crawls up the mattress, lying down flat on her stomach.

"God, the way you fuck is incredible, Daniel."

I fucking hate this part. I mean, really? Could she come up with something any more unoriginal? Was it the four orgasms I just gave her that gave it away? I hate this part because all I want is for her to take her skanky-arsed pussy out of my room and away from my bed before she gets cum all over my fucking sheets. But I don't kick her out; maybe it's cause I'm lonely, or maybe I'm just too fucking lazy to point towards the door. Either way, the bitch is taking up space in my bed, and even though I hate it, I couldn't be fucked doing shit about it.

"It's Kick," I say, rolling onto my back and pulling

a smoke from the bedside table. I light it up and take a deep drag, blowing out smoke rings. "Only my friends call me Daniel, and you are not my friend."

"Well we seemed pretty friendly a moment ago," the whore says. She snatches my cigarette and draws the smoke into her lungs. I don't try and reclaim it. The butt has ruby red lipstick all over it and I have no desire to have this whore's mouth anywhere near mine. Instead, I close my eyes and let the pull of post-orgasmic bliss drag me under.

Seconds later, some arsehole is pounding on my door.

"What?" I shout, waking up the club whore next to me. She groans and buries her head beneath the pillow.

"Time for church, kid."

Ah, fuck, my goddamned dad. I'm gonna get a fucking arse-rimming about the stunt I pulled at the rally. My dad, Robert Johnson, aka Juke, has never beaten around the bush about his desire for a better son. All my life he's told me how inferior I am, how unworthy I am of the patch, and how Ethan has always shown more promise as a prospect than I ever did. But Ethan is a traitor, a rat—at least in the club's eyes. They don't know he never sold us out; he just traded his cut for his freedom, and by the looks of the girl he was shacking up with, I'd say it was the smartest move he ever made. The club don't know about any of that, though if they did, I'd be dead, because I shot my VP in the back to save the friend who abandoned me and I took a beating to help the bastard escape. I guess I really am unworthy of the patch I wear because I chose a civilian over the brotherhood. I chose Ethan, and I'd do it again because he is more family to me than the rest of the brotherhood has ever been.

"Sometime today, arsehole," Juke hollers, banging on the door.

"I'm comin'," I shout back, bolting out of bed and sliding into a pair of stained jeans, a black T-shirt and my cut. "Hold your fucking horses, Dad. Jesus."

I slap the club whore on the arse. "Get up. I got business."

"Go sort your business. I'll be here waiting when you get back." She gyrates against the mattress, and yeah, her arse is tempting, but been there, done that, probably got the fucking clap to prove it.

I take hold of her arm and yank her upright.

"Ow, you're hurting me." She claws at my hand, attempting to free her wrist. I stalk towards the door and open it, depositing her arse in the hallway, buck naked. "Jeez, you're an arsehole, Kick."

"I learned everything I know from dear old dad here," I say, folding my arms and setting my gaze on my father. He looks just like me, but older: blue eyes, dirty blond hair, full sleeves, blond scruff, and like he's spent twenty years doing hard time. He didn't, of course. My father's too smart to be caught by the boys in blue, and he'll tell you, too. Every fucking chance he gets.

I step into the hall and pull my keys out of my jeans, locking the door behind me.

"Can I at least get my clothes?" she whines, standing now and covering herself from our eyes like she's the Virgin fucking Mary.

"Door's locked, sweetheart," I say and fold my arms over my chest again. This is sort of a defence mechanism when my dad's around. I've done it since I was a kid, and try as I might, I've never been able to stop.

Juke chuckles at the club whore—or maybe he's chuckling at me. I don't know. I don't fucking care. My father pulls the whore at my door towards him, mauling the face off of the bitch I just fucked. He's such a fucktard. Everything is a goddamned competition with him, and he bests me every fucking time. He makes sure of it.

When he pulls away, the bitch is gasping for breath. Her nipples are hard and her eyes are hungry, not for me, but for my old man. My stomach roils.

"Go wait in my room, Clara. Get that pussy warmed up and ready for me, baby. I'm gonna pull out all the shit I didn't teach junior, here." Juke smacks her arse and she giggles as she traipses down the hall. *Fuckin' trollop.*

My father turns to me with a smug smile. If I could bury my fingers in his eye sockets and still keep my kidneys intact, I would, but attacking another member unprovoked and without a club vote is suicide.

"So what's the prez need help with now? Wiping his fuckin' arse?"

Juke sucker punches me, right in the gut, no holds barred. The fucker hits me as hard as he would anyone. I bend double, coughing up my guts as he towers over me. "Show some fuckin' respect."

"Fuck you," I wheeze, squeezing my eyes tightly closed in preparation for a knee to the face. It doesn't come, and when I'm done hacking up my insides I straighten.

"What the fuck is taking you two so long?" Prez's voice rings out from the end of the hall. Juke and I both turn to him.

"Just teaching the boy some manners, Prez."

Prez smirks. "Seems like he should be old enough to have that shit down already. Now come the fuck on, I got a job for you."

"You need me, Prez?" Daddy douche asks. I don't know how my dad got his road name. I don't much care either, but mine is a constant source of embarrassment for him. A kid with bikes in his blood, a third generation Angel who couldn't remember to put up the fucking kickstand before taking off in front of a couple of insanely hot chicks is as much of an embarrassment to my old man as if I'd been born mongoloid, or black, or gay.

Dear old dad is a raving racist, homophobic bigot.

"You got someplace else you need to be?" Prez asks.

"Yeah, eatin' out my sloppy seconds," I say to Prez with a smirk. The next thing I know I'm shoved up against the wall, Juke has his hand wrapped around my throat and oxygen is in very limited supply. He tightens his grasp and gets all up in my face as I claw and buck against his hands. I might be half his age but my father is stronger than me; he makes sure of it. He's stronger in every way, and he never misses a chance to make sure I know it, either.

"Put the kid down."

Juke doesn't listen. Instead, he squeezes harder. His gaze is unrelenting and intent. If he thought he could get away with squeezing the life out of me right here in front of our prez, he would. I can see it written all over his face. I've felt it since the day I was born.

"That's a fucking order, Juke." My father drops me

KICK

and I slide down the wall, gasping for each precious breath. I shoot daggers up at him, but it makes no difference. Juke Johnson has never been afraid of a bug he could squash so easily under his boot.

"Round up the rest of the brothers and head on up to church. I need Kick's help on something."

"You do?" Juke asks, his brow pinched tightly with unease.

"I just said I did, didn't I? Now get the fuck outta here."

Juke shoots me a black look and wanders off up the hall, slamming his fist against every bedroom door on the way and calling the brothers to church.

"You alright?" Prez asks, holding out a hand and helping me to my feet.

"Yeah, nothing I haven't seen, heard, and felt before," I mutter. I follow Prez down the empty hall in the opposite direction from my father. Unease pricks at my skin as we walk out of the back entrance and down a flight of stairs that lead to a locked door. My heart pounds as he punches in a key code and we enter the dimly lit room. It's a small entryway, barely big enough for the two of us, but it's not the confined space that has the hair standing on the back of my head—it's what the dark hallway beckoning before us represents. All four rooms have their doors closed, but only one has its light on. I can see through the crack beneath the door. I throw Prez a panicked look over my shoulder. I've seen these rooms only one other time, when Ethan's dad Tiny betrayed the club. He was trussed up like a fucking Christmas ham, had his Angels tat burnt clean off of his back. And then he was gutted like an animal, his stomach and intestines spilling out over the concrete floor as he writhed and gasped like a fish on the hook. It was brutal, by far the worst thing I've ever witnessed, and when you grow up inside the MC you know brutal, inside out and back to fucking front.

He knows.

He knows I betrayed the brotherhood. He knows I shot Rocker in the back to save Ethan.

I take a step back and barrel into him, but his arms wrap around me like a vice. "Hey, hey, hey, where you goin', kid?"

He's going to kill me, though it wouldn't be a quick and painless death. The president of the Angels doesn't do quick and painless. No. He likes to stretch that shit out, savour his revenge. My heart pounds against my chest, seeking a way out of its meat and bone cage.

"Start walkin'," Prez commands. For a moment I just stand there, anticipating his next move, marking mine. And then slowly I take a step forward, and another, and another until I'm standing before the closed door of the only room in this underground torture chamber to not be sitting in complete darkness.

In the past when a brother has betrayed us, the entire club has been present. They stand guard and watch on stone-faced as the brother is stripped of their patch, their tattoos, and their dignity.

I don't know why he's doing this alone, unless they're not planning on telling the club anything. Unless he wants my death to be as quick and unmemorable as taking out the fucking garbage. A part of me doesn't blame him. If I were in his shoes, I'd annihilate me too.

"Quit fuckin' around and open the door, Kick,"

KICK

Prez says. Despite the pounding in my head and heart, despite the synapses firing a warning to every single cell in my damn body, I reach for the handle and turn it. Unsurprisingly the door is unlocked, and I'm met with no resistance. I push into the space, with fear and hatred and so much loathing for myself; for my dad being the one to indoctrinate me into this fucked-up family; for Ethan for getting me into this mess; and even for my prez, for getting to be the fucker to end my life with a single bullet to the back of the head and then go home to his loving wife and children.

My life doesn't so much flash before my eyes as it becomes a slowly spinning cycle of images — my dad's disappointment, the whore who birthed me lying dead in a pool of her own vomit after ODing, my six-year-old self not giving enough of a crap about her to even pick up the phone and try calling my father. When he'd come to see us three days later I was passed out on the lounge room floor, the remnants of a box of Cocoa Pops littered all around and cartoons blaring. My mother had never liked the TV; not because she thought it would rot my brain, like most other mums, but because she was never sober long enough to understand that what was playing out before her wasn't real. The first time I'd met Ethan and given him shit about his mum's prim and proper outfit, I'd copped a blow to the face for that one, and a broken nose. The truth was, I was jealous. I saw how his dad doted on him, how his whole family was this perfect well put-together — albeit mostly outlaw — package that I had never had, and I hated him for it. I'd been looking to stir shit, and stir shit I had. He'd smacked me out in front of everyone at an Angels' barbeque; I'd repaid the favour. Our fathers had thought it was fucking hilarious, and after the rest of the families had gone home Ethan and I were pulled aside and pitted against one another time after time, the promise of Harley's and the brotherhood dangled before us like bait on a hook. After that it was flashes of various club whores, stealing shit with Ethan, crashing cars and running riot on a town that held endless possibilities for two wannabe outlaw teenage thugs.

Prez pushes me forward into the room and I'm met with the wall of muscle that is Tank, my brother, the only brother who knows me the way Ethan once did. The only friend I have left in the world, and the only man Prez calls in to do the shit that others won't. I guess if it has to be anyone, it should be him. Him or Moose. Maybe even both.

Tank stares down at me sympathetically, pressing his lips together, his huge arms folded in front of his chest, he looks hesitant, and goddamn it, this may just be the only time I've ever seen him show remorse.

Beyond Tank, I can hear a muffled cry, and I glare up at him then behind me at Prez, trying to figure out what the hell is going on. Both glare back, stone-faced, unrelenting in their fucking crypticness. For a half second I fear the noises might be coming from Ethan. Perhaps they've captured him and have him tied up down here too, ready to dish out as much pain to him as to me.

At least I can say assuredly that my dear old dad's loyalty would never waver. For him it's always been the club; he could give two fucks about his bastard son. I give a smug nod of satisfaction when I realise this is the one thing my father has wanted since the day I was born — to snuff out the life of his arsehole, good-for-nothing son, to erase all trace of me and his ties to the stupid junkie whore I called a mother. I smile up at Tank because I know that as much as my father has always wanted this, he'll never be the one to get to do it. And that fills me with a sense of joy and courage that I've never felt in my twenty-seven years.

"Well, move out of the fuckin' way and let the kid into the room, arsehole," Prez barks, and Tank steps aside to let me see the room beyond him.

In the corner is a girl, definitely not Ethan, but not unfamiliar either. Her long legs are wrapped in leather, she's barefoot and gagged, and her face is a little banged up, but she still looks every bit as fuckable as she did when I was handcuffed and beaten with a baton by police at her feet last night.

She glares up at me and screams a long line of profanities — at least, I think that's what she's shouting behind her gag.

I spin around and glare at Prez. "What the fuck is she doing here? Are you insane?"

My heart is racing now for a different reason. What in the fuck is he thinking, abducting the fuckin' princess of the Severed Sons and stowing her on Angel property?

Prez shoots me a hard glare and steps out around me, heading for the girl. She shakes her head and yanks on the restraints binding her arms behind her back. Prez pulls his blade from the sheath on his buckle as he approaches her. The girl whimpers.

"Your daddy's been fuckin' shit up for me for a long time, sweetheart. Think it's time I pay back the favour."

"Prez," I venture. "She's got nothin' to do with it."

"But she does, Kick. See, Slayer's been fuckin' my shit up for too long."

"She's innocent."

Prez stands and whirls around to face me. "This is why I wanted you here, boy, because you're too fuckin' innocent. You wanna be worthy of that patch I gave you, then you gotta be willin' to do whatever it takes to prove you're an Angel. And Angels don't let the scourge of the fuckin' earth dictate what deals they can and can't make. Angels rise above all those other fuckers." He smiles at me, and dread creeps its way up my spine. "It's time to spread your wings, kid. Time to show Slayer what happens when you fuck with Angels. This pretty little bitch is gonna be my plaything, and you and Tank here are gonna watch her for me. Make sure she doesn't fly the fuckin' coop."

Prez hooks two fingers in around her gag and yanks it out of her mouth. She screams, and the bitch has to have the biggest set of lungs on her I've ever heard, but it won't do her any good, not down here.

"Scream all you want, little darlin'. Ain't no one gonna hear you down here. Except Kick and Tank, that is. Hell, if he's a good dog, I might even let little lover boy over there have a piece of this fine, sweet arse." Prez shoves his hand under her arse and squeezes hard. She tries jerking free, but he's not letting her go far.

"My father's going to find me and then he's going to come fuck you up," she says, and fuck me if I'm not fucking rock-hard by the determined look in her eyes already.

"Hear that, boys? Slayer's gonna fuck our shit up for

hurtin' his little girl." Prez grins, and then turns back to the woman. "I'm counting on it, sweet girl."

He leans in, getting up in her face. I can't hear what he's whispering, but I know it's not good. The girl rears back and head-butts the president of the Angels. The blow makes them both sway. Her eyes gleam with tears. Prez reels back, shaking his head free of the pain, I imagine. For a half-second he just blinks at her, eyes wide, mouth slackened with surprise, and then the tension in the room explodes as he comes up on his knees and backhands her across the cheek. Her head rocks back into the wall so hard that the sound of her skull hitting the brick is audible.

I don't think; just act.

I lurch forward, but I'm stopped by a wall of muscle. *Tank.* Tank is standing between me and my prez, between him and the blade in my hand that I have no recollection of pulling. Beyond him I hear her. The sound of a struggle, muffled grunts, the sick sound of flesh pounding flesh, and the terrified shrieks that follow as he lays into her with his fists. The scuffle as she fights to get away from him, and the sobbing that bores through my head like a fucking drill.

Tank eyes the knife in my hand. "You gonna use that thing, brother?" He doesn't bother to whisper. Prez is otherwise occupied, and her cries prove it.

"Get out of the way," I whisper, trying to sum up in my head all the ways I could take down the man in front of me. Truth is, if it were anyone else I probably could, but not Tank. No one takes down Tank.

"Think about this, man," he whispers. "You gonna go up against the prez over some bitch you don't know?"

I don't answer, I lunge instead, but Tank is a better fighter than me—he always has been. He's bigger and better in every way, and I'm caught up in his huge arms as he holds me back and forces me to watch my prez, the man who is supposed to lead us, the man who has been a better father to me than my own, shoving himself inside an innocent girl. A girl I wanted, a girl I had—no, a girl I *have* to have.

Struggling in Tank's hold, I scream, and I fight, but I'm as useless as tits on a fucking bull, just like my father told me I was all these years.

I can't see her face. Her cheek is shoved against the filthy concrete, facing the wall as Prez holds her down and fucks her from behind. I've fucked plenty of women this way before, hog-tied them and ignored their pleas when they begged me to stop, but it wasn't real. Their cries were met with harder thrusts, and their bodies betrayed their protests by cuming harder and faster than they had with anyone else. Those bitches left with breathy thanks and promises on their lips to return.

This is nothing like that, and still as I stand, rendered immobile by Tank, and unable to free myself, I can't look away, because I'm rock-fucking-hard inside my jeans, and a part of me wishes more than anything that I could trade places with Prez. I wish that I was the one filling her, and tearing her up from the inside. That's the really sick thing about it; that I'm just as hard as he is right now, watching this woman get raped.

Guilt consumes me, twisting my guts like a slab of rotten meat full of hungry maggots. I close my eyes, but I see the two of them burned into the inside of my lids: Prez on top of her, holding her down, his dick slick with blood and spit as he thrusts inside her, again and again while the woman kicks and bucks her hips, trying to unseat him.

I've seen violence. I've lived and breathed it since I was a baby. I've been shrouded in hurt, and pain, and other people's anguish for the longest time that I dared to think I was immune.

I'd thought I was safe from it. But no one in the club is ever safe; no one ever would be. Because the second you let your guard down, some motherfucker's gonna seize the opportunity to fuck you over. Especially those closest to you. Especially those you trusted.

Prez gives one final thrust, groaning as he rides out his orgasm, and sags on top of her. Beneath his bulky frame, the girl trembles. Her breathing is too shallow, too stunted. Prez rolls off of her and stands, zipping up his leathers. He pulls a pack of smokes from his pocket and lights up. The acrid stench of tar and nicotine burns my nostrils. The contents of my stomach threaten to make a reappearance.

Prez takes the few short steps towards me and glances down at my unsheathed knife that had fallen on the floor during the scuffle with Tank. He bends down and scoops it up, turning it over in his palm, testing its weight. He thrusts it towards me, just missing my arm. I don't flinch; of course I don't. Flinching would make me a pussy, and I am a lot of things, but a pussy isn't one of them.

"You got some geriatric condition I don't know about, kid?" he asks.

I don't respond because I know there's more coming, and truth be told I don't know if I can speak without losing my shit altogether.

"'Cause I can't figure how your knife came to be on the floor, at my back."

He holds the blade out and I gingerly take it from his outstretched hand. It would be so easy just to flip it around in my hand and drive it into his stomach, but with Tank here I'd be dead within seconds, because you don't betray your brotherhood, and you sure as shit don't fucking drive a knife through the belly of your prez for a bitch you hardly know. I sheath the knife and glare at him. He pulls the cigarette from his lips, and a long cylinder of ash falls away to nothing, dispersing into the air around us. Prez grabs hold of my arm, yanking me towards him and pinning my elbow in a lock that could see him breaking it if I were to try and twist free. He watches my face, grinning like a madman as he pushes the lit cigarette into my flesh at the crook of my elbow and drags it upward. White-hot pain sluices up my arm. I grit my teeth, my rage rising, building inside me like a tsunami tide, begging to be unleashed on this motherfucker. I suck in a deep breath through my nostrils, my hands clenched tightly into fists and my skin on fire as Prez draws the lit cigarette up my arm, leaving perfect circular little weals of burnt skin behind before finally stubbing it out in the centre of my bicep, destroying the thick black shading of my eight-ball tat.

Prez releases me. I'm filled with fury and hate and hot, searing pain. Inside, there's a beast raging in its cage, beating its fists against my meat and bones, demanding to be unleashed, but I stand stock-still, arms fisted loosely at my sides.

"Pull a knife on me again and I will fuck up every

inch of that pretty-boy face of yours," Prez says. "I won't leave so much as a centimetre unscarred, you got me, kid?"

"Yeah," I say through gritted teeth.

"Yeah fuckin' what?"

"Yeah, Prez. I fuckin' got you."

"Good boy." He slaps my arm in a brotherly gesture, applying pressure over the burning flesh he just mutilated. It hurts like a motherfucker, but I won't give him the satisfaction of seeing that pain reflected on my face. "Now get this bitch cleaned up for round fuckin' two. It's time you showed me where your loyalties lie."

He brushes past me, out through the door, followed closely by Tank. The door slams closed, echoing through the small unfurnished room, and I'm left staring at the trembling girl he left broken on the concrete floor, wondering how the hell I'm supposed to pick up the fucking pieces, knowing all the while that I'd prefer her broken down and bleeding before me, because that's who I am, the harbinger of torment. Just like my president, just like every other worthless piece-of-shit motherfucker in the world. I am no different from them; I'm just better at playing pretend.

KICK

I stare at the woman. She hasn't moved since we left the en suite. She stares back, still covering her bruised body with her skinny arms.

"What's your name?" I ask again, and then pause, giving her a sideways glare. "Your real name?"

"Kayla."

"You got a last name?"

"Kennedy."

Fuck. This bitch has been missing for three weeks straight.

"Not anymore. From now on, you're Indie."

"My name is Kayla," she says through gritted teeth.

"Your name is whatever I say it is, you got that?" I snap. "Kayla is dead; I knew there was a reason you looked familiar." *Besides being the spitting image of Lauren, that is.* "Your face has been splashed across every paper in the country. You've been missing for three weeks. Your family is looking for you."

She sucks in a sharp, sobbing breath and crouches down on the shitty carpet, collapsing into a ball of shaking limbs and more fucking tears than either of us know what to do with. *Christ, even Ivy doesn't cry this fucking much.*

"I just wanna go home, please? I won't say anything to anyone. I'll … I'll pretend I didn't know where I was. I won't say a thing about the others. I'll keep my mouth shut—"

"What. Others?" I demand, stalking over to her side and yanking her up from the floor. I shake her, hard. "What others?"

She sobs, twisting and fighting against my grip. Her hands grapple for purchase on my arms, her nails dig into my flesh, but she's weak, and the pain is as insignificant as her life is to my club brothers.

"Start fucking talking, bitch," I demand.

"There were more."

I shake her again. "More what?"

"More than just the dentist. There were two more men."

"Fuck," I shout and release her. "Who?"

She shakes her head. "I don't know."

"Who?" I demand.

"A cop …" she sobs, as I shake her again. "A cop, and a priest."

A cop, a dentist, and a priest all walk into a bar …

"Jesus fucking Christ."

A loud banging forces both our heads to snap towards the door. Goddamn it. Not now. I let the girl go but I'm surprised when she grabs hold of my shirt sleeve as I turn away from her.

"Who is that?"

"That's the Butcher." I glance down at her tiny fist, clutching the fabric of my shirt. She looks at her hand too, only it's as though she has no idea what the hell it's doing yanking on my sleeve. Quickly, she retracts it.

"The Butcher?" she whispers.

"He's a doctor. He's coming to look you over."

"I don't need a doctor," she whimpers. "I just need to go home." She repeats that last phrase over and over as she backs away from me and presses herself tight against the wall.

"You were just raped and tortured for a three-week period. You're seein' a fucking doctor."

I scoop my keys up off the table and head for the door. Ramming the keys into the lock, I pull it back to find the Butcher, Tank and Prez standing in the hall. The butcher is a tiny little man. He wears neatly pressed pants and a blue button-up shirt beneath a fucking white doctor's coat. In all the time I've known him he's worn that thing, which I totally don't fucking get. Dude's not even a real doctor anymore. You'd think he'd be sick to death of wearing that shit for the last forty-something years of his life, but no, he's still wearing it around like a fucking trophy. And that's the other thing; with all the backyard surgeries he performs, wouldn't it just be easier to wear a fucking rubber apron?

The Butcher made a few friends during his short stint in prison, and now he works freelance. Any and every MC has him on fucking speed dial. He's the man you call in to fix your shit. He doesn't give a damn about MC politics; he has no loyalty. He speaks only to money, and I'm about to pay a pretty price for the service he's

KICK

about to provide this bitch.

In one hand he holds an old-fashioned medical bag, the rich brown leather tended to and cared for, probably more than any of his patients ever would be. He runs his free hand through thick silver hair that's cropped longer on top with a short back and sides. His hair gel probably costs more than my fucking plasma screen.

"Patient?" he barks, looking me over as though he's assessing me for the first time. This contempt he eyes everyone with is getting fuckin' old. Especially when the bastard has fixed me up more times than I could count—fishing out bullets, resewing stitches ... in actual fact, he and Tank are the only reason I'm alive to be able to call on him again. If Tank hadn't called in the Butcher and laid out the equivalent of a down payment on a bike when I ran from Sugartown with my guts fallin' out all over the road, I'd be dead. Doesn't stop the fucker from being an arrogant prick, though.

I'm just about to answer his douchie question with a douche-baggie response when I'm barrelled into from behind. Indie tries to wipe me clean out on her way through the door. She didn't count on barrelling into Tank, or me grabbing her from behind and lifting her in my arms the way I did just an hour ago when I dragged her smelly arse to the shower. She screams, flailing and kicking, lashing out at me with her arms and kicking anyone who is crazy enough to get close to her.

"Let me go!" she wails over and over.

"Calm. The. Fuck. Down," I whisper harshly in her ear, biting off each word with the effort of keeping her restrained. I move her toward the bed, shielding her naked body from the others.

Indie sobs, but her struggling eases off a little as she whispers, "Please don't let him touch me. Please?"

I slide my hand from her waist to her throat, allowing her feet to touch the ground. Her body leans heavily against me as I coo in her ear the way I've done with Ivy countless times; the way I'd done with *her*. "I got you, Little Spitfire."

I almost have Indie completely subdued when the Butcher appears at my side, syringe in hand, and jabs her in the side of the neck with it. She jerks in my arms and turns to glare accusingly at me, and then she's falling into me like I'm her lifeline, as though she knows I'll catch her. And she's right. I've known her all of a few minutes and already I know I'll catch her, because just like Ivy knew, and Lauren before her, I'm a fucking sucker for the messed up ones, and I ain't met anyone as screwed up as this girl is right now.

KICK

TWO YEARS AGO

I breathe out a sigh of relief as my prez and Tank's footsteps echo up the hall and I slowly cross the room and crouch down beside her. She doesn't move as I undo the rope binding her arms behind her back.

"Are you okay?"

Fuck. That's a dumb question. My prez just held her at gunpoint and raped her, and I'm asking if she's o-fucking-kay. *Stupid motherfucker.*

"I gotta get you cleaned up," I say, stupidly, because what else do you say to someone after you just witnessed their rape?

I study her. There's not as much blood as I'd thought there would be. I mean, he wasn't fucking gentle — every ringing slap of flesh that bounced off the corners of the room as he pounded into her unwilling body told me that — but I'd seen his cock as it entered her again and again, and that fucker was darker than the Red fucking Sea.

The girl moves, slowly, gingerly. "Touch me and I'll cut off your balls." She rolls over and lifts her arse in the air and carefully slides her tight leather pants over her hips, and then she huddles in against the wall, her lip busted, her cheek grazed and bloody. She's the picture of defeat, and yet strangely … she's not. There's a fire in her eyes, the same one I saw at the rally, a fierce determination that screams "do not fuck with me". And I'm like a dog with a fucking bone, because all I want is to challenge her, beat her down and force her to submit to me, top dog, fucking alpha of the pack. Only I'm not an alpha, I'm a goddamn whelp, improper breeding and all that shit … inferior.

I move to the other side of the room and sit down, pulling out a packet of cigarettes from inside my cut and lighting one up. I slide the pack forward, across the filthy concrete floor.

"Why did you try to help me?"

I shrug and draw in a deep breath of my cancer stick.

"Why?" she demands in a shaky voice.

I glare at her. "Doesn't matter. It didn't work, and if I know my prez the way I think I do, it's gonna be so much worse for the both of us."

"It gets worse than having that fucker hold me down and shove his filthy cock inside me while the two of you watched on?"

I lean forward, pinning her with my gaze. "Princess, when it comes to the Angels, it can always get worse."

Tears stream down her cheeks and she whispers, "My father's going to tear your club apart. He's going to rip off your prez's dick and nail it onto his forehead. And then I'm gonna come back with a gun and blow

KICK

your fucking head off. You and the big guy, you both have a date with my Beretta and a bullet between your eyes."

I nod, because I don't doubt her for a single second. "Looking forward to it, Princess," I say, and I mean every word because it's nothing we don't deserve, and if the only redemption I receive in this life is seeing that beautiful face before I'm thrown in the fiery pits to burn for all eternity, then I'll take it. I'll take whatever this extraordinary angel of death has to offer. I'll take it willingly, and with force. I'll milk every second from that last moment of my life because her face is the only afterlife I need.

KICK

I paced the room while the butcher checked her over and then I stood ramrod straight behind him, ready to pound his fucking head in if he so much as looked at a blade while he opened her legs and examined her internally.

The butcher leaned back when he was done, stripping the gloves from his hand. He tried giving me the technical terms for what was wrong with her. I'd lost my cool and had almost pulled my piece on him to encourage the use of plain fucking English when Tank had stepped in front of me and said, "Doc, you're gonna need to use simple words so Kick here understands. He never made it outta high school."

"She's fine. Without an X-ray I can't determine whether she has multiple fractures or whether she's just badly bruised. Point is you're not taking her to a hospital, so we will likely never know. Treatment is the same for both: rest, and a good doping up to the eyeballs should do it. Her second and third molars are all gone from the top and bottom of her mouth, and she has some minor vaginal and anal tears. I felt a substantial amount of scarring inside both orifices. Either she's always liked to play extremely rough, or the past few weeks have been absolute hell on her.

"She needs rest, and a shit tonne of therapy, but I'm guessing both of those will be in short supply while she's held hostage. I'll leave a little morphine for pain management, but I'll need payment now." He pulls a bottle from his bag and doles out four little blue pills into his palm, setting them down on the bedside table.

Jesus. "Don't do it out of the kindness of your heart, Doc."

He turns his weasel-like grin on me. It's unsettling. "What heart?"

I head over to the wall safe and stand in front of it, sure to block what I'm doing from the others before I punch in the combination and pull out the standard five large for his consultation.

"By the way, my fee increased to seven last month."

"Of course it did," I mutter.

"Times are tough for everyone, Mr Kick."

"Yeah, especially serial mutilators."

He gives a lazy shrug of one shoulder. "It's hard to find good help when the company you keep is with criminals and thieves."

I shake my head. "Yeah, and I'm starin' at the motherfuckin' pirate king."

"Arrrgh," he says in a disdainful voice, and god help me, it takes everything I have not to riddle his brain with bullets. I glance at Tank who shakes his head, reading my thoughts as closely as if they were his own.

"Morphine is one hundred extra," the Butcher states quickly, before I can close the safe.

"A hundred fucking bucks for four lousy blue pills? I could walk out on the street right now and hit up some dealer selling them for ten bucks a pop."

"You're certainly welcome to try that, but then your captive would be unattended and I'm quite sure her trying to execute an escape plan would hinder any healing she might do unless otherwise suitably sedated."

In the end, I paid the money, and the Butcher left seven thousand and five hundred dollars richer. I'd cleaned him out of the entire bottle of pills.

Now, I watch Indie sleep from the arm chair I pulled up beside the bed. She's fitful; her lashes flutter against her cheeks and her mouth is turned down in a grimace as she tosses and turns.

"No," she murmurs. "Stop." She begs, tears stream down her cheeks and I shift forward in my seat, mesmerised. She startles awake, and swipes at the tears staining her cheeks. Slowly her head turns towards me, picking me out easily from the shadows in the half-light created by the bathroom door that I left ajar. She stares me down and rolls her head against the pillow, my pillow, glaring now at the stained, watermarked ceiling.

"What do you dream about?"

"What do you think?" she whispers through a cracked, raspy voice.

A beat passes, and if I couldn't see her face, see her eyes staring at the ceiling as her lashes bat away the tears, I might think she'd fallen asleep.

"The Priest—that's what they called him—he is

what I see. He had a handsome face, stereotypically good looking: light brown hair, blue eyes, and gleaming white teeth. He didn't look like a priest; more like a fitness model, like he chewed steroids for breakfast. He had a giant Roman cross, tattooed on his back—" She shakes her head. Her eyes are on me, but her gaze is soft and unfocused. "No, not tattooed ... it was branded into his skin, like a cattle brand. He liked to make me run my fingers over it before he'd rape me. Then he'd shove himself inside me and he'd whisper, 'I know your pain. Jesus knows your pain. But it's time to atone for our sins'."

"Christ."

"The cop liked to film it. He liked everything they did on film. I never understood that."

FUCK!

There was a video camera in that warehouse. The dentist had knocked it off the pedestal when he went down. Fuck. Fuck. *Fuck.* If Prez finds out we left that tape behind, he's gonna put us to ground.

We gotta go back.

I rise and stalk towards the door but before I can walk through it, I remember Indie. I can't take her out of the room. I can't risk her running, or worse her skitzing out at the sight of the warehouse she was locked up in.

"Where are you going?" she whispers.

I lean forward, pushing my forehead into the door. "Out."

Walking over to the nightstand, I pull the bottle of morphine from the drawer, shaking one out into my hand. She shakes her head, but I'm on her before she has a chance to move. I straddle her waist and endure the blows she lays on my face and torso.

"No," she screams, bucking her hips beneath mine and turning her face into the pillow so I can't gain access to her mouth. "No. Stop."

It's the easiest thing in the world to overpower her. I hate how that excites me. Hate how it makes me just like the men that took her, that the darkest part inside me relishes it too. My cock is hard as fucking stone right now; it would be nothing to tear away the sheet between us and slide inside of her. Instead, I lean down, smothering her with my weight as I use two hands to pry her mouth open and pop the pill in. I clamp her jaw shut and hold it tight until she has no choice but to swallow.

She gags. Her eyes well with unshed tears, and the horror in them rouses more than just my dick. It awakens the animal within me, that predatory instinct that a better man would push down and ignore. I close my eyes and breathe in the scent of her: fear, sweat, soap. What I wouldn't give to own her body the way her fear is owning her mind. Instead, I continue to hold her jaw closed until she's forced to swallow, and I know the pill is gone.

I release her face and stare down into her hate-filled gaze. I have this insane urge to kiss her, to taste her lips, force my tongue down her throat. I move closer, letting my breath wash across her face, daring her to fight or head-butt me again, but her assault comes in a different form than I expect.

"I'm going to kill you," she whispers, fury robbing the coolness from her words, betraying her little tough-girl act. "The second your back is turned I'm going to take that knife from your belt and drive it right through your kidney."

"Looking forward to it, Little Spitfire," I say, lifting my weight off of her and sliding off the bed. Her eyes are already drifting closed again. A doped up expression comes over her face and I wonder whether she's had a single day in the last three weeks where she hasn't been drugged. I sit on the side of the bed and watch as she gently slides into sleep.

She looks so peaceful as the drugs sweep her under—no fitful dreams, just peace. I watch her a beat longer. Inside me the beast rages to be freed, it claws and raves as flashes of me straddling her small body and smothering her with the palm of my hand clasped tightly over her mouth run riot through my mind. The images quickly turn worse as I see myself prying her legs apart and shoving my way between them, pumping in and out of her as my need builds until I can't contain it any longer and my hot cum spurts inside her even hotter cunt.

I shake my head, grabbing my keys and wallet from the table. I deadbolt the door behind me and go in search of Tank. We have unfinished business, and if Prez finds out we left evidence that could pin the dentist's death and Indie's disappearance on any of us, we're all as good as dead.

For the second time in as many days Tank and I sit in the van outside the warehouse, waiting. We've been here an hour already and there doesn't seem to be anyone moving in or outside the building, but Indie said a cop was involved, and if they're onto us then shit won't just hit the fan, it'll cover the motherfucking ceiling.

"Prez is gonna cut off our cocks and feed them to his pit bull," I murmur, fiddling with the air vent and pushing my fingers up against the broken slats to warm my cold hands.

"See, now I don't know whether you're referring to his old lady or his actual dog?"

"I mean it, man. If he finds out we screwed this up so badly we are six-feet under before we get back to the clubhouse."

"Hey, I didn't screw this up. The dentist, the girl, the fucking evidence? That shit is all on your pussy-whipped shoulders."

I shake my head and glare through the windshield at the building that looms up before us. I don't know what the fuck we're waiting for. There isn't another goddamned soul to be seen.

"How's she doing?" Tank asks.

"Indie?" I ask and shrug. "She was raped, tortured, and held in a warehouse for three weeks. How the fuck do you think she is?"

Tank shifts in the driver's seat, staring me down with a smug expression.

"What?"

"You named the bitch."

"Yeah, considering she's a missing fucking person, for shit's sake. I had to name the bitch."

"You could always shoot her." Tank shrugs when I glare at him. "It's true. If you'd let me put a bullet between her eyes, this little evidence thing wouldn't have been a problem because you'd be thinking about what to do with the body instead of leaving incriminating shit behind."

"Eat my dick, fuck-rag. You left that shit behind too."

"Yeah, but I was busy dealing with the fucking dentist you shot over a bitch you didn't even know."

I change the subject. "What the fuck are you doing with Ivy?"

Tank laughs. "Aww, you're really into this superhero complex, aren't ya, brother?"

"Fuck you."

"Nah, I don't swing that way, but put that hot new bitch of yours between us and I might be up for a double tap."

I let out an exasperated sigh, shifting in my seat. "This is bullshit. I'm going inside."

Tank chuckles quietly as I open the door and slide out into the freezing cold night. We carefully cross the road—I don't know why. There's no one around to see us at all. When we reach the warehouse entrance in the alley there's nothing more to see than a lone plastic bag caught in a drain pipe and shaking with the wind. The door is still busted off its hinges, thanks to Tank's handiwork, but when we shine our torches across the concrete floor there's nothing there—no chair, no blood stains, no video camera, nothing. It's as though the past three weeks for Indie—for Kayla—didn't exist.

"What the fuck?" Tank whispers in the darkness, and I know just by his tone that he knows I'm keeping something from him.

"We should go."

"Start talkin', brother."

I shake my head, but even as I do I know there's no way out of this. Tank won't hesitate to beat the shit outta me to get the info he needs. I may as well save myself a few fractured ribs. "Indie was the victim of a rape ring. The dentist wasn't the only motherfucker needin' a bullet to the brain. There was a cop, and a priest too."

"Jesus Christ. You didn't tell Prez about this?"

"No."

"You gotta take it to the table, brother. If there's a cop in on it, and they know we have her, we're fucked."

"Prez already wants her dead. I can't give him that kind of leverage over her."

"Why the fuck is this bitch so important to you?"

"I don't know—"

"Bullshit."

"Because I see something in her."

"You saw something in Lauren, too, and look how well that shit worked out."

I pinch the bridge of my nose and take a deep breath. I don't know why he insists on reminding me of this shit. It's not like I can forget that I'm the reason there wasn't enough left of her to bury once the Angels were done with her.

"You gotta take this to the table."

"I know—"

"You take it to the Prez, or I will," he says. "I covered for your arse before, but that was a different club and a different time. If this shit brings down the Saints, I'm gonna fuckin' put a bullet in that girl of yours. We clear, brother?"

"Yeah, we're fucking clear."

KICK

Tank walks out into the alley, leaving me standing alone in the empty warehouse. I stare down the darkness and feel the hatred, hurt, and betrayal in the room around me, and I can't help but think this is exactly where I belong. Here, in this dark room of horrors. This feeling, this warehouse, this is my heart's home, because the atmosphere in here is every bit as fucked up as the emptiness inside of me.

KICK

Walking into church wasn't my favourite experience. I'd asked Prez to call a meeting of the brothers and oddly he had, without even bothering to ask what the hell it was all about. Of course, it might have had something to do with the fact that when we arrived back at the clubhouse he was buried balls' deep in Neisha, a hot little Asian bitch who could suck cock harder than a Hoover and have you decorating her pretty yellow skin with a pearl necklace in seconds.

I enter the room, glancing at my brothers seated around our table. Tank sits with arms folded across his chest. His eyes meet mine and he nods. Beside him, Crazy—named for the crazy motherfucking look in his eyes, 24/7—chews his fingernails down to the skin. In the short time I've been a member of the Saints, I've never known Crazy to be able to sit still for a whole meeting. He's always running his hands through his jet-black hacked-off hair, chewing on some part of his anatomy, or twitching like he's on meth and jonesing for his next fix. He isn't, of course. He's just that fucking manic inside his head that he can't contain the excess energy, and so it spills out in church, and everything fuckin' else he does. Across from him the blond-haired, green-eyed Killer gnaws his bottom lip.

Killer is the newest of the brothers to patch in — and by new, I mean all of a month ago. He's probably the oddest member of all us criminals, a well-to-do rich kid from the North Shore. His trust fund is probably the equivalent of what the club makes in a year. We were all a little shocked when the dude showed up in some stiff fuckin' designer threads and said he wanted to join. Prez outright laughed in his face. Then he told the spoiled little rich kid he'd seen one too many episodes of *Sons of Anarchy*, and that we weren't into babysitting trust fund babies so they could walk on the wild side. Prez had also told him if he was serious about joining his club, or any club for that matter, he should get rid of that fucking show-pony sports bike and get himself something that at least fit the part. The next day, the cocky fucker was banging down the gates with a brand spanking new Fat Boy and packing two kg of fine-arse snow. Best fucking blow I'd ever done. Even Ivy knew the difference, and normally that girl cares for nothing but the high it gives her. Killer made it through the other hangers on, the hazing, prospecting, and then finally patched in last month.

Beside Killer sits Grim–named that because he looks like he went several rounds with the Grim Reaper and only just came out on top. The dude's in his early thirties, with dishwater-blond long hair pulled back with an elastic. His face is all jacked-up due to a run in with a rival club member and a Zippo lighter. He keeps as clear as he possibly can from Crazy, who sparks a fucking Zippo every five seconds and goes around setting shit alight.

Raphe sits beside Grim. In fact, if Raphe didn't have an old lady I would say there was some *Brokeback Mountain* shit going down between those two.

At the end of the table, One Eye leans his elbows firmly on the wood, his enormous belly protruding up and over the edge of the table. Dude might be fuckin' ancient, and might only have half the vision of the rest of the brothers, but he's still fuckin' scary as shit. He's a goddamned bear in a fight. He was built like Tank—if Tank had eaten an entire fuckin' factory full of Krispy Kremes. Despite the patch we wear, there's no love between One Eye and me. The Angels were a friend to no one, and yet One Eye knew my old prez well. Of course, no one here besides Tank knows of my affiliation to the Angels, but whether I'd seen him at a rally or he just had his suspicions about me, the fucker knew my face, and he knew my guilt, though he may not know exactly what part I played in bringing down my entire MC chapter.

Beside that cranky old fucker sits an even older one: Country. Country's grey beard hits his too thin belly. It's peppered with a tinge of ginger, proof that the ranga gene remains defiant and wilful right to the very end. Country has all but three teeth missing, forcing him to whistle when he laughs, and you never wanna stand in front of him while he's talking, unless you're into spittle in a big way. You can smell Country before you see him—he doesn't go in much for that showering shit—and his tunnel vision reached a point earlier in the year where the RT-fuckin'-A took away his license. If you can't ride, you hand in your patch; it's the way it's always been in every club since the beginning of MC history. Prez burned that rulebook and threw it out the fuckin' window when he heard the news. He's not crazy enough to let Country ride while wearing the patch, but he wouldn't take an old man's lifeline away from him either.

Prez might be a hard-arsed bastard at times, but he's a man worth following. A man whose respect has to be earned, but once you have it, you strive to make sure you never lose it. At least that's the way I guess most of the brothers see our prez. For me, I know I don't deserve it. I know if he ever found out about the Angels he'd put me to ground faster than I could blink.

Our two prospects, Diesel and Squeals, stand at the back of the room, arms folded, faces stoic. They wear cuts with their name tags on them and rockers on the back that label them with a gigantic target for slinging shit toward. Prospecting is no fuckin' picnic, and a lot of guys don't make it through their hazing. Diesel may make it. He's young, tougher than a pack of pit bulls, and has a good head on his shoulders, but I can't see Squeals making it past the first six months. Some people are cut out for the life, and others die trying.

Prez clears his throat and says, "Well, are you gonna tell us why the hell you called us into church, Kick, or are we just supposed to play Guess fuckin' Who while you stare like a fuckin' retard at us?"

"Alright, Prez, keep your fuckin' hair on," I say and

let out a deep breath, figuring the best way to say this shit is to just blurt it the fuck out.

"Tank and I tracked the Dentist to a warehouse yesterday. The plan was to capture the sick fuck and bring him in so Raphe could have a turn at him, but you guys know that didn't happen. He was torturing a woman—" I shake my head, because I don't know how old Indie is, but she couldn't be more than twenty. "A girl. The sick fuck was ripping her teeth out, knocking her out with drugs and waking her up with pain. I lost it and shot him in the back of the head."

I look at Raphe whose jaw is clenched tight. A muscle twitches in his face. I don't know whether that anger is still directed at me, or if he's imagining what could have happened to his old lady when she'd visited Dr Calder's clinic. After all, if she'd never attended that appointment–and woken up from the gas while he was busy stuffing his fingers inside her fuckin' pussy when he was supposed to be extracting a tooth–we'd never have found Indie.

"I know you know that she's stowed away in my room, and Prez has given you all a direct order to shoot her on sight if she so much as tries to leave it. She's messed up pretty bad: broken ribs, bruises, her face is banged up, so is her body, and she's completely fuckin' broken."

"Wow, she sounds like a real catch there, Kick," Crazy teases. "I bags the next go when you're done with her."

"Fuck you, man."

"Jesus Christ. Will you two toddlers cut it out? I didn't call you all here to bicker like children. I called

KICK

because according to Kick's cryptic shit, we have bigger fuckin' problems than the bitch in his room."

"The Dentist wasn't the only one. There was a cop and a priest too. They videoed their sessions. There was a camera set up in the room. A camera that Tank and I forgot to get before we left."

"Come a-fuckin'-gain, Kid?"

"We went back, just now, but the room has been gutted. Everything was stripped clean," Tank says.

"You left fuckin evidence behind?" Prez shouts. "Are you crazy? Are you fuckin' brain-dead, you little shit?"

"We were distracted with the body," I say.

"And the bitch," Tank supplies helpfully.

"So you're telling me some bitch you don't even know is the reason there's a video tape out there with your faces on it, and it's possibly in the hands of a fuckin' crooked cop? I oughtta strip both your patches for this."

"We need to find them both," I say, thinking about the bruises marring Indie's body. There's so much I want to know. How many days did she stay in that room? What did they do to her? Are any of them the same breed of monster I am? Did they force her to cum while she begged them to stop? There's so much left unanswered and the key to unravelling all of this is currently lying naked in my bed, covered only in a sheet and black bruises.

"I'll fuckin say." This is from Grim, who leans forward in his seat to stare me down across the table.

"I got an idea. Why don't we bring the bitch in here and have a little conversation with her, find out what she knows?" One Eye asks.

I glare at him across the top of my clenched fists. "She's not up to talkin'."

"Go get her," Prez growls.

"Prez—"

"Either you go get the bitch or I will, and trust me, she'd probably like that a lot less. We need to find out exactly what we're up against with this cop. I want to know everything about these two fuckers. I wanna know who they are, what they were doing with her, and what they fuckin' ate for breakfast that morning. You find out what she knows, and you find out fast. Or I'll find a way to make her talk."

I leave the room, cursing Tank for making me bring this to the club. Down the hall I run into Ivy who averts her gaze and attempts to walk right past me. I spin around, grabbing her arm and yanking her into me.

She glares up at my face, attempting to wrench herself free. "Ow. Let go of me."

"You don't even say hello to me anymore?"

"Hello," she snaps in a tone I've never heard her take before.

"What the fuck, Ivy?"

"Let me go, Daniel."

"Daniel?" I question. She's never called me that before either. "You fuckin' high, bitch?"

"No, I'm stone-cold sober, and finally seeing things clearly."

"What the fuck does that mean?" I let go of her arm and grasp her chin between my thumb and forefinger. "What are you playing at, babe?"

"I'm not playing at anything. In fact, I'm not your plaything at all anymore."

My mouth twists into a crooked smile and I can tell by the way her breath catches that we both know what she's saying is not true. "That so?"

"Yeah, that's so." She licks her lips, and I can't help myself. I back her into the wall and slam my mouth down on hers. I'm met with no resistance. How could she resist when I'm giving her everything she needs? The submission, the dominance, the animal need to fuck, the pain that stokes all her greatest and worst fantasies. I can give her all these things like no one else can, and she knows it, she craves it. It's written all over her face.

I shove my hands beneath her skirt, spreading her legs apart and grinning when I find her completely bare. I delve between her smooth, lush lips. Bitch is wet, but then I can't remember a time when she wasn't. I sink three fingers into her at once, without any preparation, and her breath leaves her in a rush.

"Then how come you're soaking wet for me, darlin'?"

I rub my fingers against the sweet spot inside her, the one that forces her legs to shudder and threaten to give out beneath her. She fists her hands in my shirt as I nip her earlobe and kiss my way down her throat and then I slide my hands free and suck my fingers clean, tasting her juices, savouring her flavour on my tongue. Ivy's pupils are huge, her eyes glazed with the need to fuck. I dig my hands into her hip and spin her around. Grasping the nape of her neck I shove her up against the wall, her cheek pressed to the peeling wallpaper, her arse tilted at an angle that's perfect for entry. She's wearing one of those tight Lycra skirts that clings to every inch of her perfect body and I slide it up and over her cheeks, revealing smooth white flesh. I bring my hand down upon her arse, relishing the sound of the slap, the red handprint it leaves behind.

"You've been a very naughty girl, Ivy. Are you ready for me to punish you?"

"Yes, oh god yes."

"Yes what?" I snap, squeezing the nape of her neck hard enough to feel the bony protrusions of her vertebrae.

"Yes, Daddy. Punish me. Please?"

I smile and let go of her neck, snagging a fistful of her hair instead and yanking it back until her spine creates a perfect arch of submission. With my free hand I release my cock and position the head at the glistening entrance to her beautiful, pink cunt.

I drive into her, savouring the resistance her swollen, slick pussy gives me when I shove inside to the hilt. She's tight, too tight. Her cunt has a death grip on my dick. She squeezes me and I almost come undone. That earns her a slap to the arse. "You trying to switch rolls, baby?"

"No," she moans.

I slide my hand over her hip, down her abdomen, and I part her lips, gaining access to her swollen clit. I circle it once and then pinch hard, much harder than I normally would. Ivy cries out; it's a sound half of pain, and half of pleasure. I thrust upward, letting go of her hair and wrenching her arms behind her back, jerking her whole body with the brutality with which I take her. Within seconds her legs are trembling again and I feel the first wave of orgasm clenching her muscles around me.

KICK

I pull almost completely out as her cunt milks my cock, but I won't fall over the edge. I won't give her that satisfaction. Releasing her arms, I wrap mine around her waist, pulling her close to me, and guiding my cock back inside her slick pussy. I snake my hand up her throat, shoving it back at an angle that allows me to see her face. "Let's get something straight here, baby doll. I can have you anytime, any way I want to, and there's not a goddamn thing you can do about it. You submit to me, not the other way around."

She tries to nod against my firm grasp, the bones in her throat straining against my calloused fingers, and closes her eyes as the tears roll down her face. Her cunt tightens around me and suddenly the position I have her in isn't close enough, I don't have enough leverage. I don't have enough power.

I let go of her throat, grab hold of her hips and smash into her body, impaling her on the end of my dick before sliding all the way out of her. She whimpers with the loss of my heat but I spin her around and shove her back until she has nowhere else to go, and then I plunge right back into her. Ivy wraps her long legs around my hips. I slam her up against the wall in time with my thrusts. Her hands slip under my cut, under my shirt, and rake my flesh, drawing blood. I quicken the pace, moving past long deep thrusts and just pushing in as far as I can get, until I'm hitting the end of her.

She's not even trying to contain her cries now; we've gone way beyond that. The two of us are nothing more than animals, scratching, and thrusting, grunting, clawing and using one another. Every second of it is perfection. It's the reason we work so fucking well together, because in this moment I own her, and in the most rudimentary way Ivy owns me too, or at least she owns my body, because I never have and I never will again give my heart to another woman but Lauren.

Lauren. I hate her so fucking much.

I hate her for loving me, despite my sick, twisted mind. I hate her for stealing my heart, for making me betray my club, but most of all I hate her for dying.

I thrust harder, punishing her, striving to make her hurt and bleed, and feel the pain she put me through from the second we met. I want to wound her. I want her heart to be the one rending open, not mine. With a growl, I let go. I fuck her mindlessly, brutally. I thrust into her body and switch off my mind, allowing my cock to do what it was built for. My orgasm rips through me. Hot cum jets out of my body and into hers, and for a brief second the bliss is so complete that I let go of the anger, but when I open my eyes and look into a pair of wounded grey-green ones instead of chocolate-brown, all the emotion, the pain, the betrayal is back, worse than ever.

"You called me Lauren," she whispers as tears slide unchecked down her cheeks.

Ordinarily, I'd watch her tears fall with a morbid sort of fascination. I'd want to know exactly what was in her head, why she fell apart every time I took her body to the brink and pushed her over the edge, but today those tears are mine. They're caused by me, and for perhaps the first time ever I'm not okay with that.

What the fuck is happening to me? Since when do I give a shit about making Ivy cry?

I lift her from the end of my cock and set her down

on her feet. "What did she do to you, Daniel?" she asks and her throat is thick with the struggle of holding back her tears.

"She died," I whisper, and then my eyes widen when I realise that this is more information than I have ever given her. Ivy clasps a hand over her mouth, holding back her sobs. She reaches up to touch my face. There's pity in her eyes. I feel hatred, and rage, and yes, even betrayal that she would try to pull this shit from me. We don't talk about Lauren. I can't talk about Lauren. Not with her.

"I'm so sorry, Daniel," she says through her tears, taking my face between her hands.

"Don't," I snap and shove her away, stalking off to my room, pushing the key into the lock and turning it hard, booting it with my foot when it won't open. I can feel Ivy behind me but I slip inside and slam the door. I press my forehead into the cool painted wood and just breathe.

Instantly, the acrid stench of vomit turns my stomach and I spin around to find Indie sprawled across the comforter, covered in the shit. The bottle of Morphine is open, and what few pills she didn't swallow and chuck up decorate the sheet beside her head.

Fucking hell. Tank was right; from one crazy-arsed bitch to another.

I take what should be a few paces to the bed in one hurried stride, leaning over her and slapping her face hard. She's completely unresponsive. Placing two fingers over her throat, I feel for a pulse. It's faint, but her chest isn't rising and falling with a cycle of inhalation and exhalation. *Indie isn't breathing*.

Time slows—at least it feels that way. Panic fires through my chest as I stare down at her. I think I hear shrieking in the hall, but that doesn't make sense. There's a pounding on my door, and Tank's voice on the other side.

"What the fuck did you do, Kick?" he demands, and my eyes roll to the door shaking on its hinges, and back again to Indie's inert body.

What did I do?

What haven't I done?

What have I ever done that's been good for anyone?

"Open this fuckin' door, or I'm gonna bust it open."

I move on autopilot and unlock the deadbolt. Tank grabs my shoulders and shakes me, hard. "Ivy's out there in the hall shrieking like a fuckin' banshee. You just ripped the heart right out of her fuckin' chest. What the hell did you do to her? What did you say?"

I don't have an answer for him. It wasn't me telling Ivy that Lauren was dead; she wouldn't be catatonic over that. No, it wasn't Lauren's death that upset her, it's that she saw the end as plainly as I did. She saw that this is it for us. She saw too far inside, and it's a chance I won't ever give her again.

Tank shakes me again, expecting an answer, but I have nothing for him. I have nothing for anyone. I see the moment when he looks beyond me to the bed, to Indie. Tank releases me and hurries to her side. "Jesus fuckin' Christ, did you do this?"

He has every right to ask, because more than anyone, Tank knows me. He knows the depths of my tarnished soul, and he knows how deep my betrayal runs. After all, how can you really trust a brother who betrays their club? Several times? Tank scoops her from the bed, carefully placing her on the floor. He wipes the traces of vomit off her mouth and starts performing CPR.

He's too rough. Her ribs are bruised, or broken; he's going to kill her.

All at once I snap to. The world ceases to move as if it's in slow motion and my heart begins pounding, beating out a furious rhythm against my organs.

Sinking to my knees beside her, I shove Tank out of the way and take over, yelling for him to call an ambulance, then I push past the taste of vomit on her lips and breathe air into her inert lungs, willing her to accept it, to take it and live, though her actions proved to me she'd rather take the out the pills offered than stay here with me.

I'm an arsehole, it's all I've ever been. A biker brat born into the arms of a junkie bitch who only cared about where her next fix was coming from, and a father who'd wished he hadn't forgotten the fucking condom. I've always been trash. I've always been nothing. I don't blame her for choosing to check out, but like I said: *I am an arsehole.* And she might fight against it, she might want it more than anything she's felt before in her life, but I'm not letting her take that way out.

In the hall, over the shrill cry of another of Ivy's mental breakdowns, I hear the rush of booted feet over worn carpet.

"What the fuck happened here?" Prez demands, appearing in the doorway. I glance at him, briefly, and then wonder why Tank is studying my face and not calling a fucking ambulance.

"Call a goddamn ambulance," I roar, but he just

continues to stare at me.

"No ambulance. Someone better fuckin' start talking."

"She's gonna die if we don't get her help."

"Tank, call the Butcher," Prez demands. "I need inside her head. I need this bitch alive long enough to tell us what she knows, but no fuckin' hospitals. We clear?"

I shake my head in disgust but continue to pump away at her chest, continue to push air into her lungs, breathing for her. It feels like an infinity, but when she finally regains consciousness, coughing and spluttering, I shift behind her and support her head on my bent knees. She vomits. I turn her head to the side and let the green bile land all over the rug. I'm covered in it. She's covered in it. My rug is covered in it.

"Jesus Christ," Prez mutters.

Tank pockets his phone. "Butcher will be here in ten minutes."

I breathe a sigh of relief and glance at Indie. She's alive; trembling, but listless, and she's already falling asleep again. I don't know what the fuck I'm supposed to do with her, but I know the Butcher is going to charge me through the nose because she's wearing the contents of her stomach like a fucking wedding gown. In the hall, Ivy is still shrieking. Tank shoots me a glare. It's full of the promise to inflict a lot of pain on me later, and then in three angry strides he's gone from the room.

I don't know what the fuck his deal is; perhaps the geriatric giant has a fuckin' heart after all. Either way, I can't be Ivy's keeper anymore. It's not doing either one of us any bit of good. Ivy never belonged to me; maybe she did in her mind, but it wasn't like that for me. And the more I try to show her that, that I'm sick, that I'm fucked in the head and full of this dark desire to hurt people, the deeper she falls. It's time that changed.

I stare down at the girl in my arms and wonder whether history isn't just on fuckin' repeat. Not just with Ivy, but Indie, too. Losing Lauren destroyed me, and yet here I am in the same goddamned situation: protecting another stupid bitch from my club and myself.

"Don't fucking touch me," Ivy screams between sobs. "Don't touch me."

The sounds of her losing her shit and lashing out at Tank filters in through the open door. He grunts, no doubt warding off each of her blows about as patiently as a bear with a thorn in its foot, and then lets out an almighty roar, "Stop. Fuckin'. Struggling. Bitch!"

The shrieking goes silent, the door beside mine opens, then slams, and the room and the hallway are swallowed by silence. I glance at Prez, who'd been close enough to the door to watch the entire scene. He shakes his head and turns his attention back to me.

"You wanna get her in the shower? I can get one of the girls to clean this shit up."

"I don't wanna move her until the Butcher gets here."

"What the fuck happened, kid?"

"It's my fault. I drugged her before I left; I thought she'd be out to it for hours. I didn't put the pills away."

"You know for someone who's as determined to die as she is, you're awfully fixated on keepin' her breathin'."

I smile, but it's full of remorse. Prez steps further

into the room and closes the door behind him, taking a seat in the armchair opposite the bed.

"You and I have never really talked about the past."

"No, we haven't."

"You came to the club, and Tank stood for you. He said if it didn't work out he'd hand over his patch and yours, and we'd never see either of you again."

"Is this the part where you take my cut and kick me out?"

"No, this is the part where you tell me what you've been hiding all this time, and why the hell some bitch you found in a warehouse is suddenly your top priority." Prez gives an amused laugh. "And then I decide whether or not to take your cut and boot you and this hot mess out on your arses."

"Let's just say there was a girl—"

"Isn't there always?"

"Yeah. Guess so." I shake my head and lean back against the side of the bed, careful not to disturb Indie, who's still sleeping peacefully on the rug, surrounded by her vomit. I place my fingers over the pulse in her neck and leave it there, focusing on the slow but steady beat. "It ended badly."

"Let me guess—with a bullet between her eyes?"

"Somethin' like that."

"What club did you belong to?"

"I didn't—"

Prez holds up a hand and the denial I have always at the ready falls away from my lips. "Don't fucking bullshit me now, kid. I know an MC brat when I see one, and you had club runnin' in your veins since you was a boy. I knew it the second I first saw you."

I stare at my prez, the man I pledged loyalty to, the man I agreed to die for if push came to shove. I meant that pledge when I took it. If I had to take it again today, I'd still mean it. I take a deep, slow inhalation and let my answer rush out with my breath, as if that could somehow lessen the betrayal I'm about to admit to. "Angels. Hells Angels."

"Sydney chapter?"

I nod.

Prez whistles low, quietly. It forces my head to snap up and glare at him. "Then you know there's still a pretty price on your head from the other chapters."

"I know it," I agree, still uncertain about my next move. In the time that's passed since I showed up on Tank's doorstep begging him to kill me, I haven't told a single living soul that I gunned down my entire club.

He grins. "You're just full of surprises aren't ya, kid?"

I shrug.

"You gonna tell me how your whole club wound up dead inside a little farm house in the country? 'Cause I know the Angels and the Banditos have been waging war on one another for several years, but from the look on your face, I'm guessing club rivalry had nothing to do with it."

"No, it didn't. But they made a good scape goat." I don't bother telling him that I wasn't the only one to survive. Or that the shit that went down with the Banditos was done and dusted long before I gunned down my club. Word was the cops had tried to cover everything up to save the big bad Bs and the Angels from an all-out war, and I wasn't about to correct anyone on that front. I'd done enough damage to Ethan and his Ana. And though I knew in my gut that the president of the Savage Saints was a good man—as good a man as any criminal can be—that was a chapter of my life I wanted to remain closed. I'd made my peace with it, and one day, if I ever crossed paths with Ethan again, how that meeting would go would depend on him. If he wanted me dead, I wouldn't stop him. It was what I deserved. It was my debt to pay for what I had done to them.

"I'll bet," Prez says, locking his hands together and cracking his knuckles. "You know how much that pretty head of yours is worth?"

"Nope."

"Fifty large. Word was that they knew someone had survived, and that the Angels were on their way to that hospital to conduct a little investigation of their own."

"I thought as much. I checked myself out early and went to Tank, hoping to check out entirely."

"And he saved your life?"

"Still can't get a straight answer out of him as to why the hell he'd do something like that."

"The Angels didn't take their change of presidency well. Tank knew that. Why do you think he turned nomad? He knew the club was on a different path, and it wasn't the one he wanted to be on. Way I see it, you did him a favour, and he brought you to me."

"What are you gonna do, Prez?"

"What else you got to tell me, kid?"

"Nothing."

He chuckles. "I believe that about as much as I believe that you're trying to rescue that girl there because of the goodness in your heart."

I glance down at Indie. I'm covered in her vomit, sitting here, chatting with my prez as though she were my drunken girlfriend who lost her guts before submitting to an alcoholic coma. I don't know what it is about her that makes me so fiercely protective and yet so completely fucking at a loss when it comes to what to do with her. It would be so easy just to wrap my hands around her slim throat and squeeze, but I don't want to, and judging by the way Prez is staring at me, he knows this as well as I do.

Prez nods toward Indie. He gives me another of his wry smiles, and I kinda wanna shoot him the nutsack for being such a cocky fuck, 'cause I'm sure I'm not gonna like what he's about to say. "That's a lot to take on, kid."

"So is a brother who shot down his prior club members."

"But here we are."

"You gonna turn me into the Angels? Collect a big wad of cash?"

"You got some issues with trust, huh?" Prez frowns. "Guess I'm not surprised. I knew your old man, and that fucker was meaner than a hornet without a nest."

"And how do you know who my old man is?"

"Because you look exactly like him. Didn't think I'd ever figure out who the hell you reminded me of; if I didn't know you were an Angel—"

"I was never an Angel, but I make a perfect Saint."

He laughs; this time it's not the carefully controlled chuckle from before, it's an all-out belly laugh.

"Yeah, you do," he says when he recovers. "But if

you fuck up like this again, I'm gonna have your balls in a vice for all eternity. You got that, Newbie?"

I smile at the use of his nickname for me. "Yeah, I got it."

"You stay with her until she wakes up, and then you find out what she knows. I need that tape, and then I need those two fuckers taken out."

"One question. Who gets to be the one delivering the bullet?"

"You do, kid. Get me my tape and they're all yours."

He opens the door and walks through it, and I spend the next few minutes wondering what the hell just happened. I just admitted to killing not one, but several of my former club brothers, an offense normally punishable by death, and my prez didn't even bat an eyelid. Either he has way more faith in me than he should, or he's dumber than I thought he was. Because if it's the only means I have of self-preservation, for Indie or myself, then I'll betray this club too.

The strange part is I'm just prolonging the inevitable. Neither one of us are particularly fond of living, it seems, though it looks like we're both stuck here for a while longer.

INDIE

Black.

That's all I see.

Darkness.

There's no white light, no pearly gates, no redemption. Just blackness and spinning and shouting, screaming. And then there's his voice above me, around me, behind me. I turn but can't escape it. I scream; I cry out and fall to my knees, covering my ears with my hands pressed firmly against the soft cartilage.

There's a sting in my arm and the world snaps into place like a rubber band from a slingshot.

I'm back in the warehouse. I'm not with the biker at all. I'm back in that warehouse, and the Dentist is pushing the needle through my vein like a hot knife through butter. I struggle. Scream. Fight. And then it's the biker's voice in my ear. "Shh, I have you, Little Spitfire."

"No!" I scream. I sob, but all I feel as I slip back

under are his arms banding around me, holding me down. Holding me captive.

"Same shit, different day," I mutter, but I don't know if the words come out right or if I just think I said them. I don't know anything anymore except that I want to die. With every fibre of my being, with everything I am, I know that much is true.

I just want to die, but he won't let me.

I wake to a cool, dimly lit room, looking much the way it was before he drugged me with the morphine, which makes me wonder if it was all a dream. I guess the fact that it didn't work makes it a nightmare, now, doesn't it?

His long body is folded in the chair. I squint into the darkness, expecting to find him asleep but though his face and posture are relaxed, his eyes are not. They study me too keenly. I close my eyes and shift, wincing when my hand sears with pain from the catheter. My eyes fly open and my gaze narrows in on the needle in my hand. Panic seizes my chest. I follow the line of plastic tubing to the IV bag hanging by the bed and instantly I begin trying to free the apparatus from my skin.

"It's just fluids," he says, leaning forward in his seat. The blanket falls away from his body, revealing a heavily tattooed naked torso. His arms are decorated with pictures of skulls and mechanical parts; his chest, too. It's painted with old-school style tats: anchors, pin-up girls … I squint at the image decorating the right side of his abdomen. The lighting is dim, and I could be seeing things on account of the drugs I've had coursing through my system, but she looks just like a 1950s, Victoria's Secret version of me. *Weird.*

The biker's blond hair falls over those hard blue eyes. He looks every bit as frightening as he did when he held me underneath the shower yesterday. "Doc says you're severely dehydrated. Been back twice to change that thing over."

Twice? How long have I been out? Days? A week?

My tongue and teeth are furry, and despite the residual tang of drugs and vomit in my mouth, my stomach growls. I want a shower. I want to scrub away every trace of their hands on my skin, but then I remember the biker touching me, sliding his calloused fingers against my arse, over my clit. Heat claws at my neck and cheeks, and I see flashes of his beautiful and terrible face twisted into rage as I tried to fight him, the smirk that played on his lips as I aimed his gun at him, the tight band of his arms around me as he cooed in my ear before the doctor knocked me out—all of these things slide through my mind. The sound of my sobs accompanies the memories. It's a soundtrack I've become very familiar with in the last few weeks. That and the piercing sound of my screams.

The Priest was fond of the screaming. I knew it, and so I would clamp my mouth shut against the pain. I tried not to give him the satisfaction of hearing my agony made vocal, but the more I resisted, the more he pushed. The more he punished. The other two liked to watch his sessions as if they were taking notes, learning from his depravity.

"You thought the Dentist was fucked up? Baby, you

haven't seen anything until you've lived inside my fantasies for a day." The biker's words play on repeat, twisting my gut with fear. Despite the aching in my body, instinct urges me to move, to fight—to run. But what's the point? He'd trap me at every turn, and I'd wind up a little more bruised and beaten up than I am already. And what would I run to? I can't outrun the last three weeks of my life and the other two animals that did this to me are still out there. They'll be watching my family, and they'll come for me. Maybe not right away, but eventually, and I would rather spend an eternity in purgatory than fall victim to those men again.

"You should have let me die," I croak. My throat is scratchy as hell; it hurts just sucking in breath. I guess downing a half bottle of pills and throwing them back up again will do that to you. I'm surprised to find my mouth doesn't feel as bruised, and my body—while certainly stiff from misuse—doesn't ache as much.

"Why are you so keen to check out?" he whispers. His voice puts my teeth on edge.

"I traded three monsters for one with a prettier face, and a heart blacker than any of the rapists I've spent the last couple of weeks with. I didn't try to kill myself for kicks."

"What happened to you?"

"What happened to you?" I counter, narrowing my gaze as I study his face.

"You like playing games, darlin'? Is that it?"

"No," I say quickly. Too quickly. A flash of the scars burned into the Priest's back jolts through my mind and sears the inside of my lids. I gasp, remembering his thick, greedy hands and the deep baritone that used to ask me repeatedly, "if I like to play games" and "if I liked what I'd become", "if I enjoyed being a whore".

My throat tightens, and my body tenses with the memory. "No. I don't like to play games."

"What do you remember about the others?" he asks, as he pulls a Subway bag from the coffee table beside him. My stomach growls loudly and I watch on with interest as he unwraps one of the largest subs I've ever seen. I can't remember the last time I ate. Thinking back, it's possibly been more than five days. They fed me periodically in that room, mostly liquids, protein shakes, to keep up my strength so I wouldn't pass out while they raped me. Repeatedly. One after the other.

The biker picks up one half of the sub and opens his mouth wide, I'm reminded of a snake unhinging its jaw in order to devour its prey. He catches me staring and lowers the sandwich. "You hungry?"

I nod slowly, wary of asking him for anything, but the sandwich smells so good and let's be honest here, right now I'd likely sell my grandmother's corpse to a necrophiliac for a single bite of food.

"Tell me what you know and I'll let you have the entire thing."

"Forget it," I croak. I'm not giving him shit until I know for certain he isn't just keeping me alive to get that tape back. Even if that is the best smelling sandwich on the planet.

He shrugs. "Suit yourself."

The bastard eats the fucking sandwich. My stomach protests the misuse and I'm forced to watch as he devours every last bite and then licks his long, tattooed fingers clean. I glower at him, searing him with my hatred, though like the others, he remains unaffected. I hate feeling this way. Like a poor, little misguided mouse, staring down a mountain lion. I hate that these arseholes have taken the control, my strength, my will to fight — my right to choose — from me.

He opens a small paper bag and produces a cookie. I can smell that too from here, and there's some half-witted response dancing on the tip of my tongue about how hogging the cookies to yourself is a form of torture worse than any other, but then I remember the Dentist's chair. The sheer delight on the Dentist's face when he'd pry my mouth open and rip out my teeth, losing himself in the small part of me he'd just extracted. And the Priest's face, hovering over me. His sweat-soaked hair brushing my forehead as he pounded into my body again and again, brutalising me. The horrifying grin as he chained me to the St. Andrew's Cross, stroking his cock through the thick fabric of his pants as he schooled the others in how to whip me properly.

And though certainly not innocent, at least the Cop doled out a form of punishment and cruelty that was easy to understand. He liked to pretend I was a bad girl who needed to be chastised and taught a lesson by the big man of the law. He was sick, just as sick as the others, but the depravity of the Priest was the thing that frightened me the most. Every day there was a new fresh hell that awaited me, and each day the punishment was so much worse than the day before.

The biker, though scary as all fucking hell, didn't really compare to those men. Maybe it was the fact that he'd saved me, not once but several times, or maybe I'd just lost my ever loving mind, but whatever the case, I

KICK

knew I was damn well better off with him than in the hands of those animals. Even if he had warned me he was worse, there's no way he could know that, because he'd never met the Priest.

"Talk, Indie. Tell me what you know and I'll make sure you're comfortable."

"That's not my name," I snap. I hate that he called me that. I'm not Indie. Indie is a girl born to hippie parents, a girl that leaves home with a couple of hundred bucks and a plane ticket to India, a girl who lives in the fucking Himalayas for a year with no technology. I'm Kayla Kennedy, born to conservative parents, the girl who aced every test she ever took, the girl who was smart enough to run from danger while all the other bimbos flirted with it. The girl who was kidnapped two blocks from her house, the girl who was raped and tortured for weeks. The girl who was taken by bikers and saved by one who was potentially just as fucked up as the monsters he took her from.

The biker lifts his brow, waiting me out, it seems; though I have no idea what it is he's waiting for. I scrub a bruised hand impatiently over my face. The Morphine has made me itchy. He bites into the cookie, one of those delicious triple chocolate ones that taste exactly the same no matter which Subway store you get them from, and I won't lie, I know they kill baby orangutans to harvest the palm oil for those cookies, but they're freaking delicious.

"I'm not going to break just because you dangle a cookie in front of my face," I spit.

The biker sets the cookie down on the paper bag and stands. He wipes the grease from his hands on the back of his worn jeans as he walks to the dresser and rummages through the open top drawer. Every muscle in my body tenses as I wait to see what his next move will be. I don't bother to try and run. What would be the point? He can't do anything to me that hasn't been done before.

The biker moves towards me and despite my prior thoughts of self-fortification, I shrink back into the pillows when he circles the bed and parks himself down on the mattress. He lunges. I shrink away, but he grabs my wrist and forces it above my head. The white-hot bolt of pain shooting down my side causes me to still, which makes it easier for him to slap one loop of a pair of cuffs around my wrist and the other to the wrought-iron bed rail.

I stare at the shiny silver restraints for a beat, and then fear seizes my chest, my heart. I thrash wildly, despite the pain in my ribs. I scream and kick, but my legs are tangled in the covers. I can't do this again. I can't. "What the fuck are you doing?"

"Relax, Little Spitfire," he says, rising from the mattress. My gaze follows him as he stalks around the bed and slips his leather cut on over a black hoodie. There's a winged skull insignia stitched onto the back of the vest and patches above and below that read *Savage Saints* and *Sydney*. When he turns around to face me I notice the small patch over his heart: *KICK*. I store all this information away for later and focus on his face as he says, "I'm not going to rape you. When you submit to me, it will be because you need to."

"That won't ever happen," I say through clenched teeth.

KICK

His eyes blaze with smug certainty and his mouth tips up in the corners. "Yes, it will. I can help you, Indie."

His statement makes me want to laugh, but tears well in my eyes again. A knot forms in my throat as I try to hold them at bay.

He can help? How can he possibly help me? How can he possibly fix this?

"You keep saying that and yet I'm still here, handcuffed to a fucking bed, held captive by another sick, twisted scumbag."

He smirks. Fucking smug bastard. One day he will let his guard down and I'll take his gun and shoot him in the head, and then I'll walk out of here, and disappear for good. I may not be able to go home to my family, but I will be free.

"The club wants your captors dead just as much as you do. Seems they have a little something that could incriminate Tank and me in your disappearance, and the Dentist's death."

I frown, not understanding what he means by that. The MC didn't have anything to do with my abduction, so how... "The tape. The Dentist was recording when you shot him. You left the tape behind?" I ask incredulously, because that is possibly the dumbest thing any criminal has ever done.

He sets his jaw and glowers at me. "Yes, I left the fucking tape behind. I might not have done that if you hadn't resisted my help."

"You kidnapped me," I shout. "Excuse the fuck out of me for not helping you execute your plan to abduct me."

"I didn't have to fucking save you, I did it because—"

"Let me guess, you did it out of the goodness of your heart?" I scoff. "You should have let the big guy shoot me if you were too gutless to do it yourself."

"Bitch, you need to fuckin' stop talking," he snaps, stalking over to the door, his shoulders tight with anger and his face twisted into a sneer.

"Where are you going?"

"Out. I got business."

"You can't leave me here like this. What if I choke? Or I need to pee?"

"You'll hold it 'til I get back. And if you choke, then I guess you're checking into the Pearly Gates early." He pulls a cigarette from the packet and lights up. Thumbing his keys from the table, he shoves them and his wallet in the front pocket of his jeans. I don't realise his gun is sitting on the coffee table until he picks it up and holsters it in the back of his jeans. "You should think about what I said, Indie. I can't erase what they did to you, but with a little cooperation on your part, I sure as shit can take down those motherfuckers."

"And then what? You're just going to let me go? Your club is going to let me walk out of here knowing what I know?"

"Pretty much," he agrees as he ashes his cigarette on the carpet. I glance briefly around the room. It's disgusting. The biker's a genuine slob. There's left over food wrappers and empty bottles of beer strewn everywhere. The room reeks of smoke and mildew. I remember coming to, covered in vomit, the biker hovering over me, and I'm both relieved and mortified that someone had cleaned me up while I was comatose—obviously it wasn't this guy, because he is a complete pig.

"You keep your mouth shut and we don't have a problem. We can put the bad guys to ground and you can live out your life however the fuck you want to, and you never see any of us again."

"And if I talk?"

He smiles. "If you talk, you see me again. And I promise you, my face will be the last thing you see." Biker winks and slips from the room. The key turns in the lock. He deadbolts the door from the outside.

I roar in frustration, yanking on the hand that's cuffed to the bed, though I know it won't do me any good. My left arm is pinned in position with the IV bag. I feel the needle beneath my skin and I long to rip it out, but for some reason I trusted him when he said it was just fluids. I don't know why, and it's a feeling that puts me completely at odds with the chills he gives me the other ninety-nine-point-nine per cent of the time. I know I can't let my guard down with him, but do I trust him enough to let him help me when it comes to finding and destroying the Priest and the Cop as badly as they destroyed me?

I don't know.

There's only one thing I'm sure about now: they have to pay. With or without the biker's help, I will hunt down both men, and I will grin like the devil as the light leaves their eyes.

KICK

If I have to sit through one more fuckin' conversation with Crazy about the brain-dead little Asian pop tart he's bangin', I'm gonna pull my gun and unload an entire bloody clip into his face.

We're sitting in the clubhouse lounge on a black leather sofa that's seen so many fucking cum-stains you'd need a Hazmat suit in order to remain unscathed. Truth be told, I'm pretty sure the seat of my jeans are wet because Killer just got done banging the shit outta Brooke on this very cushion five minutes before I sat down.

Crazy pulls the lighter from his pocket, flips the lid, rolls his thumb over the flint and watches the flame dance in front of his eyes. Jesus Christ, that's the nineteenth fuckin' time he's done that in the span of twenty minutes. He flips the lid closed and slides it back in his cut. I drink down the rest of my schooner and wish I could just lie the fuck down without some arsehole wantin' to strike up a fuckin' conversation. I haven't slept properly in days. I've gone from the floor to the armchair and back again, 'cause some bitch has been in my bed and it just isn't right.

Crazy produces the lighter again and flips back the lid; the metal *ping* and then the spark as his thumb strokes the wheel is the sound of me losing it. I completely fucking snap, snatching the lighter off of him and dumping it into the jug of beer in front of us. Then I close my eyes and sink further down into the soft leather, resting my head against the headrest.

"Dude, what the fuck?" Crazy flies into a flurry, his knickers in a fucking twist as he plunges his hand into the jug to retrieve his Zippo. Beer sloshes out the side and over the jacked-up coffee table, which has probably seen more cumshots than the couch. He pulls out the lighter and wipes it off on his shirt, flipping back the lid and rolling his thumb over the roller. It throws off a few tiny sparks and he stares at it, looking forlorn, as if he's trying to will the fuckin' thing to life. He runs the roller across the pant leg of his jeans and attempts to light it again. "No, no, no, no, no, no, no," he mutters. "You killed it, arsehole."

"It's a Zippo, you crazy fuck. It's not like you don't have a drawer full of them anyway."

"I won't forget this, Kick," he says resolutely and I chuckle, because the expression on his face is the funniest fuckin' shit I've seen all week.

"Great, I look forward to you kicking my head in later. Now fuck off, I'm trying to get some sleep."

Crazy stalks away, muttering under his breath. I swear to God, the longer I spend with my club brothers the more I wonder how Prez expects to be at the forefront of the one per-centers, leading the way in organised crime. With arseholes like Crazy and Country among our ranks the Savage Saints is closer to a fucking geriatric ward at a mental asylum than an MC.

Raine bends over in front of me to wipe up the spilled beer. I have a front row seat to the best fuckin' natural cleavage in the house. My dick stirs, but I'm bone fuckin' tired. Raine looks tired, too. She has on too much eye make-up, and her skirt's a lot shorter than anything I've seen her wear so far. She's sexy as fuck, but she doesn't need all that shit. In fact, it kinda looks like she's playing dress-up in her junkie mother's clothes.

"You need another refill, Kick?" she asks, scooping up the half-empty jug and straightening. She catches me staring at her tits and blushes. It's endearing as fuck, and on any other given day I'd bend her over the sofa and fuck her in the middle of the room where everyone and anyone could see her 'til she'd forgotten the meaning of the word embarrassment.

"Nah, I'm good," I say, kicking my feet up on the coffee table she just cleaned. She shoos me off and I see one of those rare smiles from her.

"You get your muddy boots off my table, Mister. I don't want to give Jett a reason to fire me."

"Prez isn't gonna fire you, darlin'."

"Yeah, well, I can't afford to take that chance. I can't shoot a gun and I don't ride a motorcycle, so unless I'm doing my job properly, I'm not much use to him."

I laugh, wondering how she's so completely oblivious. "I'm sure he'd find other uses for you, Raine."

She shakes her head and carries the jug and our

empty glasses to the bar, dumping them in the sink. As she clears the bar she snags the bottle of black Sambuca and then leans over to grab a clean shot glass. Her already short skirt rides up and I catch a glimpse of a white lacy G-string. I tilt my head for a better look and say roughly, "I'm sure we could all find plenty of other uses for you, darlin'."

"Stop," she warns, walking towards me on her spiky heels. There's a rejuvenated skip to her step, though. Raine sits down on the couch beside me, placing the shot glass on the coffee table. She fills it and hands it to me. I down the shot and then place it back on the table, signalling for her to pour another. When she's done, I lift the glass and offer it to her. She smiles and shakes her head. "I don't drink while I'm working."

"Drink the motherfuckin' shot, darlin'." I hold it to her lips and she tries turning her head away but I grasp the nape of her neck in my hands, tipping her head back along with the shot so that she has no choice but to open, unless she wants it spilled down the front of her top. "Thatta girl, open up and say ah."

She glares at me when I pull the shot glass away, but I'm distracted by the drop of Sambuca that's escaped the corner of her mouth and is running down her face. I pull her towards me and run my tongue along her throat, collecting the droplet off her chin. I smash my lips into hers, forcing my tongue into her sweet little mouth, tasting the liquor on her breath. She makes a sound of protest and tries to ease away, but I hold her to me until I'm done trying to wrench an emotion other than frustration from my consciousness. I draw a big fucking blank. *Surprise, sur-fuckin'-prise.*

I release her and flop back into the couch, defeated, horny, and feeling like I have a fuckin' conscience. I don't fuckin' like it.

"Kick …" Raine begins

"Nah, it's alright, darlin'." I lean forward and grab the bottle from the table, taking a hefty swig of the stuff that tastes like shit, but it keeps me from thinking about the rock-hard cock tucked away in my jeans that I'm ignoring. I pat her knee with my free hand. "I got enough bitches to contend with as it is. Besides, Prez would probably kick my arse anyway."

"Why would he kick your arse? Because I'm the hired help?"

I laugh. "Oh sweetheart, tell me you're not that fucking clueless?"

"Screw you," she says and stands, getting ready to huff off in a fucking pansy-arsed little bitch fit.

I grab her arm and yank her back down onto the couch. "The man wants in your sweet little lacy knickers, Raine."

"But he's married?"

"Yes, he is." I take another swig from the bottle.

She frowns, tucking a strand of hair behind her ear. "Did he … did he say something to you?"

"Didn't have to. It's written all over that dumb fucker's face."

She straightens her top, yanking hard on the hem, and then balking when she sees she just exposed more of her precious lacy underwear than she intended too. Her face is beet fuckin' red.

"You're a perfect fuckin' ten, darlin', just the way you are. Some of these bitches need all that shit: hooker heels, short skirts, the make-up ... you don't. You're not gonna lose your job because you're not dressing like a slut. In fact, Prez might fire you because you're trying to look like a slut. Fucker is crazy jealous."

She smiles. I'm sure deep down somewhere in that girly head of hers she's twisting my words the way women do. She's probably telling herself right now that I'm only humouring her. I'm not. I don't bullshit people unless I think I can gain something from it. Raine's legs are firmly closed to me and despite the fact that my cock is gonna be starved for pussy for fuck knows how long, I'm okay with that. I wasn't lying when I said Prez would likely beat my head in if he walked into the club and caught me fucking Raine; he really would beat the shit outta me. Her first shift he called a club meeting to tell us what was going down with her, and to let us know that if he caught any of us *going* down on her, he'd beat the holy living fuck out of us. It doesn't take a genius to figure that he was factoring his own needs into that equation.

"Perfect ten, huh?" Raine asks, jolting me back into the room.

I nod. *What, does she want it in fucking writing?*

"And what's Ivy?" She's not asking 'cause she's jealous; I don't think Raine has a malicious bone in her body, but she's gently poking buttons that she has no right to be pushing at.

A humourless laugh escapes me. "Ivy is a red-hot fuckin' mess."

"She was when you left her in the hall the other day." She quietly adds, "I've never seen her look so broken, Kick."

Ah, hell. This is why I've stayed in my room for three fuckin' days. Knowing that shit is one thing, but having to deal with the fallout? I'd rather take it up the arse with a sword than deal with that clusterfuck. "Yeah, had to be done though."

She nods. "That doesn't mean it was easy for you."

"You got a point, Raine? Or are you just gonna poke at the past and make me feel even more like shit?"

"Did it hurt?"

"Little bit, yeah."

"How's the new girl coping?"

"Indie?" I ask, rolling my head on the sofa back to look at her. "She's not. Tried to off herself in my room."

"I heard." She offers a sad smile, and fuck me, it's one of the sweetest fucking things I've ever seen. "I'm sorry."

"What the fuck is with you women? Why the hell are we talking about this shit?"

"Because I know what it's like to be alone, Daniel. It's a hard place to be."

"Jesus Christ," I mutter, shaking my head, but she's right; alone is the hardest place to be. Alone fuckin' sucks, but what can any of us do about it?

I let her words sink in for a beat, and then I let out an exasperated breath. "Can't even take a fucking nap in peace," I say, and push up off the couch.

Raine chuckles. "You're welcome," she shouts after me, and I give her the finger as I continue down the hall to my room. To Indie. I've left her to sit and stew long enough. Now I need answers; now I need her to trust me. Though that shit didn't work out so fucking well for the last woman who put her faith in me.

KICK

TWO YEARS AGO

I set my empty pack of smokes on the concrete floor beside me. My arse hurts. I don't know how long we've been here but the girl has been dozing on and off for what feels like hours, sleeping fitfully. She wakes—expecting to be somewhere else, maybe—and startles when she sees me, and then after glowering at me for the longest time, she eventually slips back under.

The door opens and the girl jumps and then skitters back against the wall, instantly awake and huddling in the corner as Tank and Prez stalk into the room.

"Time for round fuckin' two, bitch." Prez throws his arms wide, looking gleeful at the panic he's seeing in her. I wanna empty my clip into his dick but I glare at him instead, wishing I had the balls to do something to save her from him.

I'm not under any illusions; I'm no fuckin' hero. I'm the antihero here because I didn't fight harder, because I watched and I got off on it, but that doesn't mean I wanna see him do it again. She's so fucking strong, and he might hold her down and use up her body until she's physically broken and bloody, but she still won't break, not mentally. I know that as inherently as I know I deserve to burn in hell for the things I've done, and the things I'll no doubt do before I'm dead. I know that as well as I know that my prez won't give up. And I know that she'll die screaming because of it.

I rise to my feet and glance at Tank as Prez advances on the girl. Tank's face is stoic—no surprise there—but he won't meet my eyes, an action so at odds with everything I know about the man. I dart my eyes back to the girl just as Prez backhands her across the cheek. She's corralled into a corner, trying to fend off Prez's greedy fuckin' hands. He pokes at her, the way you'd poke a stick at a dead animal.

"Here, kitty, kitty," he says, lunging for her. He wraps his hand around her throat, lifting her from the floor as she struggles against him, her face contorted in pain, the wall at her back. "That sweet little pussy ready for me, yet?"

"Fuck you." She grits out the words around the fingers clasping her throat.

"No, sweet thing." I can't see his face but I know he's grinning like a homicidal maniac. "Fuck you."

Her eyes meet mine over his shoulder. They're not pleading for me to make him stop, but challenging. The bitch is fucking daring me to watch as he breaks her body. I can't do this again. I bend double and glare a hole into the floor. "Kick, get over here."

I take a deep, shuddering breath, my chest squeezing tight. My head doesn't want any part of this, but my cock

KICK

is already straining against my jeans. I straighten. Do I see a way out of raping this girl? Yeah. I could stab my prez in the kidneys, the way I would have done if Tank hadn't been here to stop me yesterday. I could beat the shit out of Prez, take the girl and run, but would Tank let me? Not fuckin' likely. If any brother but Ethan ever had my back it's Tank, but even he's not dumb enough to let me get away with that shit.

Prez turns to face me. "Sometime to-fuckin'-day, son."

Hatred burns my gaze as it bores into him. I take a step forward, my body going through the motions, but my mind is flailing around like a fish out of water, not knowing what to do. If I kill Prez and take the girl, I betray the brotherhood—assuming I can get past Tank, that is. If I go through with Prez's orders, then I'm as fucked up as him. I want this girl, but I want her on my terms, not his. If it were any other bitch, I might not bat an eyelid. I'd do what I had to, because it meant I didn't wind up with a bullet in my skull.

I stalk forward, knowing without having to make the decision what I will do because there's only one option here … to follow orders.

Prez smiles. He pats me on the back as I stand next to him. The girl begins thrashing; he has her pinned to the wall with one hand. He laughs as she strikes him. "Fuckin' feral bitch, this one. Wanna watch your cock doesn't get chewed up by that vicious little cooter of hers."

I step between them, forcing Prez's arm away, and I trap her against the wall with my lower body. She throws out her fist and strikes me across the side of the face with it. It isn't some half-arsed girly attempt; this bitch knows how to hit, and she's not pulling punches. The blow hurts like a motherfucker, my cheek throbs, and pain radiates through my skull. I catch her wrists up in mine before she can deal another blow and force them up above her head, slamming her into the wall.

I lean in and whisper close to her ear, "This will go much better for you if you stop struggling."

I hate that I'm forced to take her like this. If I could just tell her that I have every intention of making this as pleasurable as it can be for her, she may be less inclined to fight, resulting in less damage. But rape is still rape and admitting that I don't want to hurt her, that I'm forced to follow orders, in front of my prez is as good as a bullet to the brain. Gripping her wrists with one hand and undoing her pants with the other, I slip my hand inside, cringing inwardly when I feel the crusted blood over her swollen pussy. She bucks her hips, pressing herself further into the wall to escape my touch. That only aids me though, giving me a better grasp on her cunt, and the second she realises this, she begins twisting and writhing against me—no, not writhing against me, trying to get away from me. Though both my mind and body want her, I have to see this for what it is: rape. That's all it can be, because as much as I might want to slide my fingers, and my cock inside her, she doesn't want that, and this is the decision I made. This is the choice that keeps me alive—albeit a shitty one—but it is what it is, and I am who I am. I don't make any excuses for that.

"Stop. Fucking. Struggling," I whisper.

"Fuck you." She rears her head back in an attempt to

head-butt me but I snap my head back out of reach. My fingers shift inside her pants, spreading swollen lips and searching for that sweet spot. I know the second I find it because she quits struggling, at least for a beat, and then she's back to bucking like a wild animal. I rub furiously at her clit until I feel her body jerk involuntarily. Her legs tremble, her flat stomach quivers against the heel of my hand, as her muscles war with her head. She lets out a whimpering cry, half torment, half pleasure. I slow my tempo, stroking in long, sure caresses, soothing her, coaxing her pleasure from her slowly, despite the anguish she feels, despite the fact that I'm the one forcing her to feel it.

Her eyes lock onto mine, and in that moment everything slips away. Prez, Tank, her pain, the room she's held captive in—all of it. There's only her eyes on mine, and her body succumbing to pleasure under my deft hands. Tears stream down her face and her eyelids fall closed as her body jerks with orgasm. I continue stroking, petting, playing, even as she tries to squeeze me from between her legs by clamping them shut. I stroke until I feel the violence of another release rip through her, and then I pull my hand free and lick my fingers clean, savouring the taste of her arousal tinged with the tang of blood that dances across my tongue as she slides down the wall and curls into herself, her eyes synched tightly closed and her mouth open with a silent, sobbing scream.

My prez brutalised her and she may have screamed and cried for help, but even bruised and bloody and in more pain than I imagine she was letting on, she remained strong, resilient, defiant. He couldn't break her, but I just accomplished that feat in a matter of seconds. I knew the second her eyes met mine. I felt it, and I forged ahead anyway when I should have walked away. Sometimes kindness is a far worse weapon than brutality

Fury wells within me. Fury at him, at her, at myself. I take a step back. Prez laughs. It's a fake, obnoxious sound, and it makes me want to rip his fuckin' face off. He slaps me on the back. "Jesus, son, those are some magic bloody fingers."

I shrug out of his hold and put some distance between me and the girl. I don't trust myself with the taste of her on my tongue. I don't look at her but at Tank instead, who's been all too fuckin' quiet since he walked in. He returns my glare and gives me an imperceptible nod. Is he fuckin' congratulating me for not attacking our prez? I've never wanted to beat the shit out of Tank before, but these last two days have shown me a different side to my brother. A side I badly want to eradicate.

Prez pulls the girl up by her hair. I expect her to scream or cry out, but she does nothing—she just allows him to move her body wherever the fuck he wants. He spins her around to face me, positioning himself behind her as he takes hold of her throat, and his other arm snakes around her waist. Her eyes are red rimmed, glazed and vacant. The rent in her lip has opened up again and blood slowly pools on the surface. Her eye, where Prez beat on her yesterday, is still swollen shut. *Jesus Christ.* "Take off her pants. You're not done yet, son."

I glower at him, ready to tell him to go fuck himself, because I can't rape this girl, and I know that still makes me scum because with anyone else, if it were the choice between staying alive and following orders, I wouldn't hesitate. I wouldn't falter. You do what you have to in order to stay alive, regardless of whether it helps you sleep at night. But not with this girl. Not her. I slide my hand to the knife holstered at my waist and open my mouth to speak when Prez's phone rings in his pocket. And then Tank's phone rings, too. Prez tips his chin in Tank's direction, signalling for him to answer it.

Tank pulls out the phone and his deep baritone fills the room. "What?"

His brow creases–that's about the only expression you'll ever get out of the man, unless you make him really mad.

"Fuck." He hangs up and pockets the phone. "Cops are at the gate, Prez."

"Jesus fuckin' Christ? Can't a man get fucked in peace?"

"What do we do with the girl? Can't leave her here. Frogger says they've been out there for the last thirty minutes. Can't come in without a warrant, but that doesn't mean they're not getting one."

"FUCK!" he bellows and releases the girl, throwing her towards me. He stalks to the door, and then turns back to me, pointing. "Get her into the shower, you keep her in there until they pry you two apart. You don't know nothin' about no raid, you're just fucking your old lady on a lazy Sunday afternoon. Got it?"

I nod.

"And you." He turns his attention on the girl. "You make a fuckin' sound that isn't like he's just fucked the shit outta you, and once those little piggies are gone, I'm gonna let every single one of my boys bury their cock in every fuckin' hole you have to offer, bitch."

She doesn't say anything in response. She doesn't even flinch. She just continues to stare at the floor as I take hold of her arm and push her forward towards the exit. Prez and Tank are already running ahead of us. There's shit to hide, incriminating evidence to get rid of, and drugs to flush.

"Don't try anything stupid. It won't get you rescued; it'll only get you dead," I say to her as we clear the stairs. I open the door leading to the outside, and the light blinds us both. I throw my free hand up to block the sun and the girl takes that opportunity to elbow me in the guts. My reflexes kick in. I let go, because being punched in the gut always feels like someone just shattered your balls with the turn of a vice. She begins screaming for help as she runs, but she's injured and definitely not quick enough.

I bolt after her, collecting her up by the waist and slamming us onto the asphalt. It hurts like a mother fucker, winds us both, but I recover before her and climb on top of her, holding her arms above her head as she struggles. "I told you not to fuckin' run, bitch."

She spits in my face. "Go fuck yourself, you filthy fucking pig."

"If I didn't do that shit back there, it would have been so much worse. You want my dick inside you, bitch?"

"Fuck you."

"We're both still alive enough to feel the adrenaline runnin' through our fucking veins because of what I did in that room. You should be fuckin' thankin' me."

KICK

"Thanking you? For molesting me? I should be driving that god damn knife at your belt into your heart."

"This knife?" I ask, unsheathing it. Her eyes dart around wildly, looking for an exit. I take the wickedly sharp blade and slide it down the front of my jeans. "By all means, take it, Princess."

She glowers at me. I push up off her and pull the knife from my pants. Wouldn't help to cut off my cock, now would it? That might make our story a little hard to believe. I lean over and grab her arm, and half-walk, half-drag her to the door leading to the clubhouse. Her skin is scraped to hell from our roll on the asphalt. "Run again, and I will slit your throat."

She struggles, digging her bare feet into the ground. She tries yanking her arm from my grasp, desperate for escape. I tighten my hold and drag her forward. She gasps as the ground scrapes her feet. She might be tall but she's a little thing, and despite her inner strength, she's not strong enough to fend me off. I can't see the gate from this side of the compound, so they sure as shit can't see or hear us, but I still need to get her inside before the boys in blue are bangin' down our door.

I open the door to the clubhouse and shove her inside, wedging her up against the wall with my body. I deadbolt the door from the inside, then I drag her, kicking and screaming down the hall to my room before I unlock it and throw her inside.

"Get undressed," I command. I don't bother locking the door because the bastards will just kick it down, and then I'll have to buy a new lock. Instead I grab her by the wrist and lead her to the shower. I shut the bathroom door behind us. The girl stares at me. "Take your fucking clothes off."

"No."

"Bitch, I'm getting real tired of you fightin' me," I say. "Take your fucking clothes off, or I'll do it for you."

She doesn't move and even though she's bein' an obstinate little bitch, under different circumstances I'd fuckin' love the idea of having to rip the clothes from her body.

I throw her into the shower and turn on the spray, and then I strip her bare while she howls, and kicks, and scratches, and yeah, even bites. She sobs as I push her back under the water. I strip off my shirt and throw it to the floor, and then I unbutton my jeans and shove them down my hips. My cock springs free, jutting upwards, hard for this beautiful mess of a woman with her bruised body and her face all jacked up, as if she just got out of federal prison. I step out of my jeans and throw them in a sopping heap on the floor.

She's turned her body into the wall, huddling against the wet tile. A part of me wants to leave her there, but that's not part of the plan. "In order for you to get out of here wearin' somethin' other than a body bag, you're gonna need to make this believable."

I take hold of her shoulder and spin her around to face me. I push her back against the tile and spread her legs apart by wedging my knee between them. She resists, but I give her an impatient glare and drive my leg between hers until she has no choice but to open, or suffer even more bruises. "Open for me, Princess. I swear I'll be gentle."

I use the distraction of my words to slip between

her legs. Her body is pressed to mine and my cock rests against her belly. I take hold of it and slide it into the hollow V created by her thighs, her smooth pussy skimming my dick. I can feel her wetness, her arousal left over from the two orgasms I wrought from her with my hands. That might have broken her, but if anything it's only made me want her more. I rock against her body and promise silently that one day she will let me inside her. It won't be because my Prez has commanded it, or because she thinks things might go easier for her if she plays nice. It will be because she wants me there. Because she craves it—needs it. And when that time comes she won't just be a princess of an MC, she'll be a motherfuckin' queen. My motherfuckin' queen.

"When are you going to get it through that fuckin' thick skull of yours? You're going to die unless you go along with this. You got me, babe? You play nice and when I can I'll help you get outta here, but if you fuck this up, if you run again, or you don't go along with everything I say to the coppers that are about to come busting through that door there, then no one can fuckin' help you. Not me. Not your dad. No fuckin' one."

"Please don't hurt me. Please?" she begs.

"I'm not gonna hurt you, darlin'. And I'm not going to rape you. So long as you play nice, you get to leave this bathroom with your pretty skull intact."

I move my hips back, unable to resist the sensation of my wet cock sliding against her slick cunt. I know this isn't doing much for my promise not to rape her, and I wouldn't, because I've had a taste of this wildcat's surrender and it's the closest thing to holy that I'll ever get in this life, or the one after. Shoving myself inside her without permission isn't going to get me more of that delicious submission, it'll only make her fight, and while I may even enjoy that too, it's not how I want her.

I want the taste of her cunt on my tongue, I want to bury myself so deep we merge into a single being. I want her begging and pleading with me to send her over the edge, and for perhaps the first time ever, I want someone to need me, to depend on me. The arsehole, the bastard who's left a long string of whores broken in his wake without so much as a second thought. The piece-of-shit whose life was almost snuffed out by his father, who wakes every day and looks in the mirror with enough self-loathing to detonate Times Square, if only that shit was combustible. That pathetic excuse for a man wants to be worthy of someone. The question I need to figure out now is: why?

Out in the clubhouse sounds of protests, glass breaking and furniture being overturned ring out. I stare at the girl's eyes; they're wide and panicked, and I know she hears it too. I press my palm flat against her sternum, and it makes her glance down and her eyes grow wider. Her heart taps out a staccato beat against her flesh, and mine.

"Look at me, Princess," I say. Her wild gaze shoots up to meet my own. "I'm not going to stick my cock in you; not today, anyway. But I can make this enjoyable for you, like downstairs."

"Touch me again and I swear to you I will scream."

"Yeah, you will." I say. Her eyes narrow with anger, her jaw clenches tight. "Face it—I know exactly where to touch you. I know exactly how to break you in, and you like it. You don't want to, but you do. It's written all over your face, and it's here." I slide my hands down between us and slip into her slick pussy lips. She jolts away, but she has nowhere to go. I have her penned in with one arm and the other is stroking her pretty cunt, coaxing more pleasure, coaxing her orgasm from her. She sobs, but it's the sound of resignation, not pain.

I quicken my pace, lean forward and whisper, "Scream for me, Princess."

She clenches her teeth, resisting. I rise to the challenge, or I guess I bow down and kneel to it. The dirty tile hurts my knees. It's been a long time since I've been on them before another person, but I push past the discomfort and spread her thighs apart, hooking one leg over my shoulder. She struggles; when does she not? But I take that bud in my mouth, sucking hard and wrenching the screams from the back of her throat. Her thighs clench around either side of my head as her whole body gives over to the spasms, head thrown back, eyes closed, mouth open in pure blissful pleasure.

I don't stop at just one, though. I lick and suck through her twisting and twitching, her protests and punches. I delve my tongue into her hole, as far as I can reach, rubbing my coarse stubble against her pussy, making her flinch and cry out, and eventually tilt her hips toward me for more.

When the cops finally bust down my door, I've forgotten all about the fuckers. I stand quickly and capture her face in my hands. If she's smart, she'll play along; if not, this may be the only time I get to taste her, have her, kiss her. So I do that, despite the fact that I'm buck naked, she's scared out of her fucking mind and the cops have a gun trained on my head. I lower my lips to hers and drive my tongue into her mouth, forcing her to taste herself, to feel me in her mouth the way I was inside her pussy. I use the distraction to wrap my hand around the nape of her neck, realising how easy it would be to twist and snap it, and fearing the fragility of her all at once. I keep my eyes trained on her as I take her mouth. She's doped with pleasure, and her eyes are glassy—or the one that I can see is. The other is still swollen shut.

"Get your hands on your head and turn around slowly," the cop commands. I let the girl's face go and place my hands behind my head, turning with a cocky smile and an even cockier dick, considering I'm still fuckin' hard as concrete and beggin' for release. That's one orgasm I can kiss goodbye.

The cop closest to the door curls his lip in distaste. "Jesus Christ."

"There a reason you officers are busting down my door while I'm trying to make sweet mad love to my old lady here?"

"Step out of the shower, and drop to your knees, Sir."

"Listen, fellas, you might swing that way down at the station, but I don't suck cock. As you can see, I like pussy." A grin tugs at the corners of my mouth. "Mostly just her pussy, but I'm not fussy."

One of them pulls a towel from the rack and throws it at me. "Cover yourself up," he hisses, bringing his hand back to his gun.

I step from the shower and wrap the towel around me, not bothering to dry off, then I throw another at the girl and say, "Princess, go wait for me in bed, okay? This shouldn't take long, and then I can get back to fucking the shit outta that sweet cunt of yours."

She just stares at me and I have to refrain from rolling my eyes. Could she be any more fuckin' suspicious? Her gaze darts from the cops to me, and back again. She opens her mouth to speak, but I shoot her a warning look and her eyes widen. I'm shoved to the ground. The men slap me in cuffs, though I'm not read my rights, so I don't know what the fuck is going on. For a half a second I think my prez might have used me as a scapegoat, but no one rats to the cops. Not even Prez can come back from that shit. You rat, you die. It's the reason they've been gunning for Ethan's head for so long, because the Angels believe he ratted and then cashed in his get-out-of-jail-free card. I know differently, but I can't exactly tell them that, because that would open up a whole slew of questions Prez wouldn't like the answer to. Answers that would get me a bullet to the face.

The water shuts off and her little feet thud on the mat beside me. I dare a glance in her direction. She's covered by an old towel, hair plastered to her back and water beaded on her skin. I wanna lick it off. I wanna trace my tongue over every fuckin' inch of that gloriously brown body, but one of the bastards in blue hauls me up by the cuffs and shoves me forward. The towel slips from my waist. The cop in front of me lets out an exasperated sigh.

"Christ. Can we get some clothes on this fucker?"

"Just do up the God damned towel."

"I'm not going near his Johnson. You fucking do it."

I roll my eyes as the two cops fight about my junk hanging out for the world to see. Princess surprises us both, I think, when she bends down in front of me and retrieves the towel. It's more surprising still when she glances up at me from her position on the floor. Her eyes are dark with challenge. Over what? I don't know.

Princess stands and wraps the towel around me, skimming the hard muscles of my hips with her tiny fragile hands as she tucks one end of the towel into the part covering my waist. "Thanks, Princess. Now be a good little girl and go wait in bed for me."

Her hatred is a fuckin' beam that sears me right down to the core. She stands before me, not saying anything, but conveying everything with the tension in her gaze.

"Princess," I hiss through my teeth.

"He the one that did that to your face?" one of the officers asks. She just stares at him, and he turns his stupid fuckin' questioning gaze on me. He looks like a fuckin' dickhead. "You like to beat on your old lady?"

"I didn't do that, but right now I'm beginning to wish I had," I warn.

Her eyes dart between me and the cop again, and she says, "My name is Lauren Costello. My father is Slayer—" She shakes her head. "My father is Vincent Costello. He's the president of the Severed Sons' Motorcycle club. These people kidnapped me, they've held me hostage. Their president … he raped me … he beat me."

"Stupid fucking bitch," I hiss, shaking my head.

So Princess has a name, huh? I could have done without knowing what that was, because now the name Lauren will forever be tainted by the fact that I watched her get tortured. That I watched her die right in front of me and that I could do nothing to stop it. And she will die. Prez will see to that. He won't tolerate that shit. Just because a man wears a uniform doesn't mean he isn't just as criminal as the fuckin' rest of us. And even if she gets lucky and the cops do send her home, we'll still find her, and we'll gun her down and string up her insides like Christmas tree tinsel, because that's what we do to rats. You rat, you die.

"Ah, shit," the fatter of the two officers says. His porky belly protrudes over his belt, and he jams a finger through the belt loop and tugs it upward. "And this guy? He rape you too?"

She glances at me, and it's the fuckin' damnedest thing, but I think I see guilt behind her eyes. "No. He was trying to help. He promised to get me out of here."

"Stop fuckin' talkin', bitch," I shout. Every word that comes out of her whoring trap sinks me further in the shitter, and she doesn't even know it.

"Did he now?" the cop asks. Princess nods her head vigorously.

Tilting his head towards his partner, the cop yanks me out of the way while the other grabs Lauren's wrists and hauls her through my bedroom and out into the hall.

"Wait," she protests. The wall blocks my view of her but I can hear the panic rising in her voice. "Can I at least get my clothes?"

"Nope. We need them for evidence," the cop replies.

"Ow, you're hurting me."

I don't need to be told to move forward, cuffs or not. I all but sprint after them, only I'm yanked back by the officer. "There's been a slight change of plans."

"Get your filthy fuckin' piggy hands off me, motherfucker." I try twisting from his grip, but he yanks my arms up behind me, causing my elbows and shoulder blades to groan and protest the pain.

"Walk," he commands, holding my arms at bay by the chain connecting my cuffs. I stagger out into the hall as he urges me forward. The gun trained at my head is the only thing keeping me from head-butting this motherfucker and making a break for it. Well, that and the cuffs, pinning my hands behind my back.

As I clear the hall, I'm not met with my brothers kneeling on the floor, all lined up in a degenerate little line of criminals, the way we'd usually be in a raid. Instead, my prez is relaxing back on a fuckin' La-Z-Boy, sharing a bottle of top-shelf scotch with some douchie lookin' rail-thin officer of the law, and my brothers are spread throughout the front room, arms folded, guns in holsters, and fuckin' unhappy expressions on their faces. Though for some of them that's a regular expression. My father included, who leans against the wall and doesn't meet my eyes. He's probably fuckin' pissy that he didn't get an invite to Prez's "Let's Kidnap A Rival MC's Daughter And Rape And Torture Her For Fuckin' Kicks" party. *Cunt rag.*

The only people that look as if they're havin' a good time here are Prez and the fucking arsehole in blue who's holdin' Princess close to him and feelin' up every inch of her body as she struggles.

Prez watches me closely as I'm pushed towards the centre of the room. I might have my eyes glued to the fucker whose paws are all over Princess, but that doesn't mean I can't feel Prez eyeballing me harder than a whore he wants inside of. "And speaking of fuckin' pathetic," Prez says as I'm forced down on my knees before him. "I had such high hopes for you, Kick. We raised you from a fuckin' babe, we made you into a man, and then you go and turn into a snivellin' fuckin' pussy, over some fuckin' pussy."

Sniggers come from all around the room. "Have you been inside her tight little cunt yet?"

"Fuck you."

He leans forward and strikes me across the face. I rock back on my knees with the force of the blow, and then I'm shoved flat on the floor, his boot pressing against the back of my neck, crushing my upper spine.

"Get comfortable, kid," he says. "I'm gonna teach you the difference between takin' pussy and fuckin' being one."

I growl into the filthy carpet. My eyes dart wildly around the room and land on my father. He looks bored. The arsehole looks as if he'd rather be scratching his arse than standing here, watching his son debased in front of the club.

My eyes dart to Tank but he glares back at me, stoic as ever, and then he turns and leaves the room. Prez doesn't try to stop him. No, Prez doesn't care about anything but teaching Princess and I a lesson.

Her screams make me struggle. Prez lifts his foot and for a second I can breathe easier, and then he calls Frogger to his side and the fucker straddles my back, pulling my head up by the hair, my neck yanked up at a painful angle.

He leans down and whispers, "I'm gonna savour this moment forever, you little shit." He jerks on my head again and I'm forced to see it: her, them, touching her, tasting her, hurting flesh that should be mine to hurt. Punishing her cunt with their cocks as she screams and struggles and bleeds. I try to close my eyes but Frogger punches my kidneys to make me watch. Prez and the police officers take it in turns, and then Juke steps forward. His mouth turns up in a sideways grin that even the devil wouldn't touch. He lifts her up. She's bruised and beaten, covered in cum and blood and spit. She's not even crying anymore—she doesn't fight, just allows herself to be positioned wherever they want, however they want.

"Wait," I growl out. I'm surprised anyone but Frogger hears me with the ruckus of the room.

"SHUT UP!" Prez bellows, and the room falls into silence. "Kid's got somethin' to say. Let's hear it, lover boy."

"She's mine. I'm laying claim to her. Want her for my old lady."

Prez chuckles. It's a dark and foreboding sound. "You can't take a fucking club whore as your old lady, kid."

"She's not a club whore, and you know it."

"Well, if it walks like a club whore, and talks like a club whore …"

"She's Sons' property. Slayer's gonna tear this club apart when he finds her."

"Exactly; she's Sons' property, and she serves a purpose you can't even comprehend." He turns back to my father. "Take her to fuckin' town, Juke. Show the boy how it's done."

INDIE

I jolt awake. My heart pounds in my chest, and my body is slick with sweat from yet another nightmare. I'm still in the biker's room, one arm is still cuffed to the bed, and the other is still hooked up to the IV that prevents it from falling forward. I attempt to move within my restraints, but what the hell is the fucking point? My limbs prickle with pins and needles. My arse cheeks are numb, my bladder full to bursting. I blink my tired eyes and adjust to the dimness that is my hell without windows. At least in the warehouse I knew what time of day it was. Three days could have passed here and I wouldn't know if it was midnight or morning.

I know my cookie's still there, though. I can smell it.

If the biker ever comes back it's gonna be a tough decision between peeing and stuffing my face with enough trans-fats to kill off a village full of African children. I sag against my restraints. If the biker ever comes back, feeding my face is probably the least of my worries. I already know I need his help to find those bastards that raped and maimed me, both physically and psychologically, but that doesn't mean I'm going to trust him. How can I, when he's every bit as dangerous as them? I know it's not an act. He wasn't playing good cop, bad cop with me—I know a monster when I see one. I've spent enough time with monsters to know, to feel the wrongness that seeps from every single pore on his body. What I don't understand is my reaction to him. He may have saved me, but for what purpose? He can play nice guy now and pretend that we need each other to bring those bastards down, and maybe we do need each other for that, but why did he take me in the first place if it wasn't just to use me the way they did? To wring every last bit of humiliation and pain and dread from my psyche?

Jesus. All these questions are giving me a headache. Or maybe that's just the copious amount of drugs I've had pumping through my system for days. No, not days, weeks apparently.

I wonder what my parents are doing now. Are they trying to find me? Are they out walking the streets, seeing my face in every brunette they pass? Did they have any leads? Would they have ever found me if the biker hadn't found me first?

A rustling has my adrenaline spiking again. I dart my gaze all around the room but despite how my vision has adjusted to the lack of windows, I can't see a damn thing but junk, empty trays of take-out, and unwashed coffee cups. Every freaking surface is covered with filth. Biker's a pig, but it's not just that. Apart from a couple of pieces of beaten up furniture and the plasma on the wall that's probably stolen, there's nothing here to tell me anything about the man who has me chained to his bed.

The rustling is closer now, and the scurry of tiny feet along hard surfaces has icy fingers creeping down my spine. My eyes roam the room, falling on the table where the biker left the wadded up paper from his sub. The paper moves, falling off the edge of the table onto the floor, revealing a tiny grey mouse with his nose in the air. His little mouth twitches and then he practically pounces on the cookie.

My cookie.

I lurch forward, but my restraints hold me back. I buck and shout, "That's my fucking cookie!"

The mouse scurries down the table leg and under the armchair the biker had been sleeping in hours earlier, but it isn't the mouse moving around that catches my eye now — it's the biker. I was so worked up over that fucking cookie that I didn't hear or see him come in. But he moves through the room like the angel of death, all darkness and unleashed fury. He pulls the knife from his belt, crouches down and then spears the mouse on the end of the blade.

He holds it up. Blood and innards stain its short grey fur. A single droplet slides down the mouse's tail, and falls onto the carpet. Biker carries it across the room and slams his foot down on the pedal of the stainless steel bin, jiggling the knife over the rubbish until the tiny body slides off the blade and lands in the garbage. Something about his brutality, about his ruthlessness and complete disregard for life enrages me.

"You didn't have to kill it," I shout.

He glares at me. "You'd rather me let it eat your cookie?"

"You're disgusting," I hiss.

Rounding the tiny bench he stands in front of the sink, his back to me. The giant winged skull on his cut mocks me. Savage Saints MC, the patch reads. Savage is right. Biker runs the water and rinses off the blade, pulling a tea towel that's seen better days from a rail above the sink and wiping the knife clean. He slides the blade back in its sheath on his belt and turns to face me. "I can promise you that was a much quicker, and more humane death than setting traps."

"Maybe if you cleaned up this shitty room, you wouldn't have mice you had to kill."

"Gotta sink my blade into something, Little Spitfire." He smiles as he sits down in the armchair opposite me and leans his elbows on his knees. "Can't afford to get rusty with a priest and a cop to kill."

He's baiting me. I know it, and yet I can't help but rise to it. "What do you get out of helping me? Besides your tape back?"

"So you're going to tell us what you know?"

"If I do this, we take down those fuckers, and I walk away. You let me walk away."

He nods his acquiescence. His dark blue eyes glint with hunger; he's like a wolf with a prize that he knows is within his reach. I don't trust him, but what choice do I have? I tell them what I know, or I keep my mouth shut and die anyway. I'm dead if the Priest finds me, so what do I have left to lose?

"Where do we start?"

"You tell me what you know, and we go from there."

"Can I at least pee first?"

"If I uncuff you are you gonna run?"

"Really?" I ask, impatiently. "You left me sitting here for an entire day, staring at a fucking cookie and trying desperately not to think of running water and you're asking me if I'm going to run? Hell yes, I'm going to run, straight to the freaking bathroom, and then you're going to feed me, and then we'll talk."

He smiles and shakes his head, walking over to the dresser he produced the cuffs from a few hours ago. He holds the keys up in front of him as he walks forward and sits on the edge of the bed. "What I said before still stands. Until Prez gets the info he wants, if you leave this room, they will not hesitate to put a bullet in you."

"Yeah, yeah, big bad bikers come equipped with lots of guns and big hurty bullets. If you don't hurry up and uncuff me, I'm going to pee all over your bed."

He sighs and then slips the key in the lock. The sound of that tiny latch unlocking has to be the greatest noise I've ever heard. I don't remember the sound of him unbuckling the restraints in the warehouse—he knocked me unconscious for that—but I don't think even that sound could have compared to this. When he saved me from that warehouse, I wasn't truly free, and while I might be held in the tender loving care of the Savage Saints Motorcycle club right now, the fact is that once we find the arseholes who abducted me, I'm free. Forever. I'll take karate, learn how to fire a gun—I'll carry an entire bag full of pepper spray with me everywhere I go. I'll do whatever it takes to make sure another man can never enslave me again.

The knot in my belly twists and I fear that the half a pizza sitting heavily in my insides wants to revisit the outside. That could have something to do with the fact that I haven't eaten a real meal in weeks, but it's more than likely because the biker is sitting on the armchair opposite me, while I sit on this worn, shit-stain coloured couch. His dark blue eyes burn into mine. He waits, though not patiently, because the label from the beer bottle he finished almost as quickly as he opened, is torn into tiny pieces and strewn all over the floor.

"Start talking, Indie," Biker says.

"Where did that name even come from?"

"I don't know. You reminded me of the Indy 500."

"I reminded you of a car race?"

"You reminded me that we're runnin' a race."

"Shouldn't I remind you of shoes then? I could be Nike, or Puma? Now that's a bad-arse name."

He sighs. "You're wasting time. Tell me what you know."

"Where do I even start?"

"At the beginning. Before you were taken. Did you see anyone, hear anything? You were a couple blocks from your house, right?"

"How did you know that?"

"I saw it on the news. CCTV saw you get off the train at around 9:00pm. A woman was interviewed by the cops, said she walked a ways with you before you reached her door."

"Rachel. She's two blocks before me. She's a student

too; we shared a class that night, and it ran late. We caught the later train. I walked Rachel to her gate, like I usually do, and then I headed for home. Only I never made it. I didn't hear anyone behind me. I didn't see anything suspicious. I just hurried along the footpath, and then I was pulled back into a little laneway between a set of row houses. He covered my mouth, and stuck a needle in my neck. I remember seeing a garbage bin in front of me. I reached out, and pulled it over — glass shattered as the recycling spilled out. That's the last thing I remember before I passed out."

"And when you woke up?"

"I was in the warehouse. They didn't have the chair at first. The room was empty. I was suspended from a beam in the ceiling by chains, stripped naked and freezing. I could feel the cold winter air coming up from under the door. I don't know how long I was out; it was still dark outside. Or maybe that was just the blindfold over my eyes.

"The Priest was the only one there the first time. At least, I think he was alone. In the beginning, they'd blindfolded me. His was the only voice I heard that first night. I can still remember it, you know? When I close my eyes, I hear him whispering in my ear. 'And if they have a change of heart in the land where they are held captive, and repent and plead with you in the land of their conquerors and say, "We have sinned, we have done wrong, we have acted wickedly."

"1 Kings, 8:46-47. Do you know how I know that?"

Biker shakes his head.

"He'd recite those verses; every time." A short humourless laugh escapes me. "I never knew what it meant, but I think I'm starting to. And then he'd tell me that 'we were all sinners and that it was time to atone."

"They ever use their names in front of you?"

"No. They called him Father. That was it. The Cop liked to wear his full uniform when he fucked me, and you already saw the Dentist in action."

"What did the Priest do, that first night?"

"What do you think?"

"I think this will all be over a whole lot quicker if you tell me everything you remember. I can't find these guys if I don't know exactly who I'm looking for. There are hundreds of churches in Sydney; that's a lot of fuckin' clergies' doors to bust down. And the Cop could be anywhere; he could be anyone. How do you know the uniform was real, and not just part of his M.O.?"

"He was a cop," I say, resolutely. "His weapons, the rigid posture. He had special patches sewn onto the sleeve of his uniform. And a duty belt."

"You can buy that shit off eBay," he says, leaning forward on his elbows again and piercing me with that narrowed gaze. "How do you know for certain that he was a cop? Do you know the weapons were standard police issue? Did he have a badge? What did the patches on his shirt say?"

"I'm sorry, I was a little distracted by the knife he held to my throat to pay too much attention to the fucking patches on his shirt," I shout.

The biker sets his jaw. A muscle in his cheek ticks, and his eyes glaze over as he clenches his right hand into a fist. He doesn't like it when I yell. He's going to have to get used to it.

"I know this might make you a little uncomfortable,

but I need to know this shit so I don't wind up serving a sentence for killin' a cop who had nothing to do with your abduction."

"A little uncomfortable?" I spit. "You wanna know what's uncomfortable? You wanna know exactly what they did to me? He fucked my arse, until I bled out all over the floor. Then he raped me with his baton while the fucking Priest egged him on. They tied me to a post and beat me senseless. The Priest liked to quote bible passages, and call me a whore as he raped me over and over until I begged for him to kill me. Until I promised to repent for sins I never fucking committed.

"The Dentist liked to knock me out and wake me up in the middle of an extraction. He liked to hold my mouth and nose closed until I was choking on my own blood, and passing out from oxygen deprivation. And that's just the stuff my brain hasn't repressed.

"You want me to give you information that tells you for certain that he was a cop? I can't do that. I don't know the difference between a real uniformed officer and a fake. But I know in my gut he was a cop. Just like I know that priest is out there somewhere, sitting in a confessional booth, hearing the sins of his congregation, and drizzling holy water over the top of babies' heads for baptismal rites. I know I wasn't the first girl they've done this to. And unless we find them, I sure as fuck won't be the last." My breath comes in short, hard gasps. My hands shake and tears sting my eyes. Frustrated, heartbroken, and so full of rage I can taste it in the back of my throat, I stand, and instantly regret it. I dash for the bathroom and manage to get the seat up before I spill the contents of my stomach into a porcelain bowl that looks as if it hasn't been cleaned since it was installed.

The biker's shadow looms over me. He stands in the middle of the tiny room, probably not knowing what the hell to do. I vomit again, and again, and then I pause, leaning over the bowl. Hot tears sting my face. My hair is yanked back. I cry out and skitter away from his touch, wedging myself as close to the wall as possible. "Don't touch me. Don't fucking touch me."

He holds up his hands in a warding gesture and backs away. "Just tryin' to help, Little Spitfire."

I wipe the vomit from my chin with the hem of the T-shirt he'd given me. I cover my mouth with my hands. The levee, the wall I've been building to fortify my heart, my spirit, crumbles, and just like that I fall apart completely. I don't know how to deal with any of this. I can't reconcile where I am from with where I was a few days ago, and where I am now. I want to see my mum. I want to hug my dad, something I can't remember doing for the longest time.

The biker moves from the doorway. Without a word he stalks from the bathroom, through the living area and out the door, slamming it behind him. I lay down on the floor, curling into a foetal position. I thought I could give them what they wanted, and in turn he'd help me to take the Priest out, but reliving that stuff? I don't know if I can do it. I don't know if I have it in me. I don't know if I'm strong enough to face all the things I don't remember from that warehouse of horrors.

KICK

I had to help. Hearing her cry like that, hearing her fall apart, and not being able to do … something. It was rippin' me apart. Which is fuckin' ridiculous. I don't know this girl from any other bitch on the street. I don't know what the fuck I'm doing. I glance up at the late-night chemist from the parking lot.

And I don't know how the fuck I got here.

I flip the kickstand down and take off my helmet, sliding the fastened strap over the handle bars. And then I ease off the bike and head inside the chemist. It's warm in here, chasing away the wind-chill from the cold July night. My presence is announced with an annoying fuckin' *ding* and I head straight for the aisle with all the shit to fix upset stomachs. I pick up some antacids, some Panadol and then hit the fridge for lemonade, snagging a bag of potato chips on the way to the register. I pay the bored-looking chick on the front counter and then head outside and hang the sack of goodies from the handlebars. I left not knowing where or why the fuck I was going, so my backpack is back at the clubhouse. It's late, and I likely won't come across any cops in the three blocks back to the compound anyway.

When I pull in, Tank is leaning up against the outside of the garage. I haven't seen him since the incident with Ivy in the hall. Grim said he'd taken Ivy to his big fancy fuck-off house in the woods, which admittedly shocked the hell outta me. He'd be better off dropping her at the nearest rehab clinic and getting her into a fuckin' methadone program, but what the fuck could I do about it? I'm the one that left her in that fuckin' state in the first place, and everything I've done from the time I first got that bitch on her back up until the way I fucked with her in the hall has just encouraged her behaviour, given her hope for something more, when there just isn't hope — not for me, not for her, not for us.

I take off my helmet, pull the bag from the handlebars and step out of the garage. I'm met with a flying fist, a slash of pain and a pulsing eye socket. "Ah fuck!" I stagger back, drop the bag, and hold my hand to my eye to stem the pain radiating around my whole fuckin' skull. "What the fuck are you doin', cunt fuck?"

"Been dealin' with cleaning up your shit for the last two fuckin' days. Bitch is a goddamn mess. Won't eat, won't sleep, won't even let me touch her. You fuckin' broke her, man, and who the hell do you think gets to be the one left holdin' the fuckin' pieces?"

"Ivy's not your fuckin' responsibility. It's not your job to step in and take my place, brother."

"No? Who the fuck else is gonna clean up your mess and make sure the bitch doesn't OD?"

KICK

"I don't know, her fuckin' family?" I say, but I know as well as he does that Ivy has no family. Only a sick son of a bitch for a dad who fucked her up so royally in the first place. "Bitch has problems beyond what you and I can fix. She needs help, and she needs away from this clubhouse."

He shakes out his fist and throws back his head with a roar of frustration. "I wanna beat your fuckin' head in for this."

"Yeah? Why the fuck stop at one punch?"

"Don't fuckin' test me," he warns, and then scrubs a hand over his face. "I know why you did what you did. I don't blame you for it. But I won't lie, if you so much as talk to her in the future, if you build her up again and give her hope that something might one day happen between the two of you, I'll put you to ground, brother."

For a beat all I do is stare at him. Tank, who didn't kill me when I told him I'd shot down our entire chapter, the dude who feels nothing, is all fuckin' twisted up over a girl. "Fuck me, does she know your boner's the size of fuckin' Uluru for her? All that shit about kicking her out 'cause she's crying all over the place? That was all you covering up some unrequited love bullshit."

"Shut the fuck up." He turns and stomps towards the clubhouse.

I pick up my bag of goodies and start after him. "How long you been pinin' after that bitch, brother?"

"You breathe a word of this shit to anyone and I'll fuckin' gut you in your sleep. You got me? I will put you to ground so fuckin' fast your—"

"Jesus Christ, don't get your fucking panties all twisted up your arse."

"She doesn't see me that way."

"So fuckin' make her see you that way, you douche. Have you never had to chase a bitch your entire life?" I ask. "Ivy's fucked up, but she's still a God damn woman, and she needs that love and cherishment crap more than most. The other stuff? Hurtin' her and all that? It's what she's used to. Doesn't mean that shit can't be broken, brother."

"Fuck me. Who'd have thought I'd be takin' romantic advice from the un-fuckin'-luckiest motherfucker in love walking the face of the planet?"

"Yeah, well, I might be unlucky, and I might have made a dick-tonne of mistakes, but if you don't come clean with her about how you feel you're gonna regret it."

Tank scrubs his hands over his cropped hair and stares down at his feet. Sighing heavily, he shakes his head, and then turns to me; his game face back on. Back to being the bastard who cares for no one, and gives nothing away. The dicktard doesn't even fuckin' realise that if he showed Ivy this side of himself, if he made her see that he actually fuckin' cared whether or not she lived or died, he'd have that bitch in the bag. She may not love him straight away, but I know her well enough to know that despite all her fucked up needs, all she really wants is someone to care the way her father never had. She'd grow to love anyone who showed a little bit of fuckin' interest in her. It's why she thinks she's in love with me.

Game face or not, he sounds tired when he says, "Prez wants to see you. He called a meeting while you were out, something about more fuckin' mess than he can deal with right now."

"I just gotta take this shit to Indie first."

He shrugs as he opens the front door to the clubhouse and steps inside. "Your funeral."

Yeah, it fuckin' will be if he finds out I didn't head straight to church. When Prez summons his flock, the flock better fuckin' haul arse, or Prez's gonna be lookin' for someone's face to bust in.

The lounge is dimly lit, full of smoke and the smell of sex and liquor. Raine's standing at the bar, a summery dress on, next to no make-up, and her hair all piled on top of her head in a messy knot as she wipes down the bar with a rag, soaking up some spillage left by Country. He never leaves that bar except to take a piss, weigh in at church or head back to the farm once every couple of weeks to feed his fuckin' chickens.

I glance around and see that 'most everyone is sitting on the lounges instead of taking their seats in the boardroom. In an alcove across the room that houses yet another cum-stained couch, an old pokie machine, and a beat-up coffee table, Ivy is laid out on the sofa. Her skirt is pushed up around her hips, mouth slack, and her eyes are rollin' back in her head while Killer positions himself at the entrance of her cunt and slams inside.

"Oh shit" is all I manage to say before Tank is across the room, grabbing Killer in a headlock and dragging him off of her.

Killer thrashes in Tank's hold, kicking and slapping at the big-arsed motherfucker, but the truth is the kid's completely fucked. None of us are big enough or ruthless enough to take Tank down. It'd take five of us to pull him off of Killer. *Dude is completely fucked.*

"Brother, ease up," I say, punching him in the head repeatedly. He shakes it off but doesn't let go.

"She was clean, you fuck. For two God damn days she was fuckin' clean, and you go give her blow so you can get your dick wet?"

"She came to me."

That riles him even more. Killer's face turns shades of red, purple, blue and every colour in-between.

"Fuck, brother! Killer's not your problem. She is," I say, pointing to Ivy, who doesn't even look as though she's registered the fact that Killer is no longer fucking her.

His enraged gaze snaps to me and then he shoves Killer away. The kid gasps for breath, coughing and spluttering as he hits the carpet with his junk hanging out. Tank takes the few steps to Ivy and slaps at her face, trying to get the bitch to wake up.

"Jesus fuckin' Christ, it's a god damn fuckin' zoo in here!" Prez appears in the hallway having just come from his office.

Grim slinks along behind him, head down, gaze averted. His face is more fucked up than usual—blood trickles from a cut on his lip and his eye is swelling. Not my fuckin' beef, but Grim keeps to himself mostly, so I'm kinda curious as to what the hell happened to him.

"Get your arses into fuckin church, now!" Prez roars, and the boys scatter. "Tank, get that bitch to a fuckin' hospital. If she shoots up in my clubhouse again, she's out on her arse."

"Oh my god, are you okay?" Raine asks, rushing over to Grim when she sees the state of his face.

"Leave it." he growls, and pushes her away, sending her staggering back into me when she attempts to touch him. I grasp her shoulders to keep her from toppling and glance at Prez, he's watching Grim with the pitch black eyes of a man who wants to cave another's skull in.

I circle my hand around Raine's wrist and tug on her arm to get her attention. Her eyes are glistening with tears. I bristle and then remind myself that this is also not my beef to get into. "Don't take it hard, darlin'. Grim's an arsehole to everyone."

She gives me a humourless laugh. "And here I thought I was special?"

"Yeah, I'm pretty sure it's because you're special that he's sportin' that black eye." I wink and fish out my keys and place them in her hand along with the bag from the chemist. "I need a favour?"

After Raine agrees to take the shit I bought to Indie, I head into the boardroom. We're one man down and three of us are showing off some kind of injury. I don't blame Prez for losing his shit at us. I take a seat beside Grim.

"You look even more like shit than usual," I mutter.

"Shut the fuck up."

"All of you, shut the fuck up!" Prez roars. "That bitch start talkin' yet, Kick?"

"Yeah, she's started. Don't know if she's got anything useful for us, though. I think she may have tried blocking a lot of it out."

"We got a package earlier, left at the fucking gate." He throws a USB stick on the table. "It's a copy of the little tape you left behind."

"Fuck."

"Yeah, fuck is right."

"Seems the cop has done some fuckin' diggin', found out which club you ride with. There was a note with that fancy little USB stick there. They want the girl, or they release the tape and you and Tank go down for the murder of the dentist, and the abduction of Kayla Kennedy."

"If that little fuck goes down, we all go down," One Eye says. "Jesus fuckin' Christ. Why don't we just hand over the bitch, get the fuckin' tape back and wipe our hands clean?"

"We're not handing her over," I seethe.

"That's not your call to fuckin' make, kid," One Eye shouts. "I knew he'd bring the club down on it's arse. I had a feeling about you, you little shit, and here we fuckin' are."

"Eat my dick, old man," I shout back.

"Shut the fuck up!" Prez roars.

"What are you gonna do, Prez?"

"You mean after I kick your fuckin' arse for bringing this shit down on my club? I'm gonna do nothin'. You, on the other hand, are gonna do some hard-arse fuckin' suckin' up to that bitch you got stowed away in your room. You're gonna play nice, or beat the shit outta her to get me some FUCKIN' ANSWERS!" He leans back in his chair and runs a hand down over his face, letting out a loud breath. "But first you're gonna get her the hell outta this clubhouse so she's not here when that arsehole orders a raid on my club. We're not handing over the girl. I don't like fuckin' being told what to do by some gutless pig that can't even handle a negotiation properly. You bastards are gonna protect the girl like she's your own, or I'm gonna be slammin' some fuckin' heads together and putting a shitload of my club to ground. You got me?"

Murmured agreement swallows the room. The tension is crippling. One Eye stands up, knocking back his chair so it clatters against the floorboards. "This is bullshit. If he'd fuckin' shot her the way he was supposed to, the club wouldn't be in this fuckin mess."

"SIT. THE. FUCK. DOWN!" Prez roars. There's a very long pause. Both men stare down the other, and then One Eye picks up his chair and sits down heavily in it.

"You don't think they'll be waitin' for us to move her?"

"Probably. But then again, that would just bring this fucker out of hiding. Might be wise to dangle the bait a little and see who bites."

I don't like this one fucking bit, but what choice do I have? I'm the dumb-arse who got us into this situation in the first place.

"When?"

"Soon as fuckin' possible. Or else your pretty mug is gonna be splashed across every fucking TV station in this country."

"Where the fuck am I supposed to take her? *Her* face has already been splashed across every station in this country. We take her outside those gates, people are gonna have questions."

"My wife's gonna kill me for this," Prez mutters under his breath. "You'll take the girl to my house. No neighbours, no nothing but mountain air and trees.

Place is in Mia's name, so even if the cops are getting' all up in club business, it'll still take some time for them to figure where we are. I'll make sure the old lady's out of the way, put her up at the fuckin' Sheraton if I have to. Grim, you and Crazy will head up there too; take Killer with you. I doubt they'll try anything during daylight hours, but I want the three of you patrolling the grounds at night."

"We're gonna waste good men on this bitch?" One Eye asks. Dude needs to fuckin' quit before he ends up losing his other eye to my blade. "Fuckin' bullshit"

"Then aren't you lucky you're not going?" Prez says dismissively.

"Indie has no clothes."

"I'll have Raine head out and get her some of the shit she needs now, but Mia has a dick-load of boxes full of designer threads I've been trying to get her to donate to goodwill. Tell the girl to take whatever she needs from there. Be ready to ride out in thirty fuckin' minutes, boys. I want us high and tight. Kick, you and the girl will be in the middle." He bangs the gavel against the table and the brothers disperse.

We leave the clubhouse a little before dawn. It took some convincing to coax Indie from the bathroom floor. I don't think she even really grasped what was goin' on. The second I told her about the tape and their demands, she'd huddled against the wall again and begged me not to hand her over. When I finally got her out of the room she hurried through the clubhouse as if she'd had a madman gunning for her head. Which wasn't all that far from the truth.

The road had been quiet and just when we were

twenty minutes from the turn-off to Prez's place, we picked ourselves up a tail; a black van, not unlike the one Tank and I had sat in a few days earlier as we scoped out the warehouse. It wasn't obvious at first—it weaved slowly in and out of the light traffic that travelled the M4, but now it's definitely hangin' on our arse closer than haemorrhoids.

Prez takes the nearest exit and we follow suit, keeping formation despite the fact that we have to glide over to the right-hand side of the road to avoid taking out a minivan traveling at 20km an hour. *I have a bad fuckin' feelin' about this.* The soles of my feet itch inside my boots and my gut clenches, setting off my Spidey sense—and my gut is never fuckin' wrong.

The black van follows us up the off-ramp and onto a quiet country road, hanging back for a bit, but then they grow impatient, cutting off the minivan, and forcing the driver to swerve out onto the shoulder. Prez and the brothers ahead of us increase their speed, and I shout to Indie to hold on and move with me. She squeezes her whole body tighter around my back: arms, thighs, even her tits are pushed as tightly against me as they could be. I rev the throttle and we take off.

The van edges up alongside Raphe, who's riding next to me. The window lowers, and I'm staring back at the barrel of a gun. The gun goes off, and Raphe's tyre explodes. He's thrown arse over head onto the bitumen and his bike skids out in front of me. I have to do some pretty quick fuckin' thinkin' to avoid colliding with the Fat Boy sliding across the asphalt. I jerk left on the handlebars and lean with the bike, becoming an extension of the machine. What surprises me is that while Indie may be screaming my fuckin' ear off, she moves like a pro. I jerk the handlebars to the right so we don't wind up eatin' gravel and we straighten out, only now there's nothing between us and the van.

Up ahead Prez and Killer fire off shots. Someone is shooting from behind me—Grim, more than likely. I don't have time to check because Prez takes aim and fires, blowing out the front tyre on the left-hand side. The van swerves, but cuts back in close, too close. They almost take out my bike, and Indie screams as the side of the vehicle brushes our legs. I pull my gun from my holster and take aim. Indie tucks her head into my back. Trigger comes flyin' up the inside, overtaking Prez and emptying his clip into the windshield of the van. His aim isn't so fuckin' great, and a stray bullet slices the air as it whips past our faces. I don't have time to tell Indie to move, but seconds later I'm taking comfort in the fact that her trembling hands are still holding onto my waist with a grip tighter than death, it means she hasn't been hit.

Crazy fuck. We make it outta this alive and I'm gonna beat that fucker's head in.

I fire off an entire clip. One shot makes contact and the van swerves across the road, colliding with an oncoming SUV. It's airborne, and then it comes crashing down in front of us. Prez swerves out into oncoming traffic. Grim hits the brakes, but not fast enough; he's thrown from the bike and lands on the shoulder. Killer and I both manage to swerve around without incident, but I brake too hard and Indie's helmeted head smacks into mine.

For a half second I'm blinded with pain. It hurts like

a fuckin' bitch, and I pray like hell that we're not about to be rear-ended because I can't fuckin' see straight. I ease us off on to the shoulder of the road, but as I turn the bike around and see my brothers in various stages of devastation, I realise it could have been worse. Prez rides over to the upturned van followed by Trigger, who's fuckin' lucky he's not getting his face pounded in. Prez puts the kickstand down and climbs off the bike, then he leans down to look in the window, fires off several shots and opens the door with a gloved hand. A body falls out, some fat-arsed white motherfucker with his face all pockmarked with bullets. I bring us to a stop near the van, flip the stand and climb off, grabbing Trigger by the cut and slamming him into the side of the vehicle. "What the fuck were you thinkin'?"

He lifts his hands in surrender, his eyes wide with shock and his body all jittery and hopped up on adrenaline. I'm shakin' too, but I'm not fuckin' dumb enough to pull half the shit he does when the rush is pumping through my veins. He smiles. "I was thinkin' about takin' those motherfuckers down, brother. Prez said to take care of her like she was our own."

Jesus fucking Christ. He's like an over-excited puppy.

"And you thought the best way to do that was, what? To cut us off and shoot your motherfuckin' gun in her face?"

"I saw a chance, I took it," he snaps back, and my whole body goes rigid. Taking chances is what will get you fuckin' killed. I pull back my arm and punch him in the face. His head rocks back into the side of the van and I release him. Trigger doubles over, clutching a hand to his nose.

"You wanna risk your life? Fine. But don't fuckin' play with hers," I say, pointing to Indie. I glance at her. She's not freaking out, or at least she doesn't appear to be, but her wide-eyed gaze is glued to me as she sits astride my bike. I can't explain it, but I suddenly feel awkward under the weight of her stare.

"Alright you two, back to your fuckin' corners," Prez says. He points to Trigger. "You fuckin' disrespect me by riding front again and *I'm* gonna break your fuckin' nose. We clear?"

"Yeah Prez. We're clear." Trigger holds the bridge of his nose to stem the blood flow, and sits down on the asphalt.

"I'm gonna need you to take a look at these men, darlin'," Prez says to Indie. "You need to tell us if they're who we're after."

Indie climbs off the bike and takes a few tentative steps forward. I realise now that she wasn't just kickin' back on my bike a second ago; it was more than likely she was worried about standin' up and seeing the faces of the men than just tried to blow our brains out.

She stumbles a little. I reach out my hand to her and she glares at my upturned palm.

"Sea legs, darlin'. First time on the back of a bike is like stepping off a boat onto land. It goes away, though," I say, attempting to make her feel better. I glance at Prez, whose brows are raised skyward.

"Douche bag." Killer coughs into his hand. I glare at him. He coughs again and thumps at his chest, clearing his throat as though something is lodged in it.

Indie places her hand in mine and I lead her towards the van. We both crouch down to take a better look at the dead guys inside. If Trigger's bullets hadn't killed the driver than the steering wheel impaling one side of his face certainly had.

She presses a hand to her mouth and shakes her head, standing to her full height in her painfully white new tennis shoes and a pair short shorts I pulled from the pile of shit Ivy had left in my room. "It's not them."

"Well, who the fuck are they?" Raphe says, limping over to us. His shoulder hangs at an unnatural angle. I glance down the road. His bike is in pieces over the shoulder, about three hundred metres back. The minivan is pulled up beside it and the driver, a flustered-looking mother, stands taking pictures on her phone.

"Sent by the motherfuckers no doubt. Plenty of people got beefs with the Saints, but none that'd be stupid enough to pull this shit in broad daylight," Prez says. "You two better get outta here. We gotta get somewhere safe and set dumb-arse's shoulder here. There's a butt-load of witnesses too many. We need outta here before the cops show up."

Once our men are all accounted for, I jump back on the bike. Indie slides on behind me and clings to me even tighter than before. I wasn't sure that was possible, but she's trembling as she fits her lithe body around mine and tucks her head in against my back. Her teeth chatter, and her head bobs against my shoulder blade. I don't know what to say to her. What can you say to someone who has two men that want you dead so badly they'd hire a couple of dumb fucks to take you out? Beats the fuck outta me, although it's certainly not like I haven't been in her shoes before.

I rev the throttle and we take off, leaving my brothers

to clean up the shit, remove plates and hastily scratch off the serial numbers of the bikes that are too far gone to move. They'll likely give our budding photographer from the minivan a shake down too. That shit's not pretty, especially with kids in the car, but you do what you gotta to stay the hell out of lock up.

I take a slightly more scenic drive to Prez's house in the mountains. I've been here several times since joining the MC, and if circumstances were different I might even relish taking someone to a remote cabin where it'd be just the two of us, but this isn't exactly a romantic fuckin' getaway. And I'm not fuckin' boyfriend material. Been there, done that, got the scars—both mentally and physically—to prove it.

I pull into the drive. It looks like a damn mansion more than a cabin. Indie takes off her helmet and stares up at it.

"Holy shit, do they have a butler too?"

I shake my head. The bitch nearly got gunned down a little less than an hour ago, her life has gone from normal to full-blown fuckin' horror movie in a month, and she's cracking jokes? "No butler, but Prez would probably appreciate a French maid. You should definitely bring it up with Mia."

"Is she okay with this?"

"Apparently she made out like she gave a shit, but she gets a fuckin' week at the Sheraton, so I'm sure she'll live."

"She's not staying with us?"

"No, it'll just be you and me." I say, and then frown when I remember that's not exactly true. "And the three bikers outside, patrolling the grounds at night. They'll sleep in the den downstairs during the day."

She stops walking and stares at me, her face slackened in what looks like a horrified expression.

"Relax, Little Spitfire, you're safe with me." I shake my head. I need to quit saying shit like that because the truth is she's not safe with me. Not really.

"What if they find us here? What if they both come and you and the others can't fight them off?"

"Hey, you're gonna be fine. I'm not leaving your side, however long it takes. I'll be here. We're gonna have men patrolling; they're not gonna get within a hundred metres of you without us knowing about it."

"I should have gone to the police."

"And done what, darlin'?" I ask, staring her down. "This guy *is* the fuckin' police. You go to them and you'll be dead before you clear the parking lot. Come on," I say, and tentatively hold out my hand. She stares at it a beat. I let mine fall away, shoving it inside the pocket of my jeans.

I lead her to the house, unlocking it with the key Prez had given me back at the clubhouse in case we got separated. I punch in the security code to turn off the house alarm but switched it to perimeter. He had this state-of-the-art system installed after a rival club broke in and trashed the place 'cause they couldn't find Prez. They also made off with a shit-tonne of drugs. We more than made up for the money lost by taking their bikes and selling them on the black market.

I walk from the lounge to the kitchen and shove my overnight bag on the counter. There's a big-arsed box on top of the island bench with a pink sticky note attached. I pick it up.

Here are the clothes you wanted. This is gonna cost you, Jett, and if I see any of my designer pieces on those fucking stupid club whores parading around your clubhouse, I'm filing for divorce.

Also, I took your other credit card.

M.

XOX

Jesus Christ. No wonder Prez has been looking for affection elsewhere. Mia is a fuckin' head case. Indie reads the note over my shoulder before I can crumple it up.

"Wow, she sounds delightful. I'm suddenly really glad we're going to be alone," she says, and then her face heats and she moves away from me.

"They should fit you. If they don't then we're kinda fucked, 'cause I only brought the one pair of jeans with me and a couple T-shirts."

I tell her to stay put and decide to sweep the house. Kinda pointless really, seeing as if anyone had broken in since Mia left, we'd be deafened by the alarm, but it might help Indie feel better, and I sure as shit would feel better knowing some arsehole wasn't gonna jump me and blow a hole through my head.

The house is huge, and the whole sweep takes me a good ten minutes. By the time I come back Indie's changed into a pair of dark-blue jeans that hug her arse so tightly that all the blood rushes right to my cock. I lean against the breakfast bar, trying to cover my hard-on from view. Normally I'd revel in that shit, but this situation is anything but normal. If I wasn't concerned for her safety, I might consider a trip to the bathroom to beat one out. I doubt that would make her feel any more comfortable than me whipping it out right here. Instead, I lean into the cold marble and will my dick to settle the fuck down. It's gonna be a long couple of days.

I pull a cold beer from the fridge and turn to Indie as the other bikes finally pull in the drive. "You want one?"

She shakes her head, and glances out through the large glass front door at my brothers. "I thought you said it was just going to be the five of us?"

"It is. The others will head back to the clubhouse later."

She nods and collects the box of clothing Mia left for her. "I'm just going to take these upstairs."

"Okay." I turn back to the fridge and take out several more beers for my brothers. "Well, when you're done, come back down and we'll talk about the—" I turn to face her and shake my head, realising that she's already gone, and I'm left standin' here talkin' to my fuckin' self.

Yeah. It's gonna be a very long couple of days.

KICK

TWO YEARS AGO

I enter the room and slam my fist against the door the second I see her huddling into the wall. She's as naked as she was in the club lounge, only now—two days later—she's covered head to toe in bruises. I take several hulking steps forward and grab her shoulders, lifting her up and shaking her.

"You stupid bitch," I hiss. "I told you to play fuckin' nice, didn't I? I told you I would get you out of this."

Tank's arm shoots out, squeezing my shoulder until I release her. "Easy, brother, keep your shit together or I'm gonna throw you outta here myself."

"I saw a chance; I took it," she mutters. "It didn't pay off the way I thought it would."

"No, it fuckin' didn't, did it?"

Tears pool in her eyes. "Why would you try to help me?"

"'Cause you can't seem to fuckin' help yourself," I snap back, and then let out a deep exhalation. "We need to get you out of here."

"You can't take her out now, brother. Prez will be back soon, and if we leave the damn compound with her in tow they're gonna know about it."

"I gotta get her outta here."

"That's not why I brought you down here, man."

"This is the only time to do it. If Slayer doesn't come through she's as good as dead. You've seen what they did to her."

"Yeah, and you know what they're gonna do to us if they find out we let her go."

"I just need you to help me get to the gate. I need you to buy me some time. I'll get her back to her dad and be back here before Prez knows about any of it."

"And who the fuck do you think Prez is gonna come looking for once he discovers the bitch is gone? Slipping a roofie in Tag's coffee was one thing, but getting past four brothers is another thing entirely."

"What if she held you at gunpoint?"

He looks at me as if I've just grown another fuckin' head, and this one is sprouting bullshit for sonnets.

"I'm serious. You couldda tried to rape her, she grabbed your gun and led you outside."

"No one in their right mind is gonna buy that bullshit. Assuming we can get her past the other four idiots in the lounge, that is. Red's working the gate, too; he'll have eyes everywhere." The booth at the gate was mostly there so we'd have a little warning when a raid was upon us. The cameras only monitored the lot, but if we were walking around with a prisoner in tow, Red was gonna know about it.

"Then we just have to hope he's gone to take a piss,"

I say.

"Jesus Christ."

"I've never asked you for anything, brother, but I know you know this is the right thing to do."

"Fuck the right fuckin' thing to do," he mutters under his breath. "Whatever happened to the club before hoes?"

"Take your shirt off," I say.

He glares at me.

"She's gonna need clothes to leave the compound or we're both gonna get arrested. We haven't got time to run back upstairs," I explain.

"Fuck me. Last time I ever do you a favour."

"It'll be the only time I ask you for a favour."

Tank removes his shirt and holds it out to Lauren. She doesn't take it. Instead, she stares him down and he drops it on the concrete floor. She turns away from us as she picks it up and puts it on. It's huge, swamping her frail frame, and lookin' more like a dress than a T-shirt.

Tank opens the door and pokes his head out; then he motions us forward. We walk up the short hall to the door that leads outside. Tag is out cold, sittin' on the sofa in the entrance, head lulled to the side and his tongue hangin' outta his mouth. There's a line of drool running over his chin to his shoulder. "He gonna remember you druggin' him?"

"Doubt it," Tank says with a shrug. "I left before he fell asleep. When he wakes he's probably just gonna think he really needed a nap."

It's late afternoon, just on dusk, and the chill in the air has Princess's teeth chattering together, or maybe that's the fear of being caught. It's certainly no picnic for

KICK

Tank and me, either. If we get caught smuggling her out of here, we'll be put to ground quicker than either of us could blink.

So we walk with purpose—'cause nothing says you're doing bad shit like skulking around corners in a compound—and we make it as far as the garage without being seen. Riding outta here with no one being any the wiser is gonna be a challenge, though. I'm pushing my bike from the undercover garage when Red rounds the corner. Fuck, he must've been taking a piss after all, because he's just come from the direction of the clubhouse.

He's as surprised to see us as we are having to stare back at his ugly mug, but then his eyes shoot to Lauren and his face creases with confusion.

"Hey, what's with the bitch?" Red asks.

"Prez said to bring her out to the lot. Somethin' about handing her over to Slayer."

"Handin' her over to Slayer? What the fuck for? He hasn't come at a deal yet. We got the cops in our pocket, but he's draggin' his heels on the negotiations with the girl. Seems he's not willing to hand over drugs and guns for his little princess, here."

"Well maybe he and Prez finally came to an agreement." Tank shrugs, running a hand through his hair. "All I know was that he said to bring her out to the lot."

"And what the hell's he doin' here?" Red says, tilting his chin in my direction.

"Sayin' goodbye." I pull my gun from the back of my jeans and point it at Red, and then I slide the barrel back and forth between the two men, shoving Lauren behind me.

"Think about what you're doin' here, brother," Tank says, putting his hands up in surrender. Red reaches for his piece. I turn the gun on him and shoot him once, right between the eyes. Fucker falls to the ground like a sack of shit. Lauren sucks in a sharp breath. Tank checks for a pulse. I assume there isn't one—he'd have to be pretty fuckin' lucky to survive a bullet to the brain—because he fishes Red's gun from the holster in his pants and hands it to me. "You gotta shoot me, and then you gotta move."

"Yeah." He's right. It sucks, but it's the only thing that makes sense. Tank's unarmed. Hand to hand he'd take me down in seconds flat, but no man ever argued with a bullet and expected to come out standing. "Where do you want it?"

Tank shakes his head. "It's gotta be an arm shot. That way it looks like you were aiming for my chest, but missed 'cause you're a fuckin' lousy shooter."

"Screw you, arsehole."

"Hurry the fuck up. If you take any longer they're gonna be out here and we're both gonna be runnin'." He squeezes his eyes closed and waits for the bullet to hit him. It's only a graze, not enough for anyone to believe that he still couldn't take down his shooter, especially if she were a girl. He sucks in a deep breath through his nose.

"Fuck. Sorry," I say, and fire off three shots. One hits him in the bicep. The others burrow into the wall behind him.

"Ah, fuck!" he shouts, clutching his hand to his arm to stem the flow of blood. His eyes are narrowed into slits and he looks like a bull, ready to charge. "You owe me, motherfucker."

"I know," I say.

"Well, get the fuck outta here or I'm gonna shoot you myself."

He's right, I don't have time to worry about Tank because I'm guessing I have all of about five seconds before my brothers come streaming out of the clubhouse, wonderin' what the fuck is goin' on. I jump on the bike and rev the throttle. Lauren climbs on behind me, and we tear away from the garage, toward the front gate.

Jumping off at the booth in order to open the gate, I hold the handlebars steady while Princess slides into place. She could always just take off—she's spent a lifetime around the club, and I don't doubt that Slayer would have taught her how to ride, but something tells me she won't.

While she's keeping the engine running and the revs up, I hit the button for the gate and I yank out the video feed. I have to trust that Tank will remember to erase the tapes, before they cart his pansy arse off to the hospital, or we're both dead. I climb back onto my bike and we fly down the street, taking practically every back alley we can to avoid being seen. I don't think we've been followed, and all that shit with Tank was probably a wasted effort because as we tore away from the clubhouse I didn't see a single brother comin' outside to see what all the fuckin' noise was.

It's full dark when I pull up to her father's clubhouse. I flip the kickstand down and climb off the bike. Princess stumbles off, but her whole body's quaking so much that she falls to the ground. I scoop her up, cringing when I feel how cold she is. She tucks her head in against my chest. She's listless, probably from the ebb of adrenaline through her system. I'm surprised she didn't fall off the damn bike. She's been in that dungeon for only a few short days, but they must've felt like an eternity to her.

The Severed Sons don't have a booth like we do—they're a relatively small clubhouse, even though Slayer is notorious for being one of the scariest motherfuckers out there—but I know without a doubt they've got cameras, and possibly a gun trained on my head as I push the buzzer.

"Yeah?" a bored sounding voice says through a crackling speaker.

"Tell Slayer I have something he wants."

"Who is this? And what the fuck could you have that Slayer wants?" *So maybe they don't have cameras on me.* I glance up at the decrepit-looking camera above my head and notice the red light isn't flashing.

"Turn on the fuckin' video feed."

The little red light begins blinking and there's a muffled crash, like smashing glass and an, "Oh fuck."

I walk over to the gate as it's opening and wait.

One.

Two.

Three.

Ten angry mother fuckin' Sons storm me from the clubhouse. All have guns trained on my head, though if they shoot me they risk hurting Lauren, and if what Red said was true, that Slayer wasn't bargaining whatever the fuck he could to get his daughter safely back, maybe he doesn't care that the fall could crack her head open. Or that she could get hit with one of the shots intended for me. Maybe he just doesn't give a shit about what happens to her.

"You alright, baby?" Slayer says, making out like she's his number fuckin' one priority. If he really gave a shit, he woulda traded whatever the fuck he could to get her back. The longer I think about this, the more I wanna wedge a bullet into the space between his eyes. I wanna shoot that dumb fucker in the face for letting a man she barely knows be the one to risk his life for hers, when her own father wouldn't.

Lauren nods but tucks her head against me.

Slayer takes a step forward and then his gun is at my head, even though I'm the only thing keeping his daughter from cracking hers against the concrete. "What the fuck did you do to her?" he curses, getting a good look at her face.

"I didn't do anything to her," I say, though I know he doesn't believe that, and it's not exactly true. There's no telling what I would have done if that raid hadn't been so damned well-timed.

"Your Prez mustn't value your life any. He's gotta know the only way you're leaving here is in a body bag?"

"He doesn't know I'm here."

"What the fuck you sayin', boy?"

"I'm saying that I risked my life, that I'm risking it right now to get Princess away from there, which is fuckin' more than you did."

"Princess?" The big Italian dude from the rally is on my left side, also holding a gun to my head.

"Careful, kid. I got an itchy trigger finger. It goes off when people start saying stupid shit in front of me."

"She needs a doctor, probably a morning-after pill too, and screen her for fuckin' STIs."

"You saying your fuckin' Angel-scum cock has been near my little girl's pussy?"

"No, I'm sayin' every other Angel had his hands on her but the one who really wanted her, but then they made me watch that shit, over and over again. I'm sayin' she's been through fuckin' hell and back, and she needs away from everything that even remotely resembles bikers."

The Italian stows his gun and moves to take her from me but she screams and curls closer. "You gotta let go now, Princess. I gotta hand you over."

Her panicked gaze meets mine. "He'll shoot you."

"No, he won't."

"Yes, he will."

I smile down at her. "What are we just gonna stand here forever, you in my arms, your dad holding a gun to my head? If he shoots me, he shoots me. Ain't nothing I can do about that, Princess. At least I'll know I did one thing right."

She takes a deep, shaky breath. "I'd be dead if it weren't for you."

I nod, because it's true. If Slayer hadn't come at a deal, Prez would've eventually killed her, and he'd have tortured her some more first. "Promise me somethin'?"

"What?"

"Get on your feet and then get the hell outta here. Prez will come looking for you again. He's not a guy who likes to lose. Take as much money as you can, and get the fuck away from this life, otherwise you're gonna wind up filling a body bag way too young."

Lauren is wrenched away from me then. She screams as the Italian carts her off toward the clubhouse, flailing and slapping at him despite her injuries.

"Daniel!" she screams, reaching out toward me as he struggles to get her inside. Without thinking I take a step forward, but I'm attacked from behind. My knees go out from under me and I'm shoved face-first into the ground. Some heavy motherfucker sits down on my back. I buck, trying to unseat him, but I'm whacked in the back of the head until I stop.

"Well, isn't that fuckin' touching? The Angel scum, in love with my daughter? Didn't I warn you away from her once before?" Slayer asks, circling me like a predator circles prey. The biker using me for a chair shoves his gun against the back of my skull.

"Yeah, I did," Slayer continues, and he motions for the guy on top of me to force me to stand. I'm dragged up by the hair and presented to Slayer. "At the rally, where she fuckin' went missin'!" His red, blotchy face almost touches mine. He's so close I can see the blood vessels snaking out from the corners of his eyes. *He's fucking high.* His daughter's been locked up, raped, beaten, treated like a fuckin' animal over some shit that she shouldn't even have to know about, and the arsehole's gettin' high as a fuckin' kite instead of findin' her? He makes me sick. He's everything I hate about the life. And he's more than likely exactly where I'll end up, because this is what we are—this is what livin' in the club gets you: bitterness, enemies, and a shit-tonne of bad blood.

Slayer punches me in the gut. I double over, winded from the impact.

"Get up," he says, holstering his gun and shoving me until I stand upright. "So your prez doesn't know you're here, and I'm thinkin' once he learns of your betrayal the fucker's gonna put you to ground quicker than you can blink. He'll tear you up first, of course. He'll make you bend the knee and beg for your life, and then he'll gut you like a fuckin' fish. So, you know what I'm gonna do?"

"Send me home," I say, because I know how arseholes like him think.

He claps. "How 'bout that, boys? Kid's a thinker."

Stifled laughter sounds through the group of men. I stare them down and the only thing I see is dirty, worthless, piece-of-shit hard-faced criminals, just like there are in my own club. Just like me.

"I'm not fond of thinkers, see? They're the ones that start stirring up shit, givin' people hope. Makin' 'em think there's something better out there in the future, if only they could follow that fuckin' rainbow. I don't make a habit of keepin' thinkers around, and I certainly don't need no smart-arsed Angel scum fillin' my girl's head with stupid shit that'll only get her killed." Slayer sucker punches me. Right in the fuckin' nut sack, and I go down like the piece of shit that I am. "Have at him, boys. Just make sure he's got all his limbs to drive back to the clubhouse with."

I'm already on the ground when the first boot connects with my ribs. I try standing but some arsehole shoves me back down with a kick to the face. My shoulders and legs are pinned. I buck and try to wrench my arms and legs free, but with eight men beating on me, freeing my limbs makes very little fuckin' difference.

I'm not going anywhere until they let me. I'm pissed on, spat on, and swelling up like I'm in fuckin' anaphylactic shock. There's one punch after the other, the slash of knives in my flesh, and steel-capped boots kicking my face, groin and ribcage. It feels like hours, but is more than likely only minutes, and it's a small price to pay if it means I never have to watch her be beaten and raped again.

After a while the Italian comes out of the clubhouse and orders the other men away from me. I drag in a jagged, tender breath, grateful for the reprieve. He rolls me over so I'm staring up at his face, and the stars in the night sky beyond him. He lifts me by the lapels of my cut and slams me down on the concrete. I feel my skin split, and warm blood pours out. And then I'm dragged out of the gate, across the jagged concrete and thrown to the curb like trash. I close my eyes, and for the first time I don't see the terrible things I've done in my very short life as I drift into unconsciousness.

I see nothing.

I am nothing.

INDIE

Our third day in the cabin and I'd successfully eaten my way through half of the fridge's contents, and you know you have a problem when a bunch of big bikers stare in amazement at how much spaghetti bolognaise you were able to put away in one sitting.

I'm bored and restless, and the more I try and think about what went on in that warehouse, the more I try to remember about the Cop and the Priest, the less I remember. Under any other circumstances, I'd probably appreciate having my memories taken away, but when exacting your revenge is dependent upon those images, smells, sounds and details, it's frustrating as all hell. One thing I haven't forgotten is the way the Priest's face looked as he hovered over me, while he beat and raped me. I see it every time I close my eyes. The Cop's face is only ever a blur in my dreams. And though the Dentist took a handful of my teeth and played games dependent upon my fear of his drugs, for some reason he doesn't make an appearance at all.

When I'm awake I remember every detail of the Cop's face, but that doesn't mean I know where to find him. I've spent hours upon hours searching different divisions of the New South Wales Police Force and Googling churches and congregations online, but it's like trying to pick the guy in the red and white shirt from a *Where's Wally?* book.

I shut the laptop and throw it down on the couch beside me with an audible groan.

Biker—*Kick*, though I still can't get used to calling someone by a "doing" word—shifts the laptop to the table and sits down beside me. He hands me the beer he just opened, but I shake my head and wedge myself further into the corner of the lounge.

"What's up, Little Spitfire?"

I glare at him. "You need to quit calling me that."

"You need to work out some of this frustration."

"Yeah, let's do that. And while I'm running laps around the perimeter of the house that I'm not allowed to leave I'll throw you a wink and a wave. I still don't know why I'm not allowed to set foot out of this house, by the way. We've been here three days and there hasn't been so much as a freaking wallaby broaching the perimeter."

"You don't need to be on the property to be able to shoot someone. Surprisingly, bullets fly a really long way."

So Biker may be a complete arsehole, but I have to admit I'm kinda in love with his sarcastic side.

"Come on," he says, holding his hand out for me to take. It's not the first time he's done this, and I don't know why — it's just a hand, after all — but every time he does it, it's like he's testing me. Testing my faith in him. Or maybe I just have cabin fever and am overanalysing everything.

"Where are we going?"

"You've been here, what? Three days?"

"Yeah?"

"And you never thought to look around?"

"It's not my house."

Biker shakes his head. He flexes his hand in an impatient gesture and I take it. The smug grin he gives me pisses me off a little, but I let him lead me anyway — out of boredom, of course.

He guides me to a room at the end of the hall. I haven't even been in this wing yet — the rooms Jett had given us were guest rooms, side by side, and upstairs in the east wing of the house. They overlooked the driveway and the unsealed road half a kilometre away. At night I like to watch that road, when I can't sleep, or when Biker has woken me with his thrashing in the next room. I don't know who plagues his dreams, I don't know why he screams and lashes out, but some nights I lie awake hoping to find out. Some nights I just lie awake to avoid my own nightmares. Some nights I creep out of bed and lay on the hardwood floors, then I press myself against the wall and finally drift off. Some nights I'd do anything to feel a connection with another human being that wasn't born of violence, and other nights I'm so consumed with hurt, and anger and my unfulfilled need for revenge that I want to be the one dolling out the pain.

Biker opens the door and tugs me inside. I didn't

know what to expect, but a fully equipped gym wasn't it. I glance around the room. One wall is completely lined floor to ceiling with mirrors. A bank of treadmills, an elliptical machine, and different kinds of exercise bikes sit opposite. The wall on the left-hand side of the room is painted a hideous Pepto-Bismol colour, while the right-hand corner is blood red. The paint job isn't finished. In fact, it looks as though someone lost their shit entirely and just pulled out a roller and a can of whatever paint they could find that didn't make you begin exuding oestrogen from your pores and start popping daisies out of your vagina. This side of the room also houses a very worn-looking punching bag. I gravitate towards it.

Biker laughs. "So violent, Little Spitfire."

I glare at him, and then back at the bag. Imagining his cocky face is plastered to it, I pull back my arm and let fly. It's denser than I'd thought—or maybe I am—because the bag doesn't give at all and pain slams into me and radiates all the way up my arm.

"Ow, fuck!" I yelp, shaking out the hurt.

"Jesus Christ," Biker says, and the next thing I know he's in front of me, all up in my face and taking my hand in his. "You can't just go in all gung-ho. You're gonna break your fuckin' hand."

He flattens my palm and pushes my fingers back, assessing the damage.

"Ow, that fucking hurts."

"Come 'ere." He pulls me over to the wall and takes a roll of white tape off the shelf. My reaction is swift and automatic. I'm transported back to the warehouse. To the Priest binding my hands and feet with duct tape, dragging me across the concrete floor until my flesh burned and wept blood. I step back and yank my hand from his grasp. I lower my gaze, but he takes my chin in his hands and forces me to look at him.

"You need to get this shit outta your system. We're not leaving this room 'til you and I get straight. If I wanted to hurt you, I could have done it a thousand times already, in more ways than you can possibly count, and I wouldn't have needed to bring you to a fancy fuckin' mansion in the woods. So have a little fuckin' faith in me, and give me your hand, Little Spitfire."

I take a deep shuddering breath, close my eyes and stretch my hand towards him. His touch is gentle this time, far more gentle than I'd ever thought someone with so much uncontained violence to him could be.

"Spread your fingers," he commands. I do, and he lifts the roll of tape, presses the edge to my skin and begins winding it over my knuckles. I close my eyes. The strident sound of it stretching out from the roll makes me want to flee. It makes me want to run as far from his touch—from any man's touch—as I can possibly get.

The feel of the tape against my flesh, binding, holding, is so much worse. I tug on my hand, but he won't let go. My heartrate skyrockets, and sweat beads erupt over my brow and upper lip. I'm in that room again, struggling, screaming, trying to fight them off, and failing.

Biker knows it, too. His dark eyes challenge, they dare me to run, but they also implore me to stay. It's ironic that the only thing keeping me here, keeping me grounded, is the man who abducted me.

He holds my gaze. I don't know exactly what is

hidden in his dark blue one, but it suffocates the panic within me, douses it like water flooding flames. He bends his head to my hand. Taking the paper tape in his mouth, he rips it with his teeth.

I still. I soften. His gaze doesn't leave mine, not even once. Not even when he starts in on my wrist, gently biting through each piece of tape before pressing it down with his rough hands. I'm mesmerised by his mouth, the piercing, and the soft, full lips. The light catches a silver chain around his neck, something I've never noticed before — but then I try not to make a habit of staring too closely at him. Not now, though. Now I watch every twitch, every blink, every intake of breath, and every inch that is swallowed up by his mouth moving closer to my flesh.

Before long he's wrapping the last piece of tape around the back of my hand. This time when he breaks it off, the soft glide of his tongue sweeps over my skin.

I inhale. Slowly ... so I don't hyperventilate. I imagine his tongue all over me, lapping, licking, and laving at every inch of my body and a bolt of white-hot pleasure shoots through my damn traitorous vagina. What the hell is wrong with me?

Biker smirks, one corner of his mouth turning up as though he knows exactly what I was thinking. He sets the tape back on the shelf and then faces me. "I'm going to position you, exactly where I want you."

I nod, because it seems my brain is incapable of doing much else at this point. He stands behind me, pulls my shoulders back and manoeuvres my elbows so that my hands are raised face-height in a guarding position. He bends and slides his hand down the back of my thigh. I gasp. My whole body turns rigid.

"A little faith, Spitfire," he says, as he taps my knee until I step back into position. He straightens again, showing me how to make a proper fist. "I want sharp, even jabs, darlin'. You follow through, you'll wind up busting your pretty skin all to pieces, and we don't want that."

Taking my elbows he pushes one forward after another and I drive through the movement. I'm not close enough yet to hit the bag, but I can still feel what the force of those blows would do, if I were connecting with something more than just air.

"Make the movement hard and fast," he whispers in my ear.

"I. Am." Grunting from exertion already, I picture his face meeting my fists and find I work a little harder.

"Alright, Rocky," he says, resting his hands on my hips and tapping me. "I think you're ready for the bag."

I inch forward and take the same stance, and then I jab at the vinyl over and over, hitting hard and fast just the way he told me to, preening with his encouragement and bristling when he tells me I can work harder. I'm sure it's only been a few minutes, but all at once I completely run out of steam. I stop making my jabs clean the way I'm supposed to, and instead I begin following through after each punch. He's right; even with the tape, the slide of the bag against my fist pulls at my flesh. I lower my arms, and Kick steps away from the wall he's been leaning against.

"Again, Indie."

I shake my head. "I'm done."

"No, you're not."

"I said I'm done." I straighten and give him a look that says not to push me. He does anyway. He steps in front of me, until we're toe to toe. I have to look up to him, and it infuriates me. I hate the thought of being obedient, and compliant, and allowing anyone to make me feel small after what those men put me through.

"You think the Cop's done? You think the Priest is done?" he seethes. "You think they're gonna stop torturing you, they're gonna stop raping you just because you're fuckin' done fighting?"

I gasp at his words, at the wall hitting my back. I hadn't even known we were moving backwards. I hadn't known we were moving at all. "Shut up."

"Did cryin' for help work before?" he whispers, and his vehement tone has the hairs prickling on the back of my neck.

His mouth is too close to mine, and his body pens me in. Fear slides down my spine. It unfurls inside me, paralysing me. "Stop it."

"Would they have stopped? Just because you cowered and begged for mercy?" He grabs hold of my shoulders and smacks me into the wall. My head spins.

He uses my confusion to yank my ponytail, and then he is dragging me across the room, my feet stumbling and tripping over his in an attempt to keep up. He stops in front of the wall of mirrors, standing behind me. His hand is wrapped around my throat, and he holds my chin up, forcing me to see myself.

Tears burn a trail down my red face. I'm pathetic, crying and snivelling, begging him to let me go.

"This girl," he says, tightening his hold around my neck. My eyes meet his in the mirror. "Is she a fighter, or a fuckin' victim?"

"A ... f ..."

"What?"

"A fighter," I say, gulping in air. "She's ... a fighter."

"Then fuckin' show me." He releases me and I bend double, coughing as I catch my breath. From out of nowhere, I'm hit with the force of a wrecking ball, and I'm slammed back onto the mat. Kick sits astride my hips, pinning me to the ground. My arms are forced above my head.

"Stop!" I cry.

"Show me. Fuckin' hit me, Kayla. Hit me. Make it hurt!"

The use of my name jars me completely. I still beneath him. "Please, let me go."

"Not until you show me the fight I saw in you when we first met."

I squirm beneath him, twisting my wrist against his painful grip.

"Hit me!" he roars.

"Fuck you!"

"Fuck me?" He smiles and lets go of my hands, leaning back to undo his belt buckle. "If you're offerin', darlin'"

Something inside me snaps. I lose all trace of Indie, of Kayla, and I become something alien, something animal. I punch him in the face. It may not be the hard and fast jabs he taught me, but he still feels it. Hitting the bag is nothing like hitting a person, though. There's no crunch, or flesh giving way beneath your fingers to the force of the punch with a bag. This is so much more primal than striking an inanimate object.

He grunts and grits his teeth. "Again."

I hit him again in the face. He sucks in a sharp breath through his nose and my lips twist into a sneer because I know that one hurt. While he's distracted I buck in an attempt to get him off me. It doesn't work, though; my hands are bloody and raw, despite the tape, so I claw at him because he's still holding me down. I rent his flesh, and four long scratches mar his tattooed neck. There isn't much else I can do with my hands strapped the way they are.

"I knew you had it in you," he says. He's leaning over me now, his face above mine, and he's panting hard. I am too. "Now you have your attacker's DNA underneath your nails. If he has a record, the cops will find him."

I'm only half listening to what he says because the chain around his neck has worked free of his T-shirt and it gently swings back and forth in the space between us. Attached to the chain is a tooth … my tooth. I don't know how I know that it's mine. Maybe it's intrinsic. How does a baby know its mother when it's only been in the world a day? You know instinctively when you lose something that belongs to you, something that's *of* you. And that tooth is mine.

"Where did you get that?" I whisper, my eyes glued to the piece of me that he's wearing around his neck like a fucking trophy. He follows my gaze and shoves the chain back inside the collar of his T-shirt, pushing up off me and standing to his full height. He holds out his hand but I knock it away, climbing to my feet. I squeeze my hands into fists, attempting to feel only the rage and to keep the hurt and injustice of what he just did—of everything he's done to me up until this point—at bay. It doesn't work, and tears of betrayal and frustration spill over my cheeks.

"You're sick," I accuse. He only nods. "Why would you do that?"

"Because you only fight when there's fear. And you're too fuckin' stubborn, and too defiant to see when you should break and when you should fight back. I want you to be able to protect yourself. I want you to be able to fight back no matter who is involved, and who might get hurt in the process. You're not always going to have four bikers around standing between you and some arsehole that wants inside your pants."

That's not what I was asking, and he knows it. I know why he attacked me just now. I want to know why he has my tooth hanging around his neck. I also know he's not going to give me the answers I want. On this, and this alone, he's as transparent as glass. I stalk away but he comes up behind me, yanking me around to face him.

I wrench out of his hold and without a second's hesitation, I punch him in the face with as much force as I can muster. I do exactly what he taught me—I make it hard, and fast, and lethal. His head snaps to the side and he covers his mouth with his hand, collecting a drop of blood from his split lip. To be fair, he'd told me that one of his brothers had given that to him the other day, but I took a little delight in knowing I helped open it up again. He stares at the blood and smiles. "Thatta girl."

"Fuck you," I snap, and leave the gym.

In the bathroom, I strip the tape from my hands and slowly peel off my clothes. For the first time since he saved me I don't cover the mirror. Instead, I look at my body, at the healing bruises and the new ones he just created. I move closer and inspect my face. It's still a little swollen, there are dark circles under my eyes, and there is a shadow of a bruise high across my cheekbone and temple. I open my mouth, looking at the pink flesh at the back of my mouth where my teeth used to be. Where the most recent extraction came from, the one he wears around his neck.

I've endured more pain than most can even conceive. I went through all of that and I'm still standing. I might be covered in bruises that are still healing, and I might be just as scared for what the future holds as I was in that warehouse, but they didn't break my spirit. My lungs still breathe, my head still processes thought, and my heart still beats. No, those men didn't break me — those men made me strong. They forced me to see the strength that I never would have known I possessed if I hadn't lived through their torture. The Cop and the Priest brought out the warrior inside me who is going to bring them both to their knees, and who's going to smile while doing it. And though it was an arsehole move, Kick was showing me that. If he'd told me I was strong, I'd never have believed it. Now I know for certain. Now I know I could kill them both or die trying, but at least I won't be sitting around waiting for them to find me.

KICK

TWO YEARS AGO

The mattress dips with the weight of another body and the soft slide of leather and flesh over my naked hips. At first I think it's just another club whore—god knows I've fucked enough of them in the days since Princess has been gone—but then the barrel of a gun is pressed between my eyes. It's still fuckin' hot, which means it's been used recently. My head clears a little and I know instantly without having to turn on the light who is straddling me. Out in the hall I hear nothing, complete and utter dead silence, and considering this clubhouse is home to at least twelve men and doubles as a fuckin' rumpus room for a bunch of degenerate criminals who come and go at all hours of the fuckin' day, that's kinda disturbing.

After Slayer's boys had beaten me within an inch of my life, bloody and completely fuckin' broken, I'd ridden to the nearest hospital. I had a fractured wrist, broken nose, a couple broken ribs, two black eyes, and a concussion. They kept me for a few days, and by the time the club had found me Prez was well and truly out for my blood. I fed him some bullshit story about being attacked by a group of teenage thugs that I knew he hadn't bought. I could see it in the depths of his cold, black eyes, but I'm still waking every day to the same damn dreary fuckin' existence.

"Pretty brave of you to come back, Princess."

"I said I would, didn't I? That first night? I told you I'd be back to kill you."

"And here you fuckin' are, makin' good on that promise. Better get it over with then, darlin'. Mustn't keep the reaper waiting."

"Why did you help me escape?" she whispers, her game face is on. I don't need the light to see that, but that broken girl I glimpsed beneath the clubhouse, and again in my shower, isn't far beneath the hard exterior. I can feel her, fighting to slink further inside, and fighting to be freed. *Always fucking fightin'.*

"What does it fuckin' matter? You're gonna shoot me anyway."

"Why?" she demands, shoving the gun against my skull.

"'Cause I fuckin' wanted you. In my bed. On the back of my bike. I wanted you for myself. I want to fill up that pussy with my cum, I wanna shove myself inside every fuckin' hole you have, and feel you break beneath my hands. I want you shattered into pieces, so that only I know how to put you back together again. I fuckin' want you, Princess. In every way, shape and fuckin' form a man can want a woman, but what the fuck does it matter now that your gun is pointed at my head?"

To drive my point home I grind my cock against her, relishing the way she moulds to my poor misused dick. Her satin panties catch and tug on the barbell through my frenum, turning my self-control to a pile of fuckin' mush.

She's crying now. I feel it, rather than hear it. Her hot little body trembles on top of me. I move my hips in a steady rhythm, thrusting slowly forward against her and back into the mattress. She writhes with me, so I grab her hip and slam her pelvis down on me while I thrust my cock against her satin-clad cunt. I use my other hand to try and pry the gun from her hand, but she snaps to and tightens her hold, her finger hovering dangerously close to the trigger.

"Give me the gun, Princess. You didn't come here to kill me — you came to take what's yours. So take it."

"You. Broke. Me," she bites out, punctuating each of her words by driving the barrel against my forehead. "I would have stayed strong. I could have closed my eyes and pretended all of this was a bad dream, but you took that away from me—"

"I know," I admit, pathetically. "Time to repay the favour, Princess."

I wrench the gun free from her hand, but she doesn't make a grab for it, just allows me to empty out the clip all around us. I toss the piece on the bedside table and wrap my hand around the nape of her neck, pulling her body down to my level. She sucks in a sharp hissing breath when the movement forces my cock to push against her hot, soaking, fuckin' wet pussy. I take her mouth with mine, driving my tongue as deep as it will go, practically eating her alive from the mouth down. I can't get enough of her taste, of the slide of her flesh against mine.

As she nibbles on the stud in my lip, I slip my free hand under the pillow beside mine and curl my fingers around the cold metal handle, bringing it out, and positioning it at the base of her spine where I cock the pistol, my finger on the trigger. She stiffens. Her writhing stops as her mind registers the danger she's in.

"One shot would sever your spinal cord."

"That one shot could easily pass through me into you."

"That's a chance I'm willing to take," I whisper. "Now, push your panties aside and climb on top of my cock."

"Fuck you," she hisses.

"Yeah, Princess, fuck me." I dig the barrel of the gun into her back for a little reminder. I know she knows I wouldn't really shoot her, but she also needs me to take away the choice for her, because what woman in their right mind would fall in love with her captor, but not just that, what sane person would come back to exact their revenge and end up giving themselves completely over to one of the arseholes responsible for taking away her freedom? No one would. It's the shit nightmares are made of, only every god-forsaken second of it is real.

She leans up and places one hand on my chest to steady herself, while the other does exactly as I ask: pushes the satin of her panties aside—only I decide I want nothing in the way of my cock sliding into her perfect cunt, so I reach out with my free hand and yank hard on the delicate fabric. With a snap, and a muffled gasp from Lauren, the wisp of fabric comes away in my hand. I bring it up to my nose and bury my face in her scent, lick at the wetness her delicious cunt left behind.

"You're sick."

I laugh, "And you're fucking perfect." I take hold of her hip with one hand and position my cock at the entrance to her pussy. She's drenched for me, and so fucking hot. I let her control how much of me she takes inside, but I have to fight like the son-of-a-bitch I am not to drive into her and rut like a fuckin' dog.

She surprises me by sinking down hard, and seating herself in my lap. She gasps as if she's in pain, but something tells me that despite what she's been through, she needs it to hurt. I need it too. I need the reminder that whether she plans to blow my brains out next or not doesn't matter. All that matters is that I'm as good as dead anyway, because no one just up and leaves the club. Especially not for some bitch you betrayed them for. I'm dead before I even leave this room because having had her and letting her walk away again will kill me. Assuming she gets to walk away, and isn't spotted by one of my other brothers. I reach up and tug on a lock of the blonde wig she's wearing.

"I had to go blonde to get past that big dopey fucker at the gate. He was onto me, so I shot him anyway."

"Jesus Christ." There's no love lost between Frogger and me, but my princess just admitted to taking out a fucker in cold blood to get to me. Granted he'd held me down and made me watch, but he and Tank were the only ones that didn't take a turn with her. Yes, even dear old dad had relished fucking the shit out of the girl that I'd just tried to claim as my old lady. Of course he had.

"How many more of my brothers did you kill?" I ask.

"Three. Two in the club lounge and one outside. I used his key to get in."

"Fuck me." I grunt, as she rides my dick like a fuckin' pony. "Turn on the light. I wanna see my cock as it disappears inside you."

"No," she whispers.

"If you're gonna kill me, I at least want the visual before I die." She shifts, but doesn't reach for the light. I work on thrusting my hips into her, forgetting all about seeing her face for a moment.

I rub the wig's cheap synthetic fibre beneath my fingertips. I yank it off and toss it across the room. Soft auburn waves fall down her back. I run my fingers through it, pulling a couple of strands towards me until she dips her head to the side to avoid having them ripped out completely. And then I take the gun and place it on the pillow beside me, clearly within reach.

I know as well as she does that she won't turn it on me. Not now. She might have fantasised about it, but she's never really wanted to kill me. Hurt me? Yeah. I'd believe that as much as I believe my father would have aborted me from my mother's womb if he'd had the option. But Lauren never wanted to kill me; that isn't why she came here. She could have easily slipped into Prez's room and shot him while he nailed a club whore to the wall. She could have done that with any one of the brothers she sought revenge from. She didn't. She killed who she had to in order to get to me. She came to me first because she had a choice between revenge and me, and she may be the only person in the world who has ever chosen me over something they really want. I feel weightless and weighed down knowing that. It's a fuckin' heady thing to feel like another person on this huge planet wants you that much.

Or maybe it's my cock hitting the end of her, impaling her root to tip that has me pondering the fuckin' existence of my belly button. I scoop her up in my arms and fuck her like I mean it. And I do mean it, with all that I have — with every part of me I mean it.

I stop thrusting and lift her off me, laying her back on the mattress. I climb on top of her, positioning the head of my cock just inside her sweet pussy, and then drive the entire way in. I shove a hand between us, rubbing her clit, hurriedly at first, and then as she gasps for breath and her legs tremble, I slow my pace, and touch her with soft, lightly punishing strokes. I pull out and drive back in slowly, deeply. Each stroking glide of my cock in and out of her pussy tugs on my piercing, heightening everything.

"Cum for me, Princess," I whisper, as I groan in her ear. "Show me why you risked your life to come back for me."

Her soft moan, the way her hips rise to meet my thrusts, the hurried, angry kisses she places on my lips, let me know she's close. All of this makes me know I didn't need her to verbalise the answers to those questions either. "I ..." she moans. "I came to ... kill you."

"You are killing me. Hurry the fuck up, so I can fill you with my cum."

"You first," she challenges.

"Woman, fuckin' give me that orgasm or I'll take it from you by force."

"Take it," she whispers. "Take me. I'm yours, Daniel."

"I know," I growl and pump faster. Her breathing peaks, her muscles clench and she cries out as I pull that orgasm from her, and my cum shoots from my cock in hot, hard bursts.

KICK

I'm chugging back a beer and staring off into space when Indie comes back down the stairs. She pauses when she sees me occupying the lounge. I move my feet off the end of the couch and shift so that the side she favours is free, and then I kick my feet up on the coffee table. She's wary at first, sitting down like a kitten that can't decide if it's curious or fuckin' terrified.

"Does your face hurt?"

I laugh. "Yeah darlin', it hurts like a fuckin' bitch."

"Good," she says, taking a swig of my beer before setting it on the table.

"By all means, help your fuckin' self."

"Oh, I will," she replies, giving me a stubborn-arse fuckin' glare.

"You wanna help yourself to anything else of mine, then go right ahead," I mutter, staring pointedly at my crotch.

"You're a pig."

"And you're a pain in my arse." I smirk and snatch up my stubbie, downing the rest and putting my mouth to good use before it gets me in trouble.

"Thank you, though," she says, "For the lesson. It was still an arsehole move, but I understand why you did it. Next time, maybe give the rape victim a little warning before you drag her across the room, throw her to the ground and attack her."

"If I'd given you warning, you never would have known what you were capable of."

She thinks on that for a minute, biting her bottom lip as she stares off into space. Finally, she nods and says, "I want you to teach me how to fire a gun."

"Slow your roll, Spitfire. To do that I'd need to take you outside. Prez said outside is off limits."

"Your prez isn't here."

"Lucky for you, otherwise he'd beat you down for sayin' that shit. You have to trust that we know what we're doing here. If it were safe to take you outside, I'd take you out-fuckin'-side."

She lets out a sigh, opens her mouth to say something, and then closes it again.

"Out with it, Spitfire," I say.

She glares at me for a second and then her face crumples. "Tell me about the tooth, Kick."

I'm not wearing it anymore. I took it off and threw it across the gym the second she left. And then I walked over and picked it up, threading the necklace through my wallet chain and then pocketing it so I wouldn't lose it.

The roar of motorcycles up the drive has my head snapping around towards the kitchen where I can see through the front door. *Saved by the fuckin' bell.* Though I know we're not done here. She'll be bitchin' at me later to answer the god damned question.

"Cavalry's here," I say, standing up and stretching out my tired muscles.

After she'd left me in the gym I'd taken some of my self-loathing out on the bag. I'm not wearing a shirt because I'd soaked it through with sweat, and hadn't seen the point in putting on the only clean shirt I had left. I liked the way she looked at me when I wasn't wearing one, her sweet and innocent gaze roaming every inch of my tattooed flesh, as though all the answers to my secrets were written within. I didn't have the heart to tell her there was no mystery when it came to me. Just selfishness. And shit. And betrayal.

"Stay," I say, as I head for the front door.

"Where the fuck do you think I'm gonna go?" she yells after me, and I can't help but turn so I see her exasperated expression. I don't know how much longer we'll be babysitting the brat, but a part of me is gonna be reluctant to let the bitch go.

I step outside to find Killer, One Eye, Prez, Squeals, and motherfuckin' Country. I shoot a questioning glare at Prez. "The guy that wants the bitch dead, the blind old coot, and the motherfuckin' prospect? Where the hell is Tank and Raphe? Hell, Prez, even fuckin' Diesel would have been a better choice than these three fuckers?"

"Tank's out. Takin' Ivy home and attemptin' to get her clean again after this motherfuckin' idiot stuck his coke under her nose and she ODed. Again." He smacks Killer in the back of the head, who's been here since yesterday without a wink of sleep. The fuck-knuckle

KICK

mumbles another apology, some shit about not knowing she was Tank's property. "Raphe and Diesel are busy cleaning up your shit. We got more to deal with than your old lady."

My head snaps up. "She's not my old lady."

"Wearin' her claw marks on your neck, aren't ya?"

"That's not what it looks like."

"Dude, what the fuck happened to your face?" Killer says. "Did you let a girl beat you up?"

"Shut up, fuck-stick." I smack him upside the head and he sneers, slinking back to his post.

"If that's not what it looks like, and she's not your old lady, then what the fuck are we all doing here?" Prez asks. He tries to push past me, but I glare at him and tilt my chin towards One Eye.

"What about him?"

"Can I enter my own fuckin' house and sit down to a meal at my goddamn fuckin' table, kid? Or are you gonna forbid your prez from goin' near your pretty piece of flesh in there? One Eye knows what's fuckin' up and what's fuckin' down, and if he doesn't play nicely, he's gonna be ridin' off into the sunset minus a cut." He shoulders me out of the way and enters the house.

"Grub's fuckin' up, fuckers," Prez announces as he heads into the kitchen and throws a black duffle bag on the table. He pulls out two buckets of chicken and a bag containing a couple of containers of coleslaw, and sits them on the dining table. The brothers file in, each taking a seat and diggin' in. *Fuckin' animals*. I head into the lounge to warn Indie that if she wants to eat today she better haul that sweet fuckin' arse in here, but when I see her staring blankly before the TV I quit talkin' and step up beside her, giving her a little shake. She's utterly transfixed on some news programme.

There's a police officer on the screen. The expression on her face is the same one I saw earlier today, when I'd thrown her on the ground and attacked her. I already know, but I have to ask anyway. "Is that him? Is that the fucker that took you?"

She doesn't answer. "Indie!" I grab her face in my hand and she wrenches out of my grasp. "Don't touch me."

"Is. That. Him?"

The dead motherfucker talking on the TV says, "We have reason to believe that Kayla Kennedy is alive. We're investigating leads after witnesses reported sightings of the woman earlier this week at a three car pile-up with a notorious Sydney-based motor cycle gang. These people are dangerous, and shouldn't be approached. Anybody with information should come forward."

"Prez! Get the fuck in here!"

Kitchen chairs scrape against the tile, but they aren't quick enough. The image on screen has already changed to that of a middle-aged woman, with grey hair and tired-arse eyes that are puffy from crying.

Indie covers her mouth. "Mum," she whispers.

A string of pearls decorate the woman's neck. Her face is painted up with bright coral lipstick. Her makeup runs with her tears, trailing down her cheeks in black lines and splashing onto her no doubt designer threads. That's what I don't understand about rich folk. Your kid is missing and you're taking the fuckin' time to look pretty on TV instead of gettin' out on the streets and looking for her. The chump standing behind her is decked out in a fuckin' suit. He's obviously Indie's dad, because he too looks as if someone just ran him through with a fuckin' sword. Starin' at her parents, I decide if I ever meet either of them I'm gonna beat their heads together until I knock the fuckin' sense into them.

Indie's face is stricken as she watches her parents speak. New tears form in her mother's eyes as she pleads with the camera. "Please, just return our daughter to us. And Kayla, honey, if you're out there watching, come home. Please? We love you and we just want you safe."

The image cuts to a reporter standing on the deserted country road where we took down the men who were hunting her. "The police strongly advise against approaching these people. Call Crime Stoppers on 1300 —"

I hit the off button and throw the remote at the wall. "Fuck!"

Indie jumps, as if she's just now noticing me for the first time. She's white as a fuckin' ghost.

"I didn't get his name." I turn to Prez.

"So we're just as fucked on leads as we were five minutes ago?"

"Hit up the news sites. Someone is bound to have that fucker on there," One Eye says. He's standing at the entrance to the room, just behind Prez, with his massive arms folded in front of his chest.

"Someone get a fucking laptop out here," Prez orders.

"Sergeant Cole," Indie whispers.

"What'd you say, sweetheart?"

"Sergeant Cole, from the police department. He said he's been working with my parents to bring me home."

She sits down heavily on the couch and stares up at me. "You were right; I can't go home. I have no one."

"Hey," I say, ignoring the fact that my brothers are all watching this exchange. I sit down on the couch beside her and offer my hand. She glares at me, but places hers in mine. I wrap my fingers around her hand, squeezing hard so she'll feel it. "You have me. We're gonna find these fuckers, and we're gonna end them."

"You're sure that was him?" Prez asks. "We go in there shooting up coppers we're all as good as dead. We gotta be certain that's the right guy, and we gotta be smart."

"That was him. I'd know that voice, that face, anywhere."

"Alright, boys, let's go shoot another motherfuckin' rapist."

"I'm coming with you," I say, which of course prompts Indie to agree.

"I wanna be the one to take him down," she says.

"No fuckin' way. You two are gonna stay here out of damn sight."

"He did this to me." She shoots up off the couch. "I appreciate your help, and everything you've done for me so far, but I should be the one to kill him."

Prez laughs in her face. "Oh darlin', have you ever put a gun to a man's head before? It's not like throwing a couple of punches. That's the kinda shit you can't erase."

"I held a gun to Kick's head."

"And you're still fuckin' standin'?" Prez looks at me with his brows raised and a smug-as-fuck expression on his face.

"I'm sorry, sweetheart, but you're stayin' here. You and your new pussy-whipped boyfriend, get to play hide the fuckin' salami while we risked our arses with this shit." Prez turns to the boys and says, "One Eye, Grim and Killer, you're all riding with me. We'll swing by the club and pick up Trigger and Diesel. Country and Squeals, you'll stay here and guard the perimeter, though you probably won't be needed.

"I'll stay." One Eye says. "Can't have a geriatric and a fuckin' blind man on patrol, Prez."

"Yeah fine, whatever. It's only gonna take one of us to get this motherfucker alone and put a bullet in his skull."

"You can't keep me here," Indie shouts. She steps up into Prez's personal space. "I should be the one to do it."

He dismisses her, looking straight over her head at me. "Jesus fuckin' Christ, control your mouthy little bitch, Kick. Before she says some shit she can't take back."

"He'll be taken care of." I grab her shoulder, attempting to turn her so she can see the pleading in my eyes for her to let this go. "Little faith, Spitfire."

She yanks her arm out of my grip. "Don't touch me." She stares accusingly at me. "You said you'd help me find them. You didn't say you'd take the right away from me to drive the knife in his gut myself."

"There's more at stake here than just your revenge," I snap back.

"Kick, deal with this fuckin' shit," Prez says, giving us his back. "We got ourselves a rapist to kill."

"No!" Indie says and lunges at Prez, her fists up and ready for action, the way I taught her. I scoop her up and throw her over my shoulder, stalking away as she kicks and screams blue bloody murder. As I struggle with her up the stairs, I hear the laughter from my brothers below. *Fuckin' bitch*. Now I'm never gonna live that shit down. I move along the corridor all the way to her room, where I shove open the door and stalk inside, throwing her down on the bed.

"Calm the fuck down!" I roar.

"Fuck you!" she spits back, scrambling to her knees on the soft comforter. "You fucking promised and you lied."

"I didn't lie," I shout. "I meant it when I promised you and I would go get him together. Prez promised me that. But things fuckin' change, bitch. You can't go around attacking the fuckin' president of a damn motorcycle club. Shit like that is gonna get you killed. And likely me too, 'cause I'm fuckin' responsible for ya."

"You are not responsible for me. You are nothing to me," she shouts, and fuck me if it doesn't hurt.

It's not like I don't understand why she's so fucking distraught over this decision. When it comes to revenge, karma or someone else doing the job for you is just as bad as never getting your revenge at all. I felt it when it came to Lauren. I'd have likely died if Ethan hadn't lost his shit and started shooting motherfuckin' Angels in that farm house. There were eight of them to one of me, but that didn't matter. I wanted to put a bullet through the skull of my oldest friend because he took the right away from me to kill Lauren's murderers. They were all dead. At the end of the day it's the same result, but you feel that loss as keenly as a fucking noose around your neck.

Indie launches herself at me and I catch her up, stumbling back a few paces into the door. I hold her fists at bay to keep her from giving me another black eye.

"Stop fuckin' hittin' me, woman. I didn't do this. It's beyond my control. If I could have, I'd have strapped that bastard into a chair and let you exact whatever punishment you wanted, but it's no longer up to me. The lives of all of my brothers are at stake here if we don't handle this carefully."

All at once she sags against me and lets out a gut-wrenching sob. I walk us over to the bed and sit down. She curls her shins back against the mattress, so she's straddling my waist and then I lay down, taking her with me.

Is it the smartest move I can make? Fuck no. But I do it 'cause I don't have a fucking clue what else to do. I don't relish her tears the way I did Ivy's. I feel them. And I fuckin' hate that. I hate her for that, for making me feel.

When she's done drenching my shoulder she slides off of me and lies on her side in the hollow of my arm. My hand rests against her hip, and her thigh is hooked over mine … and my heart is skipping like a fuckin' schoolgirl's.

How the fuck did we get here?

I not only managed to screw shit up completely by taking her instead of putting a bullet in her head, but I went from being her captor, her tormentor, to what? A fuckin' boyfriend? Her old man? Her saviour?

Jesus Christ, I need my head checked.

I don't know how to process any of this shit. Her

tired body sags against me, and sleep takes her over as I hold her and breathe in her sweet clean scent with her hair all up in my face. I stare at the ceiling and wonder where the fuck I go from here. 'Cause any way I look at it, I'm completely fucked.

KICK

TWO YEARS AGO

As the high wears off for the third time tonight, the truth of our situation settles in. I've been selfish. I mean, I'm always selfish, but I've been particularly selfish with her safety, and that's not really a luxury I have with a clubhouse full of bikers gunnin' for this chick's head and dead Angels everywhere. It'll be sunrise soon, and we need to get her out of here. Propelled by new fears for her safety, I pull her close and kiss her forehead and then I jump up from the mattress and tear around the room, gathering together her things.

"We need to get you out of here."

"Jesus, Kick. You couldn't at least wait until my heart rate slows before you kick me out?"

"If they find you here, they'll kill you."

"Not if I get to them first."

"You're not still going through with this crazy fuckin' vengeance plan, are you?" I spit.

She snaps. I've never seen this kind of reaction from

her. She motherfuckin' snaps and lunges at me. "They raped me. They busted up my face and took things from me, and you can't even imagine what that feels like."

"I was there," I grab onto her arm and yank her towards me. "I don't have to fuckin' imagine. I saw every goddamned second of it."

"And yet you still expect me to let them live with what they've done?"

"I expect you to be smart," I say. "Every single fuckin' brother in this club can outwit, outshoot you and overpower you. Going in there half-cocked will only get you killed. Right now the only thing keeping you alive is that Slayer supposedly has you in hiding. That angle is gonna be shot to fucking shit if I can't get to the security tapes before Prez does. Not to mention the line of bodies you've left in your wake. We need to get you out of the city. I may know of someone who can help, but the only way we're gonna make it there is if we get you outta here before the rest of the club wakes."

"I'm not leaving until I've looked that motherfucker in the face and put a bullet between his eyes."

"No, you're not. You shoot him, you'll be dead within seconds. Silencer or not, Princess, you got lucky, but that pile of bodies in the club lounge isn't gonna go unnoticed for long. Every motherfuckin' brother in this club is gonna turn this house upside down to find the killer. And they're gonna start with this fuckin' room, because my loyalties have already been called into question. You have to cut your losses. You gotta get the fuck outta here."

"The only thing I'm going to be cutting is his balls off. I'm gonna start with your prez, and finish with the big guy."

"Tank didn't touch you,"

"He didn't stop them either."

"If he'd put his hands on you, I would have killed him myself."

"Like you killed the rest of them?" she snaps. "How can you share a clubhouse with them, knowing what they did to me?"

"What fuckin' choice do I have?"

"You could leave? You could have left when you helped me, and never came back."

I laugh, but it's a vile, empty sound. "You don't get it. There's no leaving the club."

"People leave my father's club all the time. When they want out, they hand in their patch."

"Your father isn't my fuckin' prez, bitch. No Angel hands in their wings; they have 'em stripped, burned off, or blacked out, but no one ever fuckin' walks away a free man. Betrayal comes at a price, Princess: a body bag and a one-way ticket to hell. The best you and I can hope for is you making it out of here in one piece. So get fuckin' dressed and let me get you out of here."

"I'm not leaving until he's begging for forgiveness on his knees."

"Let's get one thing fuckin' straight. If that's what you're after than you're never getting outta here. He is not gonna beg or apologise for ripping your life apart. He will destroy you, and there's not a goddamned thing you can do about it. You got off lucky, Princess. Plenty of girls been where you were and they never got to leave because they never had someone to fuckin' save them." I pick up the short leather skirt and the crop top she had on that exposed half of her breasts and I throw them at her. "Now, get dressed. Next time I have to tell you, I put you over my fuckin' shoulder and carry you outta here, and that's gonna draw a lot more attention than you strutting out in that skirt and wig and pretending like you're someone else. You got me?"

She doesn't say anything, but the tears runnin' down her cheeks mean she doesn't have to. I cross the room and attempt something I've never really done before; I comfort her. Or I try to. I don't know, I probably just look like an insensitive fuckrod, but I take her in my arms, I grasp her chin in my hand and force her face up to mine.

"I don't know how to do this shit," I begin, and then try a different tact when I realise her expression has turned angry. "I never had a woman before."

She gives me a disbelieving look and I hurry to finish. "Oh, I had plenty of women,"

"You're off to an awesome start, Daniel. No really, please, keep talking."

"I've had women, but none that were mine, you know?" I breathe out a heavy sigh. "I just, I wanna keep you. I've never had someone to depend on me ... until you."

"I can't let this go. I can't—"

"Okay, don't let it go. Just put it to bed for now. Let's get you somewhere safe and come up with a better plan than strutting in there and blowing Prez's head off." I kiss her forehead, her cheek, her lips. "Let's keep this pretty face intact. I've grown kinda used to it," I grin. "And I still have a billion uses for it."

"Fine," she says, pouting like a fuckin' child,

though the blazing bloodlust in her eyes is anything but childlike. "We put it to rest for now, but we come back with a plan that still involves me blowing his goddamned head off." She pulls away and slips into her skirt and top. She spends a couple of seconds arranging the wig back into place. Her underwear is a lost cause, but something about riding her on the back of my bike with her legs spread around mine and her bare cunt pressed up against my arse has my dick twitching again.

I ignore it though, 'cause honestly? I could fuck that pussy all night and still never get tired of it, but I'm not gonna have a pussy left to fuck unless I get her the fuck outta here.

When she's dressed, I lay one final kiss on her lips. It's hard not to let it take over, this need to have her, to possess every inch of her body. To teach her who owns that pussy. Who's always gonna own it.

She pushes me away from her and back towards the door. Before I can open it though she's in my arms again, wrapping her body around me. I catch her up and slam her into the door. I undo my fly and prepare to bury myself in her for a fourth time but she pulls away from my lips and shakes her head. "You bruised me. I'm gonna need a day or two to get the feeling back in my pussy, Kick."

I groan in her ear and tuck my cock back inside my pants. I don't miss what she said, and I'd find a way to see her, but I don't know if she grasps the gravity of the situation here. I can't fuckin' play house with the bitch that escaped Prez's grasp. I can't shack up with the only one that ever slipped through his fingers, and we've already established the fact that I can't just walk away from the club scot-free. That's never gonna happen for us. Which means that this thing between us is never gonna happen. Not the way she really wants it to. Not the way I want it to.

"I hope you heal quickly then," I say without thinking.

It's as if we both just deflate after that. As if my words are a pin through the little fuckin' bubble of happiness we've found in my room tonight. She wriggles out of my hold and slides down the door, shifting her skirt back into place, manoeuvring out from the space in front of me.

"We should go."

"Yeah," I say, and pull her back behind me as I open the door and peek out. There's only an empty hallway so I tug her out with me and make for the back entrance. It's the longer route, but we're less likely to be seen that way, and even if we are seen the lack of lighting in the lot, and that fuckin' hideous wig she's wearing combined with that outfit mean she probably wouldn't be recognised anyway.

All the same I hurry her out into the lot, through the door that I dragged her kicking and screaming through only a few short weeks ago, and now, for the second time in the month that I've known her, I'm sneaking her out of the compound, right under Angel noses.

When we round the building my bike is lined up alongside the others, but the lot isn't empty like I'd hoped. Tank comes storming towards me. I pause, not knowing what to do. Not knowing where we stand. It's true he helped Lauren escape once before, but he took a bullet to the arm for it, and he almost got caught doing it. He'd almost lost his life because of it. I don't know if he'd be willing to take that risk again.

He gets up in my face, stands toe to toe with me, his jaw set, shoulders strung tight with anger. "Need to fuckin' talk to you, brother."

I shove Princess behind me, only she's not so fuckin' happy about being hidden. She pulls the piece I confiscated from her out from the back of my jeans and turns it on Tank.

Tank stands with his arms folded across his chest. He doesn't flinch as she levels the gun on his face.

"Bitch, are you fuckin' crazy?"

"He let this happen," she screams, and Jesus fucking Christ I've never wanted to flatten a woman so bad in my life. She has no fuckin' respect for her own self-preservation, yelling like a fucking banshee in the parking lot of a MC than wants to see her pretty insides on the outside.

"Then so did fuckin' I," I shout back, getting in her face and forcing her watery gaze up to mine. I wrestle the gun from her. "Trust me when I say Tank is the only reason you're still standing here in this fuckin' car park, yellin' about shit you have no right to yell about."

"He's the one that took me," she spits. All at once, my ears start to ring, and the hairs on my neck stand up all fuckin' straight and tall.

"That true?" I ask Tank, weighing the gun in my hand.

His gaze narrows. "I was followin' orders."

God. I want so badly to beat his fuckin' head in right now. I wanna unload an entire clip into his chest, because he knew. At the rally, he knew about her. He fuckin' had to in order for Prez to give the order before he got arrested. That was why Tank was nowhere to be seen when the shit hit the fan—he was layin' in fuckin' wait for her.

"What are you gonna do, brother?"

"I'm leaving," I say, surprising myself. Tank's not surprised, though. It's as though he knew it before I did.

"Your bike's been fitted with a tracker. Frogger's been watchin' the feeds, though it seems your girl took care of that." He looks her up and down with an appreciative smile. "She pull on you too?"

"Yeah," I admit.

"Let me guess—you fucked her into submission?"

"Somethin' like that." I raise the gun to his head. I don't wanna shoot him. He's the only fuckin' friend I have left in this entire world, but I will if I have to. Sometimes decisions have to be made to ensure your self-preservation, and while I don't think Tank would kill me over this, if I had to choose between me and him, there's no question of who comes out on top.

"You really wanna do this? Where the fuck you gonna go, Kick? Prez is already jacked up on the idea of you betrayin' the club. He's had a tail on you for a month that you don't even fucking know about."

"What the hell are you talkin' about? You didn't wanna tell me this shit?"

He laughs. "If I'd told you, they'd be stringing my guts up like Christmas lights. I like them where they are. I knew–" He shakes his head. "I *thought* you'd be smart enough to stay away from the bitch."

"I stayed the fuck away. She came lookin' for me."

"And you couldn't do what you had to."

"Could you?" I ask, but I know that's a stupid question, 'cause Tank never cared for anyone but himself. Tank feels nothing, and right about now, I'm starting to think it's a pretty good way to be. "Hand over your keys, and get on the ground," I command.

"You really wanna fuckin' do this?"

"Not really," I admit. "But I don't have another fuckin' choice, so get the fuck on the ground before I shoot you in the head."

He tosses his keys to me and puts his hands behind his head, as he slowly sinks to his knees. "They'll find you. Can't go to Slayer; he'll take your girl and boot you out on your arse, and then he'll be callin' Prez to tell him exactly where to come pick you up from."

"Lay down," I snap, and walk over to Lauren. "Princess, if I give you the gun, are you gonna shoot him?"

"Yes," she says without hesitation.

Ask a stupid question ...

I sigh. "Wrong answer, baby."

I keep the gun firmly trained on Tank's head as I circle his huge form. The fucker knows he can take me, he knows it as well as I do, and though I'm the one holding the gun, he's the one with the power.

"Weapons, where?" I bark out, half expecting him to tell me to go fuck myself.

"Piece in my leathers, knife in my left boot."

I squat down and retrieve the gun, shoving it in the front of my jeans. I reach into his boot to retrieve the knife, but I come up empty-handed. Tank rears his foot back, throwing me off balance. He reaches into his right boot and pulls a knife, flinging out his arm and stopping its path a quarter inch from my skin at the same time as I press the barrel of my gun to his head. Behind him in my periphery Lauren stands stock-still.

"Sorry, brother, but I had to make it look believable. They watch the tape back and see me lying low without a fight, I'm as dead as Frogger is, and Red before him."

I yank the blade from his hand, push the gun harder against his skull, forcing him to lay back down on the pavement.

"Better hide well, brother. If you don't, you're a dead man." He calls to me as I back away with the gun still trained on his head, and I grab Princess, pulling her over to the custom Harley Night Rod belonging to Tank. It's a fuckin' Cadillac when compared to my 1991 Fat Boy, but it's nothing I can't handle. I throw my leg over, the gun still in my hand, as I flip the kickstand, and turn the key, revving the throttle with one hand once Princess slips on behind me.

I pull the helmet from the handlebars and hand it to her, shouting at her to put it on, over the roar of the engine. Then I pass her the gun with a warning as loaded as the chamber. "Shoot him, Princess, and I throw you off this bike. You got me?"

"Yeah," she snaps. "I got you."

She wraps one arm around my waist. The other is pointed right at Tank, but as we drive past the corner and by the back entrance to the clubhouse, Juke and Bear exit. It takes my dad all of two seconds to see the gun in Lauren's hand and Tank on the ground. I don't think he even registers who's driving Tank's bike, but that sure as hell doesn't give him pause. He pulls his piece and aims at us. I twist the throttle and we lurch forward around the clubhouse and towards the main gate. Someone hit the emergency lockdown switch from the inside. I push the bike faster, and clear the gate before it closes, but the weight's thrown off because I'm not used to driving such a massive bike, and we skid out when we hit the street. It takes me a second or two to right the bike, and it's seconds we didn't have to lose because dear old Dad and Bear made it through the gate after us. I begin weaving all across the road in an attempt to dodge the bullets they're shooting at us.

"Princess, if you want your revenge on those fuckers, now is the time," I shout over the roar of the bike. She doesn't hesitate, just holds me tighter with one arm while flinging the other out behind her and firing off several bullets.

"Fuck. I'm down," she yells, and then throws the piece. She reaches around to pull the gun from the front of my jeans. Her hand on my cock is distracting, but not as distracting as the almighty explosion I hear seconds after she starts firing shots again. I glance behind us. Juke is still riding our tail, but Bear and his bike are scattered all over the road. "Jesus Christ, Princess," I shout, but inside I'm filled to bursting with fuckin' pride and sexual fuckin' frustration, because fuck me, chicks with guns are hot.

Lauren lets out a triumphant growl that has all the blood in my body racing to my dick. The shots behind us make that pride short lived, and I switch my focus back to the road stretching out in front of me. It's early morning—three or four, maybe? Apart from the occasional car parked at the curb, the streets are completely deserted.

I weave all over the road, taking a turn at high speed that leads to the freeway. My dad follows. This is one road that's not deserted. It's not exactly peak-hour traffic, but there's a steady flow of cars, trucks, and the occasional bus. I have no desire to stay on the highway. Too many cameras, too many cops, too much at fucking stake to be a sitting duck. We fly across multiple lanes, weaving in and out of oncoming traffic. Lauren's not shooting anymore, but Juke sure as hell is. If there's one thing I know about my father, it's that he can't stand to lose. Even if it means getting flattened by an SUV. And that's the only way he'll give up, is if he's dead.

"Princess, when I say so, you're gonna need to shoot the tyres on the tanker." I shout, pushing the bike closer to the massive petrol tanker headed for us.

"What?"

"Shoot the fucking tanker."

"I can't!"

"Shoot the motherfucking truck, Princess!" I roar.

The shot rings out beside my head, my eardrums squeal their protest and I lose all equilibrium. I veer right, toward the shoulder and away from the tanker that's sliding all across the road, collecting cars in front of it, when we're sideswiped by a fuckin' Hilux. I yank on the handlebars to correct our path, but the bike slides out from underneath us and we're thrown across the asphalt. I land with a bone-jarring crack, my teeth slam together and my head whacks off of the road. My vision goes black.

I don't know how long I'm out, but I wake with a start and a searing pain in my head. In the distance I can hear sirens, but it's overshadowed by the hiss and pop of flaming kerosene. I go to speak, and black smoke fills my lungs. I splutter and roll to my side, gasping for breath, searching for Princess.

"Lauren," I shout, but my throat isn't working. Little bits of tooth crunch in my mouth when I set my jaw. I spit them out, and roll over on my stomach because it's all my stupid fuckin' abused body will let me do. Somewhere in the back of my hazy head I realise the tanker is on fire. That wasn't supposed to happen. This is real life, not fuckin' Hollywood. Even if Lauren shot the tank, that wouldn't happen unless there was a spark. Realisation slams into me the way my body slammed into the road. I glance over to the middle of the road and I spot her, illuminated by the flames. She's lying on the asphalt, Juke standing over her, his boot at her throat, and a smile on his god-forsaken fuckin' face as he tries to crush the life out of her. Princess squirms beneath him. Her small hands dig into the leg of his jeans, clawing at him. The fucker leers as he tries to snuff out her existence. I stagger to my feet. The world spins, my vision goes dark, and then there's only rage, red and thick as the blood in my veins.

I don't think. I just act.

I barrel into him, throwing him off balance and slamming him back into the asphalt. I hold my father around the throat, and slam his head into the road, repeatedly. His hands grapple for purchase as I straddle his waist and choke the life out of him.

His gurgled cries don't stop my assault, but the wail of sirens do, and we can't be caught here, or we'll both wind up in the slammer. I draw back my fist and slam it into the side of his head, and then I rise as quickly as my body, and my likely concussed head will allow. I stumble over to Lauren.

"You okay?"

She nods, but her eyes are wide with terror. It's a look I'd become too accustomed to in the time that I've known her, but it isn't one I fuckin' like.

"We gotta get outta here before the cops arrive and start asking questions." I hold out my hand and she takes it, gingerly peeling herself off the road and standing on shaky legs. One of her boots is missing a heel. I motion for her to prop her foot up on my knee and it takes some work, but eventually I snap the spike off the other one. She might not be runnin' anywhere anytime soon, but at least she won't break her damn neck.

"That man," she says, looking past me. "Is he dead?"

I glance back at the body of my father lying prone on the asphalt, and then turn back to her. I don't tell her that I just beat the shit outta my dad to save us both. I don't tell her he's merely unconscious. What would it serve but to fill her with more hatred, and anger, and the desire for revenge?

"As a doornail, Princess," I say, and take her hand. I edge us as far from the burning trailer as possible, and double back to the scene, leading her across the road to a car whose occupants had stopped to help victims of the pile up. Tank's bike is a write off, and even if it weren't, they'd be looking for it.

We climb inside a beaten-up old Charade and take off while the owners are preoccupied with watching the tanker burn. When I check the rear-view mirror, they aren't any closer to realising their car is gone, and the further we get from the sirens, the more my heart rate returns to normal. The sirens get further away the longer we drive. I glance over at Lauren and notice her shaking—no, not shaking. Her whole body is vibrating. She's in shock. I take her hand in mine and bring it to my lips, nipping and biting her clammy flesh. "Hey, you still with me?"

"Yeah," she mutters, but it's an automatic response. She's not here in this car with me.

"We got this, Princess," I say, and maybe I'm just lulling us both into a false sense of hope, because I have no idea where to go from here. We're both beaten up pretty bad. Grazes cover her upper thigh and arms, and we're both bleeding from the head, but our injuries are the last of our problems right now because everything Tank said is true. They will find us, and they'll kill us, so I'd better seek out the best motherfuckin' hiding spot, or it's gonna be so much worse than the shit-storm we just rode through.

INDIE

I jolt awake from another nightmare, my arms smacking against the floorboards. My head swims, my body aches all over, and with the way the moonlight streams in through the window, for a split second I think I'm back inside the warehouse. Crickets chirp outside, and a lonely owl calls into the night, and I know I'm not at that warehouse, because nothing had life there but my screams. I press my ear to the wall and listen for a beat. Biker's not there, or if he is he's not dreaming.

I stand, stretching out my protesting muscles. Everything hurts, but for once it's a welcome pain, because it means I've accomplished something. It means I'm stronger than I was yesterday. I wrap one of the silk robes Mia left inside the box around me. It's black and really the only thing comfortable enough to wear downstairs — not everyone can pull off designer fuchsia coloured playsuits. I've been sleeping in nothing because in that entire box of clothing there was one damn T-shirt, and I've already worn it every day this week without washing. I'm also out of clean underwear; I'll have to locate the laundry room tomorrow, because god knows Biker's clothes could do with a wash too.

I open the door and creep downstairs to the kitchen. I pull a glass from the cupboard and fill it with water. I have only a small sip when a noise from the west wing of the house draws my attention. I set the glass down on the bench and softly pad up the hall. The gymnasium light is on and the sound of flesh hitting the bag over and over again filters out through the partially open door. I push it wider.

Kick is facing away from me, tattoos on display, back slick with sweat. It drips from his hair onto the rubber mat flooring. His arms piston with his frenetic punching. One after the other, his bare fists slam the bag. He's merciless, an animal in his rage. I move forward, my feet making no sound against the mats. I can't see his face, but I feel the fury coming off of him.

What has happened to this man that he can be so full of violence and hate? Was it the same as me? Is that why he saved me? Did someone hurt him too? I've seen his scars, the perfect circular cigarette burns up his arms, the angry, jagged marks over his hard abdomen. They're covered mostly by his tattoos, and maybe an ordinary person wouldn't notice them—maybe the old me wouldn't have noticed them either—but there's a silent exchange between victims. I feel it every time we're together. I felt it the first time I met Grim. I stared at his scars and wept, because though our situations were probably vastly different, I'd been where he had, at the mercy of a monster, and neither one of us had come out unscathed.

It's different with Kick. I can't put my finger on it, but I can still feel his hurt from a mile away.

His grunts of exertion pull me away from my thoughts. His hands are damaged, the skin busted, stretched raw and bloody over his knuckles.

"Stop!" I reach up and grab his shoulder. He whirls around. One fist guards his face, and the other is pulled and ready to strike.

I suck in a sharp breath, staring at his loaded fist, waiting for the blow to connect.

"What the fuck are you doin'?"

The air leaves my lungs in a rush. "I don't know."

We're both breathing heavily, him from exertion, and me from fear. He lowers his fist, but then he uses his other arm to pull me into his body. Sweat soaks the silk robe I'm wearing. My nipples harden against his warm chest. He smells incredible, of pheromones and rage. He works his free hand around my back, tugging me closer before threading his fingers in my hair and grasping the nape of my neck.

I inhale. He exhales.

His dark blue eyes bore into mine. They're so full of violence that it should frighten me, but the longer I stare into them, the more I want every punishing touch he has to offer. He lowers his head, pushing the side of my robe apart to reveal my breasts. They're small, and under his scrutinising gaze, for the first time in my life I find myself wishing I had more. Wishing I had the kind of figure he's used to seeing around the clubhouse, the kind worthy of draping over a motorcycle. It's not the first time he's seen me naked, but it's the first time that matters.

He lowers his head and nips at my clavicle, kissing and biting his way down to my breast, taking my nipple in his mouth and sucking hard. My body goes electric, humming from the roots of my hair to the tips of my toes. I arch into his touch, into his mouth with its cool metal piercings. He releases me with a loud sucking sound. I moan, threading my hands through his sandy-coloured hair. My flesh is on fire, and he is the balm. He licks a path to my other breast, consuming me as he would his favourite meal. There's violence and worship in his touch, and I'm drowning in both. Swallowed. Consumed. I savour it. Revel in being handled, being venerated, being something worthy of the kind of hunger reflected in his gaze.

Biker kisses my neck, across my jaw, but he doesn't kiss my lips. He pauses instead, pressing his forehead to mine.

He breathes. I breathe.

I slide my hands from his hair, down his powerful shoulders and across his chest. I toy with the barbell through his nipple, and he makes a low growling sound in the back of his throat, as if he's barely keeping himself contained. I wish he'd let go. I want his violence, his pleasure — I want whatever horror he is hiding inside of him. I want it unleashed, if only to be able to understand him better.

He grinds his erection against my thigh. I run my hand down his hard stomach, luxuriating in the feel of each rigid indentation, and then I seem to lose control of myself entirely and run my hand over his denim-covered cock.

I'm not the only one losing control. Biker's lips smash down on mine, his tongue pushing inside, tangling with my own and drawing a desperate, needy cry from me.

Next thing I'm weightless. My knees go out from under me and I'm slammed back against the rubber mat in much the same way I was earlier today, only now he's not holding back. Now we're not fighting so much as ripping and tearing at one another, seeking refuge in our bodies. His hand slides between us and yanks hard on the sash holding my robe together. The black silk falls away and I'm completely exposed to him, my pale flesh, my bruises and my scars, all of it laid before him.

He leans up on his elbows and pushes himself up from the floor. At first I think he's just standing to take his jeans off, but the dark glint in his gaze forces my heart into my throat. Tears prick my eyes as I come to see his actions for what they are: a rejection.

I can't breathe.

"I don't know how to be gentle with you," he whispers, but it sounds more like a hiss than an admission, and then he's gone.

And I'm left alone again.

It isn't long before sobs wrack my body, and I'm pulling my robe closed and curling into myself in the empty gym.

KICK

TWO YEARS AGO

Five hours on the road, and I can barely keep my eyes open. I blink and then swerve when Princess screams at me to get back on the road. I gently ease in to my lane, thankful that there was no one else driving at this hour, and then shake my head to clear it.

"Sorry."

"It's okay. I shouldn't have fallen asleep."

"You've been out for hours."

"Oh my god, where are we?"

"Just outside Port Macquarie. I woulda just pulled over and slept by the side of the road, but we can't run the risk of the cops stopping to ask questions. Owners would have reported the car missing at the scene. We'll have to ditch it soon, find another ride."

"Where are we going?"

"Sugartown, about three hours north of here." She nods, but I doubt she's taken any of this in. "We're gonna have to stop for the night. Sleep, tend to our wounds—god knows we have enough of them. I doubt we'll find a chemist open this late, but there's bound to be a servo somewhere."

We pull into a service station about ten minutes later and I wait outside while she uses the toilet. When she emerges, she's wiped the dried blood from her face and tamed her hair into a ponytail. She winces when she sees me, and I realise I must look like shit so I push her back into the stall and closed the door behind us.

"What are you doing?" she asks.

"I gotta clean up before I walk in there covered in blood and I'm sure as hell not leaving you alone at a rest stop in the middle of the night." She nods, and I can't help but smile. "I should endanger your life more often. You're much more agreeable."

She gives me a sad smile and I figure it's probably way too soon for jokes. I turn to the mirror and look at my face. Jesus Christ, I look like I just came shuffling out of a Romero film. I run the water and splash my face, wincing when it stings the cut on my forehead. I tear off a couple sheets of paper towel and pat my face dry, but Lauren takes it from me and begins cleaning up the spots I missed on my ear, my neck and even a little on my cheek.

"You have to scrub it a little. Tell me if I'm hurting you."

"Take a lot more than that to hurt me, Princess," I say automatically, but even as the words leave my mouth I know that's not true. This woman could break me with her fuckin' pinky finger and she doesn't even know it. I gave her that power over me, and now I can't take that shit back. And worse still? I don't want to.

She cleans me up as best she can, and disposes of the paper towel. Before she turns, I grab her arms and pull her into me. It's weird how much we feel considering we know so fuckin' little about one another. I take her chin in my hands and tilt her face up to mine.

"We'll be okay, Princess. I'm gonna take care of us."

Though now I'm kinda thinking I have no idea how to do that. I got some money saved in the bank, but it's nothing compared to the cash in the safe back in my room. I wanna smack my head against the mirror for not fuckin' thinking straight. I kiss her quickly on the mouth, and then head for the door.

Once inside the servo, we grab as many packages of Band-Aids and Neurofen as we can find, and two of the overpriced first-aid kits. I throw them on the counter with a box of donuts and a couple of packets of chips, a bar of chocolate, some water bottles and a tin of breath mints. The dude behind the counter just stares at our loot and then begins ringin' everything up as if someone suddenly lit a fire beneath his arse.

I pay for the shit using my card because I've got no damn cash on me, not really something I'm used to, and we hobble out to the car. Twenty minutes later we're walking through the door of some seedy-arse motel to bunk down for the morning. It's almost daylight now, so we'll have to wait for nightfall before we can steal another car.

Lauren and I take turns bandaging each other up. The cut on my forehead won't stop bleeding, and I could probably do with a stitch or two, but I tape a band aid over it instead and hope it closes up soon—or at least crusts to a point where blood doesn't drip down my face.

When we're done, we undress and fall into bed. She curls into my side while I drift off.

The metallic click of a bullet sliding through a chamber wakes me. My eyes spring open, but the bite of cold metal against my temple forces me to hold completely still.

Until I see her, bound and gagged on the worn motel carpet.

Her body quakes as Tag kneels behind her. Her face is contorted with fear. Pain. Tears stream down her red cheeks. Her mouth gapes open in horror around the gag. Her eyes stare accusingly at me as his dick slams in and out of her.

I explode.

I don't think. Just act.

I launch myself up off the bed, but I'm shoved back down with a boot to my gut. It hurts like a motherfucker, but I dodge the next kick and come back swinging, slamming my fist into the side of Prez's face. He laughs, as he grips my shirt and head-butts me.

The thin bones in my nose snap, I taste copper on my tongue. Pain lances through my skull. My head spins. Blood drips from the wound in my forehead, blurring my vision. Prez smashes my head into the grimy concrete walls. "You know what disappoints me, son? Is that you never seem to fuckin' learn. I gave you a home, a roof over your head, a seat at my goddamned table, and my patch, and you throw it back in my face. You shit all over it for a filthy fuckin' whore!" he bellows, slamming my head into the wall, punctuating each word with a sharp blow to the skull.

"You know what hurts even worse though? Is that my boys all seemed to have gotten soft. Ethan, Tiny, you, and even your dearest old dad."

I don't know how I didn't register the others in the room. My dad is in the corner, bound and gagged and surprisingly, the look on his face isn't one of disappointment—it's sympathetic. Not once in my twenty-seven years have I ever seen that look from my dad.

"See, I'm beginning to notice a pattern here," Prez continues. "First the kid deserts, and then the father follows. Only problem with that scenario, is that all of you bastards owed me something, and it's time I fuckin' collected. Tiny stole something very valuable from me. Fuckin' cockhead over there—" he turns and points to Rue, who's standing guard at the door. "He killed the bastard before I had a chance to reclaim it. But there's a way to get it back, and that lies with you."

"Let her go," I plead. "I'll give you whatever you want; I'll tell you whatever I know. Just let her go. Please." Tears stream down my face. Saltwater stings the cut on my cheek. I close my eyes, not wanting to see him thrusting inside her, not wanting to witness her being hurt all over again.

Prez slaps my face. "Open your fuckin' eyes." He points to Lauren, whose face is twisted with anguish and pain. "This is what your betrayal costs."

My heart splits in two.

That fucker explodes inside her, thrusting his cock

in and out of her body one last time, and pulls out, shaking the last drops of cum and blood from the end of his dick. Then he tucks himself inside his pants and stands. Lauren sags against the floor, weeping behind her gag. I struggle against Prez's grasp. He slams the flat of the gun against my temple, knocking my head to the side.

"Uh, uh, uh," Prez says, and Tag automatically lifts his gun and aims it directly at Lauren's head. He doesn't even bother to turn it on me because that fucker knows. He knows I have no concern for my own self-preservation, I only care about hers.

"We're gonna play a little game. It's called Which Loved One Do You Want To See Die First? Now, seeing as you only have one parent left, Daddy dearest had to make an appearance. Can you believe he actually fuckin' said no to me? Told me about you beating the shit outta him in the middle of the road, and he still refused to be the one to come and get you. To be honest, I probably woulda killed him already, but then we wouldn't get to play this little game. So what's it gonna be, Kick? Your daddy, or your girlfriend?"

I take a deep breath. There's no question here in my mind who I'd save. My father was nothing but a sperm donor, a worthless piece of shit so full of hatred and cunning and bitterness. And I'm exactly like him, because despite all that blood-is-thicker-than-water bullshit, I choose the option that I can live with.

"Juke. Kill Juke," I say. My dad steps back and into Rue's arms. I can tell by the look on his face that he's not surprised by my decision. His eyes meet mine across the room and for perhaps the first time ever I see acceptance in them. I stare at his face until I hear the shot ring out ... only he doesn't fall.

Lauren does.

"Oops," Tag says, smiling at me.

No. No. No. No. No!

My heart stops.

I can't breathe.

I lurch forward. Prez lets me go and I clamber across the bed and fall down onto the floor. Her eyes are wide open, but she's not breathing, she's not gasping for breath or fighting to hold on because there's a huge hole blown out of the side of her head. Fragments of bone litter the carpet, and her blood and brain tissue paint the ceiling.

My chest squeezes, and a howl rips from my gut as I gather her lifeless body in my arms. I cradle her head in my lap, my fingers slip into the gaping mess of her skull, and a little more bone chips away.

I wanna die. I wanna die more than I've ever wanted anything in my entire life. Right now, all I want is to check out, but I know when I move, it'll end the last time I ever touch her. Tears stream down my cheeks, and cries of anguish rip from my body until I'm choking on the sound of my own heart breaking. I'm sinking in blood and sweat and betrayal, and yet it's as though I've learned how to breathe underwater, because for all the pain I feel, I still haven't drowned yet.

I don't know how long I stay like that, cradling her in my arms. But eventually Prez comes over and claps a hand on my back. "It's for the best, son. Can you imagine the two of you working after all you've done to her, after all she's been through?"

I explode, pushing Lauren from my lap and slamming Prez's body against the carpet. I wrap my hands around his throat and attempt to choke the life out of him. I'm knocked back with a kick to the side of the head. I don't even feel it; not really, not the way I felt the bullet that took her life as if it were my own body that'd been hit. Tag lunges and pins me beneath him. I struggle, and then I realise there's nothing left to fight for.

"Help him up, Tag," Prez says, rubbing his hands over his throat. "Nice try, but we're not going to kill you, Daniel. You're way too valuable. You're going to lead us to Ethan, because I know you know where he is, and we're gonna keep Daddy dearest here until you come through."

"Then you're gonna be waiting a fuckin' long time," I seethe. "Shoot the fucker; shoot me. I don't give a fuck."

"I think you will," Prez says, leaning over and tapping my cheek with the side of his hand. "I can be pretty persuasive. Rue, get Juke out to the van." Rue nods and starts walking forward.

"Tag, clean up your fuckin' mess. And bring the body. We've got a delivery for Slayer."

"Don't fuckin' touch her!" I bellow, as I climb to my feet and charge Tag, but I'm knocked back down again by another blow to my head, and then the nothingness I'd longed for so badly finally swallows me up.

KICK

I slam the door and stalk away from the gym. I only make it to the kitchen before I lose my shit entirely.

"FUCK!" I roar, and swipe the empty pizza boxes off the counter. I'm full to fuckin' bursting with violence. I need to punch, and hit, and feel bone crunch under my fists. I need to choke the life out of something. I need to fuck, to smash into a woman's body over and over again. I need … *I need her*.

I didn't wanna fuckin' need her. I don't wanna need her. I never wanted to feel this shit, this helplessness again. I already gave one bitch the power to break my heart and she tore it all to fuckin' bits when she died, and now Indie's in there, trying to tape that shit together, trying to see something more inside me than I deserve. And I can't fuckin' do it. I won't.

I stomp toward the front door and gather up my keys from the bowl in the foyer. I need to get the fuck outta here. I need a real motherfuckin' drink and I need a bitch that hasn't been all jacked up by some psychotic priest to ride my cock.

Jesus Christ. I wasn't fuckin' lying when I said I was attracted to the fucked-up ones. I'd thought Ivy was bad, but there ain't no hope for that bitch in the house.

Country's sitting on the front step when I walk outside, shotgun in his lap and whistling some fuckin' old-timey tune, no doubt. I ignore him as I walk over to my bike.

"Where are you going?"

"Out," I say, sliding my helmet from the handlebars and putting it on.

"There's blood on the moon, boy."

"Gonna be blood fuckin' everywhere if I don't get up inside a motherfuckin' pussy soon." I shake my head at the fuckin' crazy old coot and mount my bike, flipping the ignition switch and twisting the throttle until she roars to life. The V-Twin Revolution engine purrs and my balls pull up against my already hard cock. I walk her back a few paces, away from the other bikes, and then I give her some kick and ride off. I can't open her up the way I want to on the unsealed road, so I head out to the highway and just ride.

After a while I grow tired of thinking, and I head back towards the quiet little town of Leura. I pull up outside the pub and park my baby, stroking her dark orange racing stripes. I miss the ride; lately I've been nothin' but a glorified babysitter. I hang my helmet over the handlebars and walk inside, ignoring the faces who stare me down when I take a seat at the bar and order a JD with no ice. The bartender is a weary lookin' dude, rail thin, save for the beer gut, with greying hair almost as bushy as his eyebrows. He grunts and takes my money, and then disappears once he's handed me my drink.

I glance around the bar. There's a hen's party at a booth in the corner. The bride-to-be is decked out in a pink feather boa and a crown with pink plastic penises attached to it. They're all drunk as fuckin' skunks. Sadly, Princess Penis is the only one hot enough to put a ring on, but then I'm not looking to be tied down. I'm just lookin' for a quick, hard fuck.

I pick up my drink and sit in the booth in front of them, and then I wait.

It takes about five minutes of girlish squeals and murmuring before a plucky blonde comes and falls into the seat across from me. I'm pretty sure she meant to sit down, but I'm guessing she doesn't realise how drunk she is.

"You're hot," she slurs, with a flirty smile.

Jesus fuckin' Christ.

"You're drunk." I smirk, and bringing the glass to my lips I check out her cleavage over the rim. I chuckle when she feigns innocence. We both know why she sat down at my table, and it wasn't to tell me that she thought I was hot.

I don't understand regular people. In fact, this bitch is why I hate people that aren't attached to the life. At the clubhouse, if you want your cock sucked, there are always willing mouths available. There are twenty fuckin' club whores to the ten of us. There's no pretention, no lead up, just pure, fuckin' unadulterated pleasure.

I down the rest of my drink and stand up, offering

my hand to the ditzy blonde who I'm hoping has a mouth like a fuckin' Hoover and a snatch tighter than a vice. "Come on, darlin'."

"Are we going for a ride?"

"You're gonna be riding somethin', but it ain't gonna be my bike."

Her painted red mouth turns up in the corners, and she puts her tiny hand in mine. I think of Indie when she does that, of me doing this same very thing, and daring her to take it. Daring her to trust me.

Pissed off that she's invading my fucking thoughts again, I yank on the blonde's arm and lead her past the whoops and exclamations of 'go get him tiger' from her friends, out into the crisp mountain air. I try leading her around the corner, but the second she sees my bike she heads for it. "Can I sit on it?"

"No," I say, too sharply. She frowns and glares at me. "You don't just sit on the back of a biker's ride. You have to be invited."

"Don't you wanna invite me?" she says, stumbling a little on her ridiculous heels.

"Bitch, the only thing I want you ridin' is my cock."

"You bikers are so aggressive. I love that." She glides over to me, dancing to music only she can hear. I snatch up her hand and drag her around to the side of the building. It's an alleyway, it's dank and cold as fuck, but it'll do. She moves closer to me, her eyes on my mouth, but I have no desire to taste her lips so I grab her chin with my hand and turn her head to the side, kissing her neck. She tastes like perfume, and after a couple of seconds I'm gagging from it. Her hands are busy with my jeans. She unzips my fly and takes my cock in her hand, pausing when she feels the piercing.

"Are you—?"

"Why don't you take a closer look?" I push on her shoulders so she'll get the fucking hint. I almost praise fuckin' Jesus when she goes down on her knees before me. The bimbo takes me in her mouth and I close my eyes, leaning my head back against the brick wall. My fingers rake her hair into something I can hold onto. I pump my hips forward, shoving my cock to the back of her throat until she gags.

The blonde leans back, taking only the head of my dick in her mouth now. Probably smart, 'cause I'm kind of an arsehole, and I'd likely only try choking her with it again. She quickens her pace, and though I know how good it's supposed to be, I feel nothing. Nothing like the need I felt when I had Indie in my arms. I'm numb. I'm furious, and I'm fuckin' lagging.

I shove the girl off of my limp dick, she falls in her stupid fuckin' heels and lands on the seat of her arse on the hard concrete. I tuck my cock back inside my jeans.

"Hey," she protests.

As I make my way over to my bike, all I can think about is the way Indie looked spread out before me, asking to be accepted, to be wanted. And I wanted to. God damn, did I want to take her, and shove inside her, and show her that even with her scars she was fucking perfect—or that maybe, she's perfect because of her scars. Maybe that's the reason I want her so fuckin' much. Because she's been through hell and she looks like a fuckin' warrior. But if she's a warrior, then what does that make me?

Warriors don't need saviours.

Warriors save themselves.

INDIE

I wake with a start and I have no idea where I am. The doorknob turns and I glance around, realising I'm still in the gym. I watch the door and at first I think it's Kick coming back to apologise, but then I get a good look at the guy, and while it's definitely a biker, it's not my biker.

"There she is." The biker with the eye patch announces. I scramble to my feet, pulling the robe closed and wishing Kick hadn't yanked out the sash. I clutch at the soft silk holding it tight, and then when the Cop follows the biker through the door and closes it behind him, I forget all about my robe and clamp my hand over my mouth to keep from vocalising my horrified gasp.

"Hello, Whore," the Cop says, pulling his gun and taking aim at my face. "Father James is very disappointed in you."

"Father James can suck my big fat clit," I retort.

The biker laughs and moves towards me. "Can I

suck your big fat clit too?"

"Don't touch her," The Cop orders, and the biker turns to stare incredulously at him.

"Don't fuckin' touch her? You wouldn't have her if it weren't for me. I took out my brothers for you," he says, pulling his own gun from the back of his leathers. "I think it's time I took a little piece of the fuckin' action."

Oh god. Kick.

I make a move towards the front of the room but both men turn their guns on me.

"Not another step, sweetheart," the biker says.

He edges forward, but I refuse to be herded. If he gets the wall at my back, I have nowhere to go. As it is I have no weapons; all I have is fear and fight, but they won't be enough.

I scream, as loud as I can. I scream Kick's name and hope to hell that he hears me, but I know he more than likely won't, because if this biker was smart he would have put Kick down like a dog. He'd be stupid not to.

The biker circles me, stopping at my back. He leans in and sniffs my hair. One hand holds a gun to my temple, the other tries to slide inside my robe. I clench the material tighter in my fists, but he bats them away and grabs my breast in his big calloused paw. He presses his lips to my hair and I turn away, but he shoves the gun against my head. Tears prick my eyes, and threaten to spill over, but I won't be that pathetic girl I was in the warehouse. I won't be the girl that Kick stood in front of the mirror, crying and begging him to stop.

"This girl. Is she a fighter or a fuckin' victim?"
"A fighter. She's a fighter."
"Then fuckin' show me."

"Take your hands off the whore," the Cop says through gritted teeth. His gun is no longer trained on me. It's on the biker.

"I don't think I will," the biker with the patch says. He takes his gun from my head and points it at the Cop. "See, I already got my money. You can have your girl when I'm done with her, Sergeant."

I spin while he's distracted and fist my hand just the way Kick taught me, and I punch him with all that I have, right in the nuts. Shots ring out, and blood blooms on the biker's shirt. He lets out a strangled cry and falls to the ground, and then I'm left in the room with the Cop. The man who tortured me for weeks. The man who tried to break me and failed.

The gun falls from the biker's lifeless hand. I reach out to grab it, but the Cop kicks me in the stomach. I try to curl in on myself, try to protect myself, but he rolls me onto my back, straddling my waist as he shoves the gun up under my chin. Beneath my hand I feel the silk sash from my robe and I slowly gather it up in my fist.

"You can't hurt me anymore," I whisper.

KICK

When I get back to the house, everything feels off. Country is no longer on the front step, but there's a shitload of blood where he was sitting and the front door is wide fuckin' open. I take off my helmet, park the bike and pull the gun from my pants, creeping quietly across the drive. I climb the front stairs, glancing down at the patch of blood, and then at the bloody handprints on the door. I keep low to the ground and move inside, walking through the kitchen, but when I clear the island I almost trip over Country. He's dead, propped up against the bench. His shotgun is gone, taken from him likely, and he has a bullet hole in his chest, just below his clavicle.

I turn around, but a hand reaches out and grabs my leg. I spin, my gun aimed and at the ready. "What the fuck, old man?" I whisper. "I almost shot your fuckin' face off. Where's Indie?"

"Gym ... she's in the gym. Crawled in here, haven't

… made it no further … though."

"How many?"

"One Eye." He takes a ragged breath in. "Cop."

"Where's Squeals?"

"Dead."

Gunshots go off, and I forget all about being quiet, 'cause my fuckin' girl is in that room. I kick open the door; fuckin' idiots didn't lock it. One Eye is dead, the Cop has Indie on the ground, and his gun is shoved up under her chin.

"Shoot me, and she dies," he says, glaring up at me.

"Shoot her and you die," I challenge.

"I'm not going to shoot her, and I'm not leaving without her. He wants her back. He's not finished with her. You took her from us."

"Oh, he is finished with her. I can promise you that. The Priest is finished, period. Girl belongs to me now, and I don't appreciate people trying to take what's mine."

"You can't stop him. He's higher than you or I could ever grasp. He's on a holy mission, sent down from God to save us all."

"By abducting women and destroying them? That's his holy mission? It's been a while since I was in Sunday School—no, wait, scratch that, I've never fuckin' been to Sunday School—but I'm pretty sure your definition of worship is fucked."

"You can kill me, but God's plan, the Father's plan cannot be undone."

"Fuck God's plan." Indie jerks forward, wrapping a long black piece of fabric around his neck and yanking it tight. I don't have time to think. I just aim and shoot the way I have with so many other mother fuckers. I fire off three bullets between his eyes, hoping and praying like hell his finger wasn't actually on the trigger. He slumps forward on top of her.

My heart stops as I wait.

I can't move.

I can't breathe.

His body jerks and then he's rolled to the side as she emerges. I stalk over and fire off several more shots, emptying my whole clip into that fucker's face. Indie covers her ears and squeezes her eyes tightly closed.

"Fucking zealots," I mutter.

Indie stares up at me for a moment, and then the levee breaks. She covers her eyes and sobs while I stand there like a fuckin' tool with no idea how to comfort her. I wanna pull her into my lap the way I did once before, but for the second time tonight I'm considering someone other than myself. Country is in the kitchen; he risked his life to save her and it's only fair I repay the favour. I scoop her up in my arms and carry her out of the gym. Before we clear the door, she glances over my shoulder at the man who tortured her.

Country looks like shit. He's pale, the wrinkled skin beneath his eyes as ashen as his beard.

"Not ... too shabby ..." He wheezes. "For a blind ... geriatric, hey kid?"

"Yeah, if you'd actually hit someone, maybe." I smile at the old man and nod. "I owe you, brother."

"Nah, I'm just ... pissed ... didn't get to shoot ... some stupid-arse mother fuckers."

"You need to stop talking," I warn him. I set Indie on her feet and she sits heavily on the tiles.

"You okay, babe?"

"I don't ... I don't feel anything," she says, staring at the open door of the gym. I walk over and pull it firmly closed. "I thought I'd feel ... something, but there's nothing. I'm just numb."

"I know," I say, taking her in my arms. And I do know. I didn't feel retribution, or elation, or even satiated when I killed the Angels' president. I felt numb, because it was way too late to save Lauren.

"He needs a hospital," she says tilting her chin towards Country.

"He needs the Butcher."

"Fuck the Butcher ... get me a goddamned spoon ... I'll get it out ... myself."

"Shut up, old man." I pull my phone from my pocket and dial the prez. He answers on the first ring and I tell him what went down while I was off trying to hide my fuckin' feelings with a stranger sucking my cock. I leave out that last part. No point in upsetting Indie further. He promises that the Butcher will be here soon and orders me to stay with Country.

Forty long minutes later, the Butcher's Porsche pulls into the drive. I take Indie upstairs because she doesn't need to meet the man who jabbed her with a needle and knocked her out cold to examine her.

Grim and Killer arrive, reinforcements sent by Prez. I'm not fuckin' sure what the hell we're supposed to be "reinforcing"? We already shot dead the motherfuckers, and something tells me that though this fuckin' nutty Priest wants Indie back to fulfil his stupid-as-fuck prophecy, he will wait her out.

I wait until Country is stitched up, and I help put

him in the den downstairs to sleep it off. Prez must have agreed to pay the Butcher a pretty fuckin' hefty sum because I've never seen the bastard doll out medication so freely. I snatch up two pills from the bottle of morphine and pocket them in case Indie needs something.

"I didn't get a chance to thank you," I say, half hoping Country's asleep already so I don't have to do this shit.

He's not. That old fucker is wide awake and gloating like a stupid son-of-a-bitch. "Seems like you had plenty … of chances. You're just a stubborn dickhead … when it comes to tellin' people how you feel," he says, grinnin' like a fuckin' yokel at me. "Besides … you'd do it for me."

I wondered if that were true. I didn't think so, not up until this point, and though I was grateful, maybe not even after this point. That was just who I was. Or I thought that was who I was. But honestly? I don't even fuckin' recognise myself when I look in the mirror anymore. Lauren had changed me, and Indie seems to have picked up where she fuckin' left off. I didn't wanna feel shit; I didn't want to put others before myself, before my wants, before staying alive, but I did. I was, and I am. And it scares the ever-loving shit outta me. When you patch in, you pledge to die for your prez, for your brothers. It's all part of the code, but can I make it *my* code? I don't fuckin' know.

When I open the door, Indie is still sitting on the bed. She's staring straight ahead; I don't even think her mind has registered that I just walked in.

"Come on," I say, grabbing her hand. She doesn't even flinch, which is really fuckin' rare for her. "You need a shower. You've got blood in your hair."

I lead her across the hall to the bathroom we've shared these last few days. I shuffle her into the room and lock the door behind us. Turning on the spray, I undress and then I slowly peel the ruined robe from her shoulders and edge us both in. I take the showerhead off of the wall and hose her down with it. It's so much like the first time we did this—her mentally checked-out, and me going through the motions—and yet it's completely different.

After a few minutes of thawing out under the warm spray, she takes over, scrubbing her face with soap, lathering up the shampoo and washing her hair. There's a bench seat in the shower, and I sit and watch her body move as the water runs over it. She soaps up her hands and slides them all over herself. I don't even know if she understands how fuckin' crazy that shit is making me. I close my eyes and exhale slowly. I can't do jack shit about the huge fuckin' hard-on I'm sporting, but she doesn't seem to notice, she just continues scrubbing, so hard I think she might be taking off skin.

"It won't come out, darlin', and the blood is long gone."

She stares at me with tear-filled eyes. I give her a sad smile, knowing exactly what she's feeling: as if she's a bad person for wanting them dead, as if she's a monster for wanting to see his blood spilled out all over the gym floor. As if there's something wrong with her for being the one left standing.

"It won't come out, but it gets easier."

"Is that supposed to make me feel better?" she whispers.

"Nope, not really. It's just the truth of it." I shake my head. "You're not a monster; you're just human."

"What does that make you then?"

"A little of both."

She stares at me for a beat. "No. I think it makes you human, too."

"A regular guy wouldn't be hard as fuck watching a woman wash blood out of her hair."

"Maybe not, but that doesn't make you any less of a man."

"Yeah, that's exactly what it makes me," I say, and it's more than just my cock that's frustrated. "I don't know what you want from me, Indie?"

"I don't know either," she admits. "I've told myself over and over you were a means to an end, but now I don't know how I feel. I want you to touch me. I want your hands on me. And I'm pretty sure you want that too, or I was before—"

"I can't be what you need, baby. I'm so fucked up there aren't even words for the shit I see in my head. All the things I wanna do to you? They're not normal. I don't do vanilla; I don't make love. I fuck. And I fuck hard. And I can't do that with you. I don't know how to be any other way."

I don't know what someone like me can offer her. I don't know if I can offer her anything but a life of disappointment and danger. It certainly hasn't been smooth fuckin' sailing so far, and shit's only gonna get worse. If she's in my bed, on the back of my bike and wearing my patch, she's a target for anyone who wants to get to me.

"Can I ask you something?" She interrupts my

thoughts. "What were you thinking when he put that gun to my head?"

"I was thinking I couldn't be the reason you died. I promised to protect you; I wanted to protect you. I didn't want your blood on my hands, too."

"Too?"

Jesus. This bitch and her questions. I wish I could shove my cock in her mouth and get her to shut the fuck up. "I've been here before, and it didn't end well for her. She died; a brutal and bloody death, the same kind you woulda had if you'd been left in that warehouse."

She reaches out and touches my hair. I glance up at her, grabbing her wrist and pulling her gently into me. I kiss her stomach, the flesh over her hip. She's been steadily putting on weight since we pulled her from that warehouse, and she looks fucking amazing. Plump arse, fuller tits, her arms now contain a little muscle, and even that is hot as fuck too. I pull her down onto my lap, spreading her legs apart and shoving her pelvis down against my cock, groaning when her pussy slides over my piercing and the head of my dick. And then I kiss her mouth the way I wanted to earlier tonight. I take her hard with my mouth because I can't with my body.

When she breaks away she's panting for breath. "I want you inside me, Biker."

"You can't say that shit to me, Indie," I groan. "I'm not a man with self-control. I take whatever the fuck I want, when I want it, and I want you so fucking bad I feel like I might explode, but I don't trust myself not to hurt you."

"I trust you."

"Fuuuck," I growl and then grab my dick, positioning

it at the entrance of her sweet pussy. Later I'll take my time exploring what makes her wet, what she likes, what she doesn't. I plan on getting real fucking friendly with that gorgeous cunt, but for now I have to bring us together. I have to bury myself deep, and feel her clench around me as she rides me hard.

She reaches between us and takes hold of my cock, sliding it back and forth through her wetness. She toys with the piercing, touching it with gentle strokes, and then she's pumping me hard and fast with her soft hands. It feels fuckin' amazing. She guides me inside her body, gasping as she stretches to accommodate me, and I feel as if I'm gonna explode. The sweet, slow burn, the drag and slide of flesh, her walls squeezing me tightly. It's fuckin' killing me. Slowly.

"So fuckin' tight," I murmur in her ear. I let her control the pace, and my hands roam over her tits and down her back to cup her arse. She rocks her hips back and forward, sliding her sweet cunt up and down my shaft. Her face is soft with pleasure, but I want to own that look. I could be anyone filling this void for her, making her forget all the things those men had done in the past. I grab a fistful of hair and force her eyes on me.

"Look at me." Her heated gaze locks onto mine. I challenge her, a little game we've come to love. "I want you to look at me while I fuck you. I want you to remember who owns you."

"No one owns me."

"I own you. You belong to me. You let another man near that pussy of yours and I'll gut him like a fuckin' fish while you watch. You gonna ride on the back of my bike? Be in my bed? Then I own you, Spitfire. You're mine, and there's not a goddamn thing you can do about it."

"Jeez, Biker, you really know how to ruin the mood," she whispers, but the bitch is still riding me hard, so I know she's not as put off by that as she says she is.

"I take what's mine, and I take care of mine. Are you mine, Indie?"

She moans and closes her eyes, tilting her head up toward the ceiling.

"Look at me," I command, wrapping my hand around the nape of her neck. "Are you mine?"

"Yes. I'm yours."

I exhale, and reward her by sliding a hand between us to toy with her clit. She bucks wildly on top of me, squirming away from my touch. I hold her still, digging my hand firmly into her hip.

"Stop, I can't ..." she breathes. "Not my clit."

"I own this pussy, baby. I'm gonna make you cum, and you're gonna milk me with your gorgeous fuckin' snatch, and then you're gonna cum again and again, until I say you can stop."

"No."

"Shh, let go," I whisper in her ear and I pump my hips in time with her rocking. "Fuckin' cum for me, baby."

"Biker ..." Her moans leave her in breathy pleas that I feel every-fucking-where. I feel her give a little, and I want more of it. I want all of her. I want every thought, every breath, every orgasm, and every fucking moan.

I shift both hands under her arse and stand, taking her with me and moving us under the water, then I slam her back against the glass and let it have her weight. I press my hands against the wall and glide in and out, taking her slow, and driving us both towards orgasm. I don't think I've ever fucked like this. Not even with Lauren. I wasn't lying when I told Indie I like to fuck, and fuck hard. But right now I care more about her pleasure than my own, which is another thing that I've never felt before. As I sink inside her again and again, I don't care how long it takes. I just want her to feel something other than pain.

What the fuck has this woman done to me?

That alone should make me want to punish her, to hurt her, to fuck the shit outta her tight little cunt and feel her break beneath my hands, but it doesn't. *Jesus Christ*. I'm like every other fuckin' idiot stupid enough to get attached to someone, to care about someone other than myself.

Prez was right. I'm fuckin' pussy whipped.

"Biker?" she asks in a whisper. "Is this really happening — oh god, right there. Don't stop doing that."

"Yeah, babe," I grunt. It's no fucking picnic trying to hit that sweet spot of hers over and over without losing my shit altogether. "It's really fuckin' happenin'."

"What are we doing? What happens when the water runs cold?" She bites on her lip and I spear her with my gaze, forcing her to stay with me, though I can tell already how much she wants to let go.

I'm not dumb enough to think this is the kinda shit that lasts forever. How can it? I abducted her. I held her captive. I drugged her, hurt her. I did shit I had no right to do because she wasn't mine. She'll come to see that one day for what it is. She'll come to see that anything between us was, and can only be a beautiful lie. I'm no

Prince Fuckin' Charming. I'm an arsehole. I'm cruel, and I'm a criminal with no moral compass. Or at least that's who I was. I have no fuckin' clue who I am right now.

"Then we shut the water off and keep fuckin' in the bedroom," I say, thrusting in a little harder, a little faster, until she's throwing her head back against the glass and panting like a fuckin' bitch on heat. I kiss her neck, her jaw, working her into a frenzy with my lips and tongue, and my cock that's buried balls' deep, and then she surrenders. Body and fuckin' soul, she gives me all of her as that tight pussy milks my dick with her release. And it's fucking glorious.

Her surrender is the only religion I need.

KICK

It's 10:00am when I hear the van and the roar of bikes as Prez and the rest of the boys pull in the drive. Indie's sleeping soundly so I slip my arm out from beneath hers and ease off the bed, shoving my legs into my jeans and throwing on a fresh shirt. I snag yesterday's clothes from the pile on the floor, along with Indie's. They'll all have to be burned. She was covered in blood and brain matter when I threw her in the shower last night. I shake my head. I really need to stop shooting fuckers at close range in front of her.

I head downstairs and meet Prez as he's entering the kitchen. "You okay, kid?"

"Yeah. Indie was a little shaken up, and the old coot wouldn't take any of the morphine last night. I haven't seen him this morning, so he's probably dead by now."

"Speak for your fuckin' self, you little fuck," Country shouts from the hall. I turn to see him exiting the gym, arms full of loot: wallets, police baton, and One Eye's cut.

I turn to Prez. "Jesus, the fucker doesn't die, and he has supersonic hearing?"

"Yeah, I'm fuckin Batman, kid. I've already been for a run, taken out a couple bad guys, and made Gotham City safe again this morning while you lazy bastards slept the day away. Though by the way you two was screaming last night, can't say I blame ya."

I roll my eyes. Country sets his loot down on the kitchen bench and begins emptying out the wallets. "You mind if I keep this shit, Prez?"

"Baton and gun gotta stay with the body, Country. They're police issue; we don't want no one asking questions about where they came from. Burn the cards, but you can have anything else."

"What do we do with the bodies?" I ask.

"I got a chainsaw out back. We'll chop 'em up, weight 'em, and dump them in the dam. It's far enough away for no one to go lookin'."

"Even One Eye?

"He's a traitor, ain't he?"

"And Squeals?"

"I gotta go tell the kid's poor girl that he died protecting an innocent woman. He wasn't patched, but he'll have a club funeral. I'll see to that. I already called Shady. He'll be here later to pick up Squeals' body." Shady was another freelance healthcare practitioner that the club had on speed dial—if by health care you meant freak of nature who liked to play with dead things. He worked the crematory near the clubhouse, and for the right amount of money he'd happily fire up the machine after hours. We call him Shady, 'cause he's shady as fuck. What other man do you know that sits alone in a crematorium jacking off to the scent of burning bodies?

Come to think of it, Crazy would probably go in for that shit.

As though he's reading my mind Prez says, "I got Crazy out in the paddock setting the cop car alight. Fucker's like a kid on Christmas morning."

I hadn't seen the cop car last night, which means he must have parked it at the back of the house while I was out.

"Listen, kid. We searched the Cop's house this morning. Found a secret room hidden beneath the garage. He had a fuckin' shrine dedicated to your old lady. Pictures, hair, teeth, video tapes stacked all neatly in a fuckin' row. I haven't seen anything' like it before. And she wasn't the only one. There's a fuckin' slew of bitches they been doing this stuff to. Sickest fuckin' shit I ever saw. I removed any trace of her, got our fuckin' tape back too." He takes a deep breath and then says, "I found your priest. He's yours if you want it. Otherwise I'll pull Tank from junkie duty and send him—"

"I want him," I say, resolutely. The need to destroy this fucker burns through my veins like acid. I want so badly to meet him face to face and put him to ground knowing he hurt what was mine.

"You have to take me with you," Indie says from the lounge room. I didn't even see her come down the stairs. "You promised me, Daniel."

"Yeah, I know," I say, shaking my head as she comes into the room wearing another of Mia's expensive outfits, this one a silk sundress. It's the first time I've seen her in a dress, and I immediately wanna take her back upstairs and remove it.

"You sure you're ready for that, darlin'?" Prez asks.

Indie glares at him, her eyes glinting with bloodlust. It's a good look on her, but I know better than any that that kind of hunger comes at a cost. "I'm sure."

"Babe, you don't need to go. I can put that fucker to ground and you never have to see him again."

Turning to me, she frowns. "I have to do this. I thought you understood that?"

"I do," I say, avoiding her angry gaze. "Doesn't mean I have to fuckin' like it."

"I need to do this, Daniel."

"You can't take the bike. Too noisy; too fuckin' showy. Cops are already watching the club for her."

"What do you mean they're watching the club?"

"They're watching every fuckin' club. That's why I wanted her arse inside and away from the fuckin' windows."

"I don't get it," I say. "If he knew where she was why didn't he just bring the whole motherfuckin' squadron in here and snatch her up?"

"Because then I'd be in the system, and he couldn't have me for himself," Indie whispers. "I could have spoken up and pinned my disappearance on him. If was safer to wait me out.

"Makes sense," I agree, because what else is there to fuckin' say?

"There's a Dodge Charger in the garage," Prez says. He walks around the centre island to the pantry and opens the door. Near the light switch sits a key holder with about ten different coloured keys on it. He lifts a black fob from the hook and hands it to me, reluctantly.

"If you destroy my favourite car, I'll put you to ground, Newbie."

"I'll treat her like she's my own," I say, smiling at him.

"Yeah, I seen that piece-of-shit bike you drive, you little fuck."

"A Night Rod Special is not a piece of shit, Prez."

"No, a Night Rod Special isn't, but yours sure fuckin' is." Prez shakes his head and turns to Indie. "Make sure he doesn't drive like a maniac."

"I'm not sure that's possible."

"Got you here in one piece, didn't I? Come on. You need a jacket and then we'll head out."

"We're gonna do it in broad daylight?"

"No, we're gonna do it tonight. But we can't just walk in there and start shooting the motherfucker. We have to watch, make sure no one is around to witness it. We have to do this shit right or I'm gonna wind up in jail, and you're gonna be sent home, right where he can find you again."

She lets out a deep, shuddering breath.

"Little faith, Spitfire. He'll be dead by the end of the day, and then you'll be free to live the rest of your life. Move to another city, or another fuckin' country. You'll be free."

Tears well up in her eyes and she nods. "Yeah, why don't I just move to fucking Ibiza and forget any of this ever happened." She storms up the stairs and I'm left wondering what the fuck I said to make her so fucking antsy. I'm not expecting her to forget what they did to her. She could live a lifetime and never forget that, but Jesus Fucking H Christ, if it were me, I wouldn't ever wanna set foot in that city again.

"Fuckin' hell, you're an idiot," Prez says with a laugh.

"What?"

"What?" he says. "Are you fuckin' missing a couple brain cells there, Kid?"

"Fuck you."

"The bitch is probably feelin' a little bit fuckin' vulnerable. She's been abducted, tortured, raped, mutilated, she's lost teeth and fucking years off of her life in a few short weeks and you fuck her, you make her feel as if she finally has somethin' good and stable to fuckin' hang on to, and then you go and tell her to move to another country?"

Country comes back from the gym, hauling another load of shit that belongs to the two dead guys. "Didn't your dad teach you nothin' bout women, boy? They're strong as a brick shithouse and fragile as a flower, all the same time."

"What Country's trying to say is that the girl needs someone to be strong for her. She's done a bang-up job on her own, but sometimes you gotta be able to fall apart and know someone is there to pick up the fucking pieces. Don't be a dick."

"Is that what Raine does for you, Prez? Picks up the pieces when you fall apart?"

"Get outta here, fucker." He shoves me, and it's not so playful. Think I hit a nerve.

I don't bother getting my shit from upstairs; I don't know where we'll end up tonight. I guess that depends on whether we put the Priest to ground or not. I have some ideas about what I'd like to do to him, but ultimately, that decision is up to her. I meet Indie at the door. Her face is red, as if she's been crying, and she's hiding it behind her hair.

"You nervous?"

"No, just impatient."

I lift her chin until her eyes meet mine. "You don't have to do this. I can do this for you. I don't know what you want me to be, but whatever that is I'll try. It might not work, but I can promise you right now I can take care of this for you."

"I have to do it myself. I have to see the fear in his eyes that he put in mine. I wanna watch him burn, and then I'm going to dance in the ashes."

"Whatever you need, baby."

She smiles up at me, but it's hardened and doesn't touch her eyes. She's not the girl I joked with on the couch yesterday, she's not the broken woman I held in the shower and she's not even the sweet satiated woman I lay in bed with this morning, because revenge is sweet. Until it isn't.

INDIE

I stand in front of the sign that reads St Andrew's Catholic Church. My stomach roils. My hands shake. It's a little past 7:00pm. It's taken two days of waiting, of watching, and planning to get to this point. Biker puts his hand in mine. "It's not too late to back out."

"I know."

"I take it that means you won't."

"No. I won't." I exhale, and I feel as if I can't get enough oxygen into my lungs. "I may throw up all over my shoes though."

"Try not to. It's evidence."

"O-kay." It frightens me how concerned he is with being invisible, though I guess when you spend your life killing, drugging and abducting people, that's a given. My head swims a little at that thought. If he'd never left that tape behind, if he hadn't needed me to find out who these men were, would he have let me go? Or would I still be locked in that room of his at the clubhouse?

Would his brothers have killed me? Would he? "Let's just get this over with."

He squeezes my hand. My palm is clammy against his. We walk towards the doors and I let him lead, mostly so my face is covered, but also because I don't know if I can walk into a room housing that man.

The second I set foot in the church the walls close in on me. I feel the blackness, the horror, the shame, and the weight of what he did choking me. I can't breathe. I wrench my arm from Kick's but he grabs me and shoves me into a pew at the back of the church.

The Priest seems completely unfazed. He continues with his sermon, and his voice presses against my skin like a thousand tiny needles. "It is because we are all sinners, that we must atone," he says, and though it's not said with the same intent or malice behind it as it was in that warehouse, I feel so much of what he did to me. My breath comes in raspy gulps, too fast, too much. I'm going to pass out and blow our cover. I'm going to ruin everything we've spent the last two days working toward. And I'm never going to have this chance again.

Biker leans closer. "You need to control yourself."

I snap my head towards him, incredulous that he just said that to me. He takes my hand and squeezes it hard. "Remember why we're here. Those things he did to you, to the other girls before you — all of that can end here. But you have to keep it together. He might not be able to hear you breathin' like an emphysema patient, and he may not be able to see your knees knocking together, but that wig you're wearing is shaking like a fucking leaf in a strong wind. So pull your shit together, and let's put this bastard to ground."

An elderly man about three rows ahead turns to shush us. Kick gives him an apologetic nod and straightens, yanking on his tie. If we weren't here to kill a rapist I might be able to appreciate how incredible he looks, even if they are just basic dress clothes from Target. I'm wearing pants, a conservative button-up shirt and heels, though I have no idea why I thought the heels were a good idea. I can barely walk as it is, much less try to balance on an extra three inches. Biker shaved his stubble for the occasion and he looks young, so much younger than he does with it. He's also incredibly beautiful. I mean, obviously there was an attraction there to begin with, but I never noticed before how gorgeous he is, even with the piercings, tattoos, and gauges in his ears. Looking at his face helps me ignore the scene around me; it helps me drown out the voice belonging to the man that tried to destroy me. Kick glances over. His gaze holds mine before turning back to the Priest.

I tear my gaze from Biker and look at the Priest. He looks exactly the same, only when he had me locked in that room his eyes were black as the night outside, and now they're almost jovial. The thing that surprises me most is how animated he is, how normal he seems in front of his congregation. And as I look around at the packed church, I see people of all ages and all walks of life who appear to love this sick, sadistic bastard. They know nothing of my suffering, of the suffering of the girls before me. I know Kick probably would have preferred I didn't know that, but I heard everything his prez said.

I don't know what he did to those tapes, or the pictures that I remembered them posing for—when

KICK

I was out of my mind with grief and pain, they lined up, one after the other and posed with me like I was a fucking trophy, like a hunter would with a deer he'd shot, or a large fish wriggling on a hook.

All of these people have no idea what their beloved pastor is capable of, and the worst part is they'll never know, because exposing myself means exposing the murder I'm about to commit, and I'll be damned if I spend any more time in captivity. I can't let that happen. I won't. So while what I'm about to do to the Priest is justice stripped down to its purest and rawest form, to the people sitting around us, this will be an atrocity. I almost feel bad for them that this charming, good-looking pastor has them so convinced he's a person worth following.

I stare at him for a long time. He doesn't look at me once throughout the service. I don't know why, but a part of me wants them all to know. A part of me wants to stand up and call him out in front of his congregation when he begins talking about sinners again, and that line he used to whisper over and over in my ear as he raped me. I'm weightless. I stand, only to be pulled back down onto the church pew.

"Sit the fuck down, Spitfire. You ruin this at the last minute and you'll hate yourself forever."

He's right. I hate that he's right. I hate that he's holding me back from exposing this sick bastard. I snatch my hand from his and remain in my seat, my head down, gaze averted. In my head I try to think of good memories from my past: summers at the beach house, fleeing the water as it swept up the sand after me. I think of my first kiss, the first time I got drunk at a high school party, receiving my acceptance letter to Sydney University, Biker teaching me to fight, the power and pride I felt afterwards, Daniel inside me, his arms wrapped tight around my body as he tried to erase everything the Priest had done to me. Before long though, the Priest's voice cuts through those happy memories, and rattles around in my skull like my missing teeth in a jar. Rage rips through me from my head down to my toes.

The Priest finishes up his sermon, and a boy in robes carrying a processional cross leads him down the altar. I stare at the object, and I feel a sick sense of recollection. He raped me with it. A gasp leaves my mouth, and I cover it with my hands and suck in air, though I don't feel it filling my lungs. I can't do this. I can't …

The sobs leave my mouth, creating some sort of wounded animal noise. I can feel the congregation's eyes on me as they file out after the Priest, but I can do nothing to stop the sounds escaping my body. The fear and horror demands to be unleashed.

He didn't even look at me as he passed.

"Is she all right, dear?" an elderly lady stops at the end of the pew, resting a hand on Kick's shoulder.

"She lost her mum today. Needed to feel closer to God."

"Oh, I am so sorry for your loss," the woman says, and she's genuinely upset for me. In some ways her sympathy hurts worse. I don't know her. I've never seen this woman before in my life, but the fact that she stopped enough to care for a complete stranger guts me, and I fall apart completely. "Did she suffer long?"

"Yes," I manage through my sobs. "She suffered …

in the worst way imaginable."

The woman doesn't know I'm referring to myself and not my own mother, though I'm sure as much as my parents led me to believe I was an inconvenience, that there was some part of them that cared I was missing. I'd like to believe that, and they certainly painted a good picture of grieving parents in the media, but that was likely more for show than genuine concern for me.

The woman pats my hand but I yank it away. I can't have anyone touch me right now. "God bless" she says, and I don't know if she's talking to me or to Kick because I can't look at her anymore. My eyes are tightly closed, my fists clenched.

"I have to go," Kick whispers. I open my eyes to find he's standing in the pew beside me and the church has emptied, save for us. He bites the piercing in his lip. His gaze locks onto mine, and I see so much buried there that he can't say. He's torn, and somehow so much older in this moment. He takes a deep breath and lets it out. "Everything you're feeling right now, use it. Channel it into something useful because if you don't, this opportunity escapes us forever, and I can't live with that."

Neither can I.

Without another word, he leaves through the main doors. The blade pressing into my lower back is cool against my fevered flesh. I take a minute to breathe, and then I remove my heels, and my wig, and I unbutton my top and fold it, stowing my belongings under the seat so I'm left in only my black singlet and pants.

And then I wait.

It feels like an eternity before the plump, sweaty altar

boy comes striding back in, and the Priest follows. He doesn't seem surprised when he sees his church is not empty. "You go on home, John. I'll take that," he says to his protégé, holding out his hand for the processional cross he raped me with. "Please tell your mother I said thank you for the biscotti."

"Thank you, Father, I will. Good night," John says and hurries out of the church. The Priest walks over and closes the doors, sliding the heavy wooden bar across them.

The sound is so final, so weighty that it's deafening. I'm completely alone with my rapist. I try channelling my fear and rage into something useful, like Kick told me, but honestly I can't make up from down. I don't feel numb like I did before the Cop put his gun to my head. I feel everything.

"I knew you'd find me," he says, sitting down in the pew beside me. "I've been waiting for you, Kayla."

I cringe when I hear my name on his tongue. The whole time I was locked in the warehouse I'd believed they had never known it. They'd certainly never used it; they referred to me only as the whore. I'd thought I was just some random girl they'd plucked from the streets, but now I realise just how dumb that was. They chose me because I looked like I belonged to somebody. Someone would report me missing and they would know exactly where to go if I ever escaped. *Had they done that with the other girls?*

"The other's failed God's mission, but not me. I am his light, his beacon in the darkness of this hell we call earth, and I will not fail, because I shall be called into the arms of the Lord." He leans towards me and his cologne — no, not cologne, it's the scent of sandalwood and myrrh, the smell of this church — infiltrates my nose, it invades my mind, and memories rape me. The Priest places his big hand on my knee. I flinch.

"Shh, shh, shh, you serve a greater purpose than you know. You are the key to redemption, Kayla."

"There is no redemption for you, you sick fuck," I say and pull the knife from my back. I slash against the arm holding my leg. He gasps and yanks away, and then I'm racing down the aisle toward the altar. His robes whisper as he casually follows me.

"That's something you don't know about me, Kayla." His booming voice fills the church. I feel it boring into my eardrums, scratching, clawing, and settling into my bones. "That I love to hunt. We never got the chance to play that game, you and I, but I think now is as good a time as any to begin. Don't you?"

I run past the pulpit, past the altar, and reach the door on the right side of the room, but it's locked. Panic seizes me as I realise *I have the wrong door*. I glance at the Priest, and then at the opposite side of the church, to the vestry.

He smiles. "Will you get there in time or won't you, Whore?"

I bolt for the door, but only make it as far as the altar before he is on the other side, taunting me with which direction he's going to move in. I knock over the goblet of wine and a handful of other sacred objects. The Priest sees red and lunges across the marble table at me. I sprint for the vestry, but he yanks me back by the hair and throws me on the ground, my head smacking against the marble steps of the altar. I scream as he bends over me. He works the knife from my hand, slamming my wrists repeatedly against the marble until I let go. He presses the blade to my throat. He can cut me, he can slice me open any way he wants to, but I know something he doesn't.

"Time to meet your maker, motherfucker," Kick says, cocking the pistol before he shoots him in the back of both knees. The Priest screams and drops to the ground beside me. Blood is everywhere, pooling out of his body as he trembles in shock. Kick offers me a hand and I climb to my feet with his help. He pulls me against him with one arm, keeping the gun in the other hand firmly trained on the Priest's head. "You okay?"

Of course I'm not okay. I don't know if I'll ever be okay again.

"You'll burn for this … the two of you will burn," the Priest says.

"Shut the fuck up." Kick fires another shot into the Priest's shoulder. It's fitted with a silencer, but guns are loud. The Priest's screams are even louder. The church isn't in a residential area, and that's maybe the only reason we could pull this off, but I still cringe with the way the sound bounces all around the room with the acoustics.

"Hold the gun." Biker hands me the gun, and I point it at the Priest. I still have no fucking idea how to use one of these, but I've seen Kick do it enough.

I just stare as Kick binds the Priest's hands together, stuffing the tie in his mouth. He screams as we move him to the altar. If Kick had a stronger partner it might've gone easier, but we both wind up covered in blood. Biker pulls the long stretch of rope from the garbage bags he brought in through the vestry. He ties him to the altar with a series of complicated knots. I don't ask how he knows how to do that. I don't want to know, not really.

I stand beside the Priest's head. The darkness in his eyes has returned, but there's fear in there too. The human mind is such a fragile thing. We can feel so powerful one moment, and so small the next.

"All this time, I'd built you up in my head," I say. "I'd see you in my dreams, hovering over me, pushing into me. I'd feel your sweat. I could feel how evil you were, and each time you came inside me I wanted to die." I level my gaze on him, feeling the shift within me. The victim takes a back seat. He feels it too. I see it in his eyes.

"I don't want that anymore. You're just a man, and for the first time since you took me, I'm going to sleep soundly tonight, because I got to hear you scream. I'm not afraid of you anymore. I found something bigger than you."

He laughs. It's a fake and showy sound. "Your biker?"

"No. *Me*."

"And there's the girl we were trying to find." He smiles. "There's the woman worthy of being called the sacrifice. If we hadn't found you, you'd have never found that. You should thank me."

"Oh, I plan to. I plan to repay every single scream that left my mouth."

Kick shoots me a look, questioning whether I want to go through with this. I've never been surer of anything in my life. I nod. He hands me his knife — not the tiny one I cut the priest with before, but the kind you know is really a knife, with a wicked blade, sturdy handle, and a deadly sharp point.

"How do you like hunting now, Father?" I ask, as I take the knife and thrust it into his abdomen. Blood spurts out and sprays my face, my hair, my body, but I don't care. I drive it in to the hilt, relishing the way his body jerks, savouring the screams.

Kick just stares at me. It's as though he's drunk on euphoria, and then he closes the distance between us and I'm caught up in his arms, my face in his hands, and the barrel of the gun grazing my cheek as he holds it. He kisses me, full on the lips, and then he releases my face with a smile.

I can't think about that right now, the fact that violence excites him. This isn't about gutting a man for kicks. This is retribution.

I pick up one of the three cans of gasoline that Kick had brought in. I unscrew the cap and douse the Priest in it. He screams as it hits the wound in his belly. Kick takes the other two cans and begins splashing kerosene through the church, over the aisle, the pews, the statues, everything. When he's done, he moves behind me and begins pouring the second can around the marble altar. It really is a beautiful cathedral, and once upon a time I may have been repulsed by the thought of anyone destroying such a sacred place, but this place isn't sacred. It's just a building, and it's tainted with the evil of its priest. It's no longer a place in which to worship God, it's a place for *him* to be venerated, and I'll be dead before I ever let that happen.

"I remember you used to go on and on about how

you were born of fire when your father gave you that cross, when he burned your tiny little body with a cattle brand. It's another thing I never stop seeing in my dreams, that scar on your back. But you should be careful what you reveal to people, Father." I lean in and whisper, "Especially when it comes to your worst fears."

His face slackens with horror and realisation. I smile and pull the matchbox from the pocket of my pants. "Are you ready to be born of fire again?"

"You can't touch me ... I am God's servant and you are the sacrifice. You cannot interfere with divine intervention."

"There is no divine intervention, not for you — only death. You picked the wrong girl to sacrifice. I'm not a lamb you can lead to the slaughter, Father, I'm a motherfucking lioness." I stand back and strike the match. It feels as if the world spins in slow motion as I throw that tiny flame on his body. The screams begin, and I close my eyes. The flames are bright behind my lids. I don't need to see to savour this moment. I *am* this moment. And I'm glorious in my destruction.

Somewhere in the back of my brain I register Kick screaming at me to move, and his arms on me tugging me back from the pyre, but if he was drunk on euphoria after I stabbed the Priest, I'm drowning in it. I'm pulled back through the vestry and my feet are burning, but I'm not as worried about that as I am that I won't get to hear him scream.

Then I realise it's not the Priest's shouts of horror I'm hearing at all, but Kick's. The Priest has already stopped moving, stopped breathing. He's no longer there, and I'm no longer exultant in my revenge.

I'm shaking.

I'm broken.

I'm on fire.

Kick drags me through the vestry and out onto the grass behind the burning church, digging up the earth with his bare hands to douse the flames on my feet. The flames licking my pant legs have already gone out. I don't tell him that, though. Instead, I bury my head in my hands and sob. I let go of everything that that monster did to me, everything I remember about those hands, and the delight in those eyes as he shoved himself inside me. I let go of me.

"We gotta move," Kick says, crouching down beside me. "Can you walk?"

I nod, and let him help me to my feet. They hurt, my burned flesh smarts, but it's not the worst pain I've endured. I stare at the flames, and then Kick and I make our way towards the car parked across the street. He uses the fob to unlock it and climbs in the driver's seat. I reach for the handle, but see my reflection in the passenger's side window. I'm surrounded by flames. They lick against the night sky as the woman stares back at me. Her eyes are vacant, devoid of anything … soulless. Her face is covered in blood, her hair matted with sweat. I can't be sure, but I imagine this was what I looked like when Kick found me, only then the blood covering my face was my own.

Kick gets out of the car and glares at me over the roof. "Hear those sirens, babe? That means the cops are coming. Get in the car."

I glance at my reflection again. This woman isn't me. I'm not a killer. I'm not a warrior, or a goddess resplendent in her havoc. I'm just a girl who did what I had to in order to sleep at night. I'm a monster. I'm exactly what they all made me. Even Kick.

"No."

"Get in the fucking car, Indie."

"Let me go, Daniel." He's on the other side of the vehicle, but I know he knows I'm not talking about him releasing me physically.

"Are you fucking crazy?"

"Maybe." I shrug, staring at my reflection again. I feel like Alice through the looking glass, as if I'm staring at a different me in a different world, and wondering how I get back to my regular life. "What does it matter? I'm walking away, regardless."

"Get in the goddamn car before you get us both arrested."

"You promised when this was all over you would let me walk away."

"Then I fuckin' lied," he snaps, coming around the side of the vehicle. He grabs the tops of my shoulders and shakes me hard. "You don't get to walk away from this."

"You can't hold me, anymore, Daniel." I push his hands away. "This is done. We're done. I just want my life back."

"So that's it, huh? You just used me to get to your Priest, and that's all I'm good for?"

"No. I used you to get strong." I shake my head. Tears slide over my cheeks. I feel my body going through the motions, but I don't *feel* anything. "And now I'm a damn iron pillar."

I don't wait for a response, I just turn away. I walk

away from everything they made me. Everything I felt last night with Daniel inside me, everything I've felt for him since I learned he was only trying to help me, that he was seeking some sort of redemption. Since I realised that he was worthy of it.

I walk away, because I'm finally free.

INDIE

THREE MONTHS AGO
OCTOBER

I miss him so much I can't breathe. The nightmares stopped for a little while, but now they're back. They usually involve Biker strapped to the altar while I throw the match. But by the time I realise what I've done, it's too late. He's on fire. I'm on fire, and all I can do is stand there and watch him burn.

Watch us *burn.*

And then I wake, gasping for breath, terrified and alone.

INDIE

NOVEMBER

"Hey girl," Kimba says, ringing up a regular's cheque. "You're late."

"I know." I head for the back of our tiny café and hang my bag up on the hook, switching it out for my black apron that reads, 'Death Before Decaf'. "Sorry, the trains were down."

"Nah, don't worry about it. I'm just messing with ya, because I can," she says, winking at me. Her bright red lipstick is perfect, even at 8:00am. She's sort of an unconventional boss: tattoos everywhere, jet-black Dita Von Teese-style hair, pin-up dresses in crazy prints, gauges, piercings—the list is endless. I love her take-no-prisoners attitude when it comes to the long line of men queueing up to get their morning coffee. She's gorgeous and she owns that, a serial flirt, but not a whore. If I felt anything even remotely sexual towards woman—and really, considering all I've been through it's a wonder I haven't switched teams, already—I'm sure

I'd have myself a little girl crush. It's not like she hasn't propositioned me enough times. Kimba's one of those rare people that swings every way. Man, woman, she's not fazed about gender, only personalities.

"See you ladies tomorrow," Michael says.

"Looking forward to it, Mr Wilcox." Kimba winks, blowing him a kiss and then turning to me once he's gone. "And speaking of Cocks ... this morning when he came in, I swear to god he was stiff as my grandmother is rigid, and it was huge. You picked a hell of a day to be late, lady."

I laugh, despite how uncomfortable this subject makes me. Truth is, in the month I've worked here, Kimba's never been particularly good with boundaries. I didn't think I'd be okay sharing a space again with someone who hugged me, or casually touched my shoulder when they walked past, but surprisingly I am. Kimba makes me feel better; less lonely somehow. And already she feels like more than just a boss — she's a friend, which is something I don't really ever remember having before. Not like this.

Of course, she knows next to nothing about me, aside from what the media had broadcast all over the airways when I showed up on my parents' doorstep after a month of being missing, looking as if I'd just escaped a horror movie, covered in blood, with first-degree burns on my feet and left leg, and a severe case of "psychogenic amnesia".

I spent a month recovering at home, seeing every shrink my parents could throw at me, applying every cream, balm and whatever other product my mother wanted to ply my scars with, as if she could erase them.

As if they could be as easily removed as lifting a stain from a shirt.

I couldn't stand the silence in that house. I couldn't stand to look at the crucifix over the mantel in our lounge room. I couldn't see that wooden cross with its painted sorrowful little Jesus without seeing that room, or the church on fire, or the pain on Biker's face before I walked away. After the month was out, I went and found myself a studio apartment in the city and I moved out the very next day. I haven't really seen them since. Their daughter returned to them safe and sound, but she wasn't the same, and neither one of them concerned themselves enough with trying to help me get better. They were just keeping up appearances.

"Wow," I say, realising Kimba is still waiting for my reply. "I'm kinda sad I missed that."

"I knew you would be," she says, and heads back to the register to serve another of our regulars when he steps up to the counter. I glance at the line of customers and head to my usual place behind the coffee machine to start making orders. Several hours later Kimba pops out to run some errands, and while we're slow, I head to the tables out front to wipe them down. I'm just getting done with the second table when I feel as if I'm being watched. I straighten and glance at the customer behind me.

He's sitting at the small table that was unoccupied just seconds ago. He lights up a cigarette and I inhale sharply, missing the scent of him, the sight of him, drinking in every detail I can from his black jeans and leather jacket to his boots and hair, and the stubble that's regrown on his face.

"You can't smoke here," I say quietly.

"I'm out-fuckin'-side," he says.

I nod. "I know. Still can't smoke here."

He shakes his head and stubs the cigarette out on the sole of his boot. The biker I knew would have done it anyway, proving to me that I'm not the only one who's changed.

"What are you doing here, Daniel?"

"I been askin' myself the same thing all mornin'." Reading my confusion, he tilts his chin to the park across the street. "Been psyching myself up all fuckin' day." He shakes his head and gives a bitter laugh. "All fuckin' week, actually."

I sit down heavily on the stool beside him.

"You doin' alright?" he asks, and he seems as though he's taking every opportunity to drink me in the way I was with him.

I nod, but then my face crumples, and I bite my lip to stop the tears from spilling out. I shake my head. "You?"

"Yeah, I'm alright."

Of course he's alright. Why wouldn't he be?

He keeps smoothing his thumb over the knuckle of his middle finger. There's an indentation there, and a tan line from what must be a very thick ring, though I don't remember him wearing a ring before. Panic seizes my chest for a second, but then I realise that while it might be the right hand, it's the wrong finger on which to wear a ring of any significance.

"I would have called, but I didn't know where to find you." I lie. I don't know why I said that, and it only seems to have made him angry.

"Then you weren't openin' your fuckin' eyes, babe. I've been following you around like a lost fuckin' puppy for months."

"Why?" I whisper.

"Now isn't that the million-dollar fuckin' question."

"I don't know what you want from me, Kick."

"Then you're stupid." He shakes his head and stands to leave. "I want you, Kayla. That's all; just you." And then he turns and walks away. I watch his back until tears blur my vision, and I can't see anything anymore.

"Oh honey, what happened?" Kimba asks, squatting down in front of me. She grasps the tops of my arms and I flinch, and suck in a sharp breath. "Sorry, I forgot you don't like to be touched. I'm a hugger by default, so I'm going to have to work on that."

Kick and Kimba have been the only ones I've felt comfortable enough with to let touch me since I was taken. But right now I'm too raw. I'm too full of feeling, too full of hurt. It's ironic that I just let the only man who I'll probably ever feel comfortable with walk away.

"Did that guy say something to you?" Kimba asks, giving me a little space and staring at the retreating figure of my biker as he walks away.

"No," I say, wiping my eyes with the backs of my hands. I stand and straighten my apron. "No, I'm just having a bad life."

Kimba laughs, and then she snaps her mouth closed when she realises I'm not kidding. I have a pretty good feeling she knows that I haven't forgotten what happened to me; she's pretty intuitive that way. "Come on, it's nothing that a sugar coma won't fix," she says and steps inside the café.

I glance once more up the street, hoping to catch a final glimpse of biker, but he's gone. I follow Kimba inside, breathing in the warm, rich scent of her special mocha. In a way this café feels more like home than my own apartment does.

A part of me would love to just head home and curl up under the covers right now, but another part knows that the minute I do, I'll fall apart. Only this time, there will be no Biker to put the pieces back together. And I miss him so much. With everything I am, I miss him. I just don't know if it really matters anymore. He's a criminal; he made me into a killer and it excited him. Either way, God or no God, religion or no religion, I'm going to suffer for the things I've done, if not in the afterlife, then in this one.

KICK

EPILOGUE

DECEMBER

I sit in the lounge, downing my fifth beer for the night and listening to Crazy flick another fuckin' Zippo while we watch some shitty fuckin' *National Lampoon* movie that they've played a hundred fuckin' times this month. Ordinarily, there'd be a party on a night like tonight. There'd be more blow and bitches than you knew what to do with, but I guess even club whores need a day off. Prez's old lady usually hosts a barbeque at the house on special holidays—not that the bitch has ever cooked a meal in her life—still, it might've been nice to have somewhere to go other than this stinkin' fuckin' clubhouse.

It's been a pretty fuckin' miserable Christmas, but it's not as if I were expecting Santa to stuff my stocking with a hot brunette. No. The only hot brunette I want doesn't want me back. Ivy may not be around anymore, but there are plenty of other whores I could take to bed, and it's not without trying, believe me. But I'm so fuckin' pussy-whipped I can't even sustain a hard-on with another bitch. I think even my fuckin' cock misses Indie.

"I don't know what you want from me, Kick."

Kick. Not Daniel. And not Biker—a nickname I'd grown kinda fond of—but Kick. The name that everyone else calls me.

I watch Raine fill Crazy's beer. She's bent double and her tits are in my fuckin' face again, but I don't even feel the hint of a stirring in my dick. She leans across the table to grab my glass, but I shake my head and sit up.

"Fuck this shit. I'm going to bed."

"You okay, hon?"

A bitter laugh escapes me. "Darlin', I'm so far from okay that I'm in my own fuckin' postcode."

Flick. Flick. Flick.

Crazy is killing me with that fuckin' shit. One day I'm gonna ram a Zippo up his arse and with any fuckin' luck, he'll light up like a fire cracker and piss the fuck off.

"Oh, the girl I kidnapped up and left me," he says. "Wah, wah, wah. Tell him he's a whinging fuckin' little bitch, Raine."

She shoots him a reproving glare. I lean over and punch him in the side of the head.

"Ow." Crazy stands and shakes away the pain, his jacked-up hair falling in his face and swallowing up the red cheek I just gave him. *Maybe this Christmas didn't suck after all.* "That hurt, you dumb fuck." He stares at me as if he's waiting for a goddamned apology, and then he flicks that fuckin' lighter again three times. Exactly the same amount of times I'm going to punch him in the head if he doesn't quit that shit. With a recalcitrant look on his stupid-arsed face he presses his thumb to the wheel.

I glare at him. "Do it again and this time, it goes up your arse."

He scowls and stalks off towards the door, pulling it back like the pissy little bitch he is. Jesus, he's worse than a girl. Raine and I both follow his spack attack and then she shakes her head and turns to me.

"You could be nicer to him. I don't think Crazy is firing on all cylinders."

"I don't think he *owns* all cylinders, babe." I down the rest of my beer and stand up, towering over the top of her. "You gonna be alright out here on your own?"

"Yeah, I'll be okay."

"You know Prez is working' in his office. I'm sure he'd appreciate a little wench in his stocking … or *in* stockings."

She slaps me on the chest, and I must be getting kinda soft 'cause it fucking hurts. "Never gonna happen, Kick. At least not while that ring is on his finger."

"So it might happen if we off the wife? I'll get the shovel."

Raine gives me a sad smile. "You're a good man, Daniel."

"No, I'm really fucking not, but I appreciate you tryin', babe." I toy with the ring on my left hand. Indie's tooth winks up at me from the hammered white gold casing. I had it made just after she left. Held a jeweller at gunpoint until he finished, 'cause I didn't wanna let the fuckin' thing outta my sight.

"She'll come around, you know," she says with

certainty, reaching up to kiss my cheek. She slaps it gently and then leans over to pick up our dirty glasses. Her dress rides up, exposing the backs of her thighs, and still I got nothin'. Can't even muster a fuckin' semi.

"No, she won't. And I don't blame her." I shake my head. I can't stand anymore of this sentimental bullshit. I head over to the bar and snag up the entire bottle of JD.

"Merry Christmas, Kick," Raine says, as I head for the hall.

I lift the bottle in the air and salute her with it. "Merry fuckin' Christmas, darlin'."

Once inside my room I shut the door and go in search of a glass. The place is a fuckin' mess. There's shit from one side of it to the other: empty takeaway containers, wet towels, clothes that need washing, and dishes covering every damn surface of the kitchen and coffee tables. Fuck me. I'm gonna need a damn Hazmat team to clean this shit up. I can't find a clean glass, and I can't remember buying any washing-up detergent for months. It's probably a good sign that I should throw all my shit in the bin and start again.

I stand by the couch for a beat and think about turning on the TV, but what's the fuckin' point? It'd just be the same shit that's on out in the club lounge. I carry my bottle to the bed and plan on getting well and truly shitfaced. I wanna drink until I forget. I wanna grab her by the fucking hair and drag her back to my bed. I wanna shove inside her like I did that night at Prez's house. I close my eyes, remembering exactly the way she tasted, the way she felt in my hands.

I don't know how much later it is, but I'm woken by a quiet tapping on my door. I jump up thinking it must be Raine, because no other fucker in this clubhouse ever knocked so timidly on my door in the middle of the night. I answer it, shirt off, jeans unbuttoned, hair a fuckin' mess probably, and sleep crusting the corners of my eyes.

Indie stands in my doorway. It's a sight I never thought I'd see again, but I can't get my hopes up that she's here for me. She probably just needs help killing some other motherfucker that did wrong by her.

She pushes past me into the room and glances around. "Jesus, you're a slob. You know there's this new thing that all the cool kids are doing nowadays. It's called cleaning."

"Woman, don't fuckin' come in here tellin' me what shit is what. You got no business getting all up in my face about the way I keep house," I say, scrubbing my hand over my beard. I've let it get too long again, and I probably look like a fuckin' hobo. I don't think that's why she's giving me that timid look she's got plastered all over that sweet face. "What the fuck are you doing here?"

"It's nice to see you too, Kick."

"You need me to kill someone else for you? Is that it? You got some other bad guy stashed away needing a bullet to his brain that you can't deliver?"

"I couldn't stay with you, Daniel."

"Get the fuck out. I don't have time for this bullshit."

"Let me finish." She gives me those fuckin' doe eyes that I can't say no to, and like a douche canoe I just stand there, staring at her goddamned face which has all healed now, save for a tiny scar over her eyebrow. I kinda like it, though; it makes her look bad-arse. "I couldn't stay because it wouldn't be fair. I wasn't whole; I wasn't who I was supposed to be. They took the life from me, Biker. You put it back, but it was all off, you know? I wasn't me, and I wasn't strong enough on my own."

"And what, you run off for a couple months, see some fucking shrink and now you're Superwoman?"

"Hardly. I can't make it through the night without waking up screaming."

"Join the fuckin' club."

"The nightmares were better when you were there. They never stopped entirely, but they were easier to deal with." She sighs and sits down on the edge of my unmade bed. "I felt you, you know. Before yesterday. I don't know how, but I felt you near me. Even when I couldn't see you."

"What the fuck do you want, Kayla?"

"Actually, it's Indie now. My shrink advised me to change it. Kayla has too much pain attached to it. I'm not that girl anymore. I tried to be. But I've changed; you changed me."

"What do you want, a fuckin' medal?"

"Actually, I was hoping for a biker. One about yay high …" She holds her hand about a foot above her head. "Blond hair, dark blue sinful eyes, bad attitude, with a fondness for Subway cookies and killing mice the humane way."

That pulls a reluctant smile from me. I run my hand through my hair, which I've also let grow way too long.

"I want you, Biker. I had to leave you to be sure."

"And now you're back? So what? You're sure now, but you weren't when I came to see you a month ago?"

"Honestly? No." She sighs. "I didn't know if there was an us outside of my revenge. I didn't know if I could love that side of you when I wasn't dependant on it."

"And now it's all rainbows and fuckin' kittens? I can't change who I am, babe. I'm not leaving' the club and I can't promise I'm not always gonna come home with a guilty conscience and blood on my hands, because that's who I fuckin' am. That's what life in the MC gets ya."

"I know." She takes a deep breath and exhales slowly. "I know I'm not always going to like everything you do, and I'm sure there will be days I want to punch you in the nut-sack — god knows there's been enough of those already — but I can't be without you."

I close my eyes. My chest hurts as if I just took a bullet to it. My stoic expression crumples into a scowl that I attempt to cover with my hands as I tilt my head up to the ceiling, but then she's there, in my space, crowding me, tugging on my arms, wedging her way into my bruised and broken heart. I don't wanna let her in. I've been feeling so fucking miserable for months, and I've grown used to wallowing in the emptiness inside of me. It's more than that, though. If I let this happen, if I let her in, if I allow her to fall in love with me, I'll only end up hurtin' the both of us because I'm shit, I'm the fuckin' king of betrayal, and no matter who's on the back of my bike and in my bed, no matter how much I might want her and love her, I'm eventually going to fuck it up. I'll eventually betray her, one way or another, because it's what I do. What I've always done.

"You turned it into a ring?" she says, tugging on the white-gold band around my finger.

I pull my hand out of her grasp and stare down at her accusingly. "It's the only thing you left behind."

She gives me a sad smile. "Not the only thing, Biker."

I scratch at my beard. "I can't stand the thought of losing you again, Little Spitfire, and if we do this, I'm probably gonna mess shit up so bad that you threaten to leave me at least once a week."

"Probably. I do have one hard limit, and if I find out that you ever crossed this line, there will be no second chances. You're mine, Biker. No one else's. Just mine."

"Baby, I haven't wanted up in anyone's pussy but yours. Can't even hold a goddamned hard-on without you being in the room."

"Does that mean you're hard for me now?"

"Not fuckin' yet, but keep talking."

She laughs, and it's fuckin' music to my tired-arse ears. I walk over to the bed, reaching out a hand to cup her face, and forcing her to look up at me. "I've never been good at this shit. I'm probably not gonna bring you flowers, and take you out on dates, and pick out fuckin' drapes. But if you're on the back of my bike, if you're in my bed, then that's it for me. I don't need no one else, just you, Spitfire."

She leans into my palm. "Drapes and dates are overrated, Biker. I'd much rather stay home and screw you with the windows wide open."

I push her back on the bed and climb over the top of her, supporting my weight with my forearms on either side of her head. "I fuckin' missed you, babe."

She smiles up at me. "Missed you too, Biker."

I wedge my hips between her legs, grinning like a fuckin' tool when my cock finally snaps to attention.

'Bout time fucker. It's only been six months. Jesus Christ. I couldda gone and joined a monastery in that time.

I slide my hand up her shirt, smiling when I feel her bare breasts, her nipples hardening beneath my fingertips. I come up on my knees and lift her shirt over her head. Those tits are just the way I remembered them: pink upturned nipples on pale white flesh that's never seen a suntan a day in its life. I lick her rosy nipples, tugging on one gently with my teeth.

She arches into me, and I slide my hands underneath her back, all the way up to the nape of her neck. I trail kisses over her tits, up her neck and finally across her cheek to her mouth. She opens for me, allowing my tongue entrance. She kisses me back tentatively at first, then much faster, much harder. I grind my hips into the hollow created by her legs and pull away, unbuttoning her jeans and sliding the tight denim off of thighs that are much fuller than they were when we first did this. She's still slim, only now she's got an arse I can dig my hands into, and thighs that can squeeze my hips when I'm rocking back and forth inside her.

I remove my jeans and hurry out of them, climbing back on the bed. I position myself between her legs, lifting her hips with my hands beneath them, and then I lower my head to her cunt and lap at her clit. She slams her legs together—or at least, she tries to. Her effort is kinda hindered by my head between her thighs. Her hands wedge themselves between me and her pussy, and I glare up at her.

"You starve a man for six fuckin' months, show him the all-you-can-eat buffet and then yank the rug out from under him, and close up shop before he even gets a taste?"

"Not that." She shakes her head.

"Why not that?" I challenge.

"Because I don't want you to see ... I don't—"

"I've already seen it, babe. Believe it or not but a man usually looks at a cunt before he sticks his dick inside it, especially one as perfect as yours."

She closes her eyes and lets out a shaky breath. Then she sits up. "Maybe this wasn't such a good idea."

"Lie the fuck down," I order. "This is the best fuckin' idea you've ever had. I don't care what shit is goin' on up in that pretty little head of yours, ignore it."

"Ignore it?" she says, riling up again. "You want me to ignore what they di—"

I reach up and clamp my hand over her mouth to get her to shut the fuck up. "That shit has no place being mentioned in my bed."

Her eyes grow wide, and then narrow in fury.

"Woman, I haven't been inside a pussy in over six months. I'm tellin' ya to ignore whatever self-conscious bullshit is goin' on in your head because your pussy is perfect, and right now I want a taste, and then I want inside of it. So stop fuckin' talking, Spitfire, let the fuck go, lay back and enjoy my mouth on you, 'cause I promise you're gonna fuckin' love it."

She stares at me for a beat, this incredulous fuckin' expression on her face. "Lie. The. Fuck. Down," I command.

Indie glares at me for another second before flopping back on the bed with an irritated huff. She can be as damn angry as she wants—don't matter. 'Cause I'm gonna eat out this fucking gorgeous pussy, and I'm gonna push into her, and take all day bringing her to the edge, and holding her back from fallin' if I want to, and there's not a damn thing she can do about it. Maybe it won't be today, or in another five years' time, but I'm gonna make her forget that anyone but me ever laid a finger on her, and she's gonna love every second of it.

Because I might be a fuck-up. And I might be a criminal, and I might be a worthless piece of shit, just like my dad always told me I was, but that never stopped me going after what I want. And like I told her at that café, she's all I want.

Just her.

ABOUT THE AUTHOR

Carmen Jenner is a thirty-something, *USA TODAY* Best Selling Author, doctor, pilot and CIA agent.

She's also a compulsive, flagrant prevaricator who gets to make things up for a living.

While Sugartown may not technically exist, Carmen grew up in a small Australian town just like it, and just like her characters, she always longed for something more. They didn't have an Elijah Cade, though.

If they did, you can be sure she would have never left.

Stay up to date with Carmen at
www.carmenjenner.com

ACKNOWLEDGEMENTS

This stuff never gets any easier, so I'm just going to dive in and hope we all make it out without losing a year or two off our lives! ;)

Firstly to my darling non-husband Ben, you, Mister are my life! Here's to many more years of beautiful, imperfect, aggressive barn dancing!

Ava and Ari, I love you more than … CHICKENS! Thanks for being the best kids walking the planet! I love you guys so much! Don't ever grow up! It's unnecessary, and I'm pretty sure it's a trap!

To all the women in my family: Mum, Chrissy, Nan Higgins, Nan Jenner, Ma, Leila Teys Bates, Barb Habner, Lauren Jenner, Sue Jenner, Trudy Duncombe, Zoe Duncombe, Simone Ellis, and all of my beautiful Aunts, thank you for teaching me that a strong woman comes in all different forms. From warriors to healers, and everything in between. All of you are superheros!

To Sydvegas, you girls save me from myself — and let's be honest, you save me from making even more of a tool out of myself on the internet — every day! I'm blessed to have each one of you in my life! Thank you for cheering me on in everything from books, to life, to just generally getting out of bed in the morning. I don't know how I'd cope without you and the few short weekends we get to spend together throughout the year are never, ever enough! #FLYFF #I'mBatman

Special thanks to my beta readers, Kristine from Glass Paper Ink Bookblog, Alexis from Reality Bites! Let's Get Lost!, Ali from Black Heart Reviews, Simone

Nicole and Jennifer Ryder.

Kristine and Simone, Gah! You girls know what I went through while writing KICK! He tore my heart out, stomped on it, and shoved the mashed up pieces back inside my chest cavity, and then he smacked my arse and sent me on my way. You both travelled that road with me, and held my hands, and I think you saw Kick as clearly as I did, and you felt all the things I felt about this book! Thank you for being the first to lay eyes on him in all his messy, fucked-up glory, and for telling me I had something worth fighting for here!

Kristine, woman, I fucking love you! From Deen Peen to M.A.C, I never get tired of our rambling conversations. I love how much you see into my words, sometimes even more than I've picked up on. You don't read books, you feel them. I hope every author you beta/review for realises how damn lucky they are! I see very big things for you and Glass Paper Ink, sweet! And I'm so freaking excited!

Simone, thank you for loving my boy as much as you do! For taking time away from your own writing schedule to ease my fragile, insecure mind! Your encouragement and cheerleading on Kick's story means more than you will ever know!

Alexis, damn girl, I value your feedback so much! Your advice is always thorough, always concise, and always leaves me feeling like I'm on the right track. And your quote, "Dark, Sexual Chaos", has to be one of the best things that's ever been written about any of my books.

Ali, my little Alicat. I miss your damn face, lady! I'm so grateful to you for being the first person outside of my family to tell me I could do this. You won't ever know what your words mean to me, and how much I depend on your friendship, and your feedback! Now, move your arse to Aus and everything will be awesome.

JJ, thanks for waving the pom poms, lady, and for taking time away from your own work to read and revel in the madness of my boy!

Super humongous squishy cuddles of thanks to my incredible editor Lauren McKeller (#McStellar), it becomes more and more difficult to tell you with each book just how much I value your work, because what can I say but: YOU MAKE MY BOOKS BETTER! I'd be lost without you! I don't know how you do it, but thank you for putting up with me—and for not showing me how many of those red crosses on your calendar belong to me pushing back deadlines, and asking to be fit in elsewhere. I can't imagine ever working with another editor! Somehow you're always simultaneously making me feel like Hemingway and pushing me to write better—not better than Hemmo, cause that's kinda impossible, but better than my last book—and I can't thank you enough for that. I'm gonna win my Hoover back, baby! :P

Arijana Karčić from Cover It! Designs, otherwise known as; the Greatest and Best Cover Designer in the World, thank you for creating such beautiful masterpieces! Working with you is a dream, lady!

Heartfelt thanks to Emily from E. M. Tippetts Book Designs. You and your team always make time to not only fit me in whenever I need you, but you also manage to produce such gorgeous interiors. I never have to question whether the pages of my book are going to come up to par with the amazing covers Ari creates, because I know without a doubt you have that down, lady!

To my Sugar Junkies—and I guess now also my Kick Cave Crusaders—I don't have enough words to express my gratitude to you ladies! From those of you who have been with me from the beginning to those of you who have just joined, you'll never know what your love support and supreme pimping skills do for me! I'd love to thank you all individually, but I'd hate myself if I forgot any of you, so please forgive my blanket thanks, and accept my offering of more delicious tattooed man candy!

To the A is for F*cking Awesome girls, each of you gorgeous ladies inspire me every day! I'm so glad to have a safe place to go play on the internet where there is no judgement, just a handful of smart, hard working women who want to help one another and see each other succeed. "Girls compete with each other, women uplift one another." I don't know who said that phrase, but I look at our little corner of the internet and I can't help but feel so much this!

Thanks to TRSoR for an incredible Cover Reveal and Blog Tour with KICK! I'm thrilled to have had you girls on this book!

Kylie from Give Me Books you are a freaking superstar! Thank you for taking on my Cover Reveals, Release Day Parties and Blitz's! You go above and beyond, lady, and I'm so thrilled to be working with you and your GMB and One-Click Addict girls!

And finally a huge, heartfelt THANK YOU full of cupcakes, lipstick and sexy bikers—three of my favourite things—to the readers and bloggers who follow, support, pimp, review, talk me up, and become as excited as I am about each of my releases. Without you I wouldn't get to do what I love, live and breathe!

Go back to where it all began with the Sugartown series

Sugartown

Book #1 Sugartown Series by Carmen Jenner

Ana Belle never wanted anything more than to hang up her apron, jump on her Vespa and ride off into the sunset, leaving Sugartown in the dust.

Elijah Cade never wanted anything more than a hot meal, a side of hot arse and a soft place to lay his head at night where he could forget about his past.

But you know what they say about wanting: you always want what you can't have.

Nineteen year-old virgin Ana is about to discover that's not quite true because a six foot three, hotter than hell, tattooed, Aussie sex god just rode into town. He's had a taste of her pie and he wants more– no really, Ana bakes pies for a living, get your mind out of the gutter.

She'd be willing to hand over everything tied up in a big red bow, there's just one problem; Elijah has secrets dirtier than last week's underwear. Secrets that won't just break Ana's heart, but put her life at risk, too. When those secrets come to light, their relationship is pushed to breaking point.

Add to that a psychotic nympho best friend, an overbearing father, a cuter than humanly possible kid brother, a wanton womanizing cousin, the ex from hell and more pies than you could poke a ... err ... stick ... at.

And you thought small towns were boring.

Welcome to Sugartown.

Content Warning. Intended for a mature 18+ audience. Contains explicit sex, violence, oodles of profanity and a crap-tonne of AWKWARD.

*More from
Carmen Jenner*

REVELRY
Taint #1 by Carmen Jenner

Cooper Ryan is living the dream. Between the parties with rock royalty, booze, groupies and performing to crowds of thousands with his band Taint, life seems pretty sweet. There's just one thing missing: the feisty little red-head that took his baby and ran off with his heart. Throwing himself into music is the only thing keeping him sane.

Until a run-in with a nonplussed, package-wielding PA throws everything off balance.

Ali Jones is having a craptastic life. Her grandmother died, leaving her homeless, penniless, and alone, and her boyfriend left her for a tramp who takes her clothes off for money. That's why when she lands her dream job at a record company it seems like it's too good to be true.

Because it is.

Slapped with an ultimatum, Ali must decide if facing the horror of the unemployment line is a fate worse than going on the road with four rowdy rockers hell-bent on making her life misery.

He's adored by millions.

She's not even loved by her cat.

Can they ignore their hatred long enough to survive the tour from hell? Or will their chemistry force everything to come crashing down around them?